Dennis Lehane is the author of eleven *New York Times* bestsellers, most of which have been made into films, such as *Gone, Baby, Gone, Mystic River, Shutter Island* and *The Drop*. He has won the Shamus Award for Best First Novel, the Edgar, Anthony and Barry awards for Best Novel and the Massachusetts Book Award in Fiction. His work has been translated into twenty-two languages. Lehane was born and raised in Dorchester, Massachusetts, and he and his wife, Angie, currently live in California with their children.

DENNIS LEHANE

WORLD GONE BY

Little, Brown

LITTLE, BROWN

First published in the United States in 2015 by William Morrow,
an imprint of HarperCollins
First published in Great Britain in 2015 by Little, Brown

13 5 7 9 10 8 6 4 2

Copyright © Dennis Lehane 2015

The moral right of the author has been asserted.

Grateful acknowledgment is made for permission
to reprint lyrics from 'Stolen Car' by Bruce Springsteen.
Copyright © 1980 Bruce Springsteen (ASCAP).
Reprinted by permission. International copyright secured.
All rights reserved.

A CIP catalogue record for this book
is available from the British Library.

Hardback ISBN 978-1-4087-0669-5
Trade Paperback ISBN 978-1-4087-0670-1

Printed and bound in Great Britain by
Clays Ltd, St Ives plc

Papers used by Little, Brown are from well-managed forests
and other responsible sources.

MIX
Paper from
responsible sources
FSC
www.fsc.org   FSC® C104740

Little, Brown
An imprint of
Little, Brown Book Group
Carmelite House
50 Victoria Embankment
London EC4Y 0DZ

An Hachette UK Company
www.hachette.co.uk

www.littlebrown.co.uk

For Keeks
Of the blue eyes and the billion-dollar smile

. . . I'm driving a stolen car
On a pitch black night
And I'm telling myself I'm gonna be alright.

BRUCE SPRINGSTEEN, 'STOLEN CAR'

Prologue

BEFORE THE SMALL WAR BROKE THEM APART, they all gathered to support the big war. It had been a year since Pearl Harbor, and they came together in the Versailles Ballroom of the Palace Hotel on Bayshore Drive in Tampa, Florida, to raise money for troops stationed in the European Theater. It was a catered affair, black tie, and the evening was mild and dry.

Six months later, on a muggy evening in early May, one of the crime beat reporters for the *Tampa Tribune* would come across photographs from the event. He would be struck by how many of the people who'd been in the local news lately for either killing or being killed had attended the fund-raiser that night.

He thought there was a story in it; his editor disagreed. But look, the reporter said, *look*. That's Dion Bartolo standing at the bar with Rico DiGiacomo. And over here? I'm pretty sure that little guy in the hat is Meyer Lansky himself. Here—you see that guy talking to the pregnant woman? He ended up in the morgue back in March. And there—that's the mayor and his wife talking to Joe Coughlin. Joe Coughlin again, in this one, shaking hands with the Negro gangster Montooth Dix. Boston Joe, rarely photographed his entire life, but that night, he was photographed *twice*. This guy smoking a cigarette by the dame in white? He's dead. So's that guy. The guy out on the dance floor in the white dinner jacket? He's crippled.

Boss, the reporter said, they were all together that night.

The editor mentioned that Tampa was a small town disguised as a medium-size city. People crossed paths all the time. It was a fund-raiser for the war effort; those were the *causes de rigueur* for the idle rich; they drew everyone who was anyone. He pointed out to his young, excitable reporter that plenty of other people who attended that night—two famous singers, one baseball player, three voice actors from the city's most popular radio soap operas, the president of First Florida Bank, the CEO of Gramercy Pewter, and P. Edson Haffe, the publisher of this very newspaper—were all quite unconnected to the bloodshed that had erupted back in March and stained the city's good name.

The reporter protested a bit longer but found the editor intractable on the subject and so went back to researching rumors of German spies infiltrating the Port Tampa waterfront. A month later he was drafted into the army. The pictures remained in the photo morgue of the *Tampa Tribune* long after anyone who was in them had passed from the earth.

The reporter, who would die two years later on the beach at Anzio, had no way of knowing that the editor, who would outlive him by thirty years before succumbing to heart disease, was under orders to end the paper's coverage of anything to do with the Bartolo Crime Family; Joseph Coughlin; or the mayor of Tampa, a fine young man from a fine Tampa family. The city, the editor was told, had already been tarnished aplenty.

The participants that night back in December had all been engaged, as far as they understood it, in a wholly innocent union of people who supported the soldiers overseas.

Joseph Coughlin, the businessman, had organized the event because so many of his former employees had enlisted or been drafted.

Vincent Imbruglia, who had two brothers in the fight—one in the Pacific and one somewhere in Europe, no one would confirm where—ran the raffle. The grand prize was two front-row tickets to a Sinatra concert at the Paramount in New York at the end of the month and first-class carriage on the Tamiami Champion. Everyone bought rafts of tickets even though most assumed the wheel was rigged so the mayor's wife, a huge Sinatra fan, would win.

The boss of bosses, Dion Bartolo, showed off the kind of dance moves that had won him prizes in his adolescence. In the process, he gave the mothers and daughters of some of Tampa's most respectable families stories to tell their grandchildren. ("No man who dances with such grace can be as bad as some have claimed.")

Rico DiGiacomo, the brightest star in the Tampa underworld, showed up with his brother, Freddy, and their beloved mother, and his dangerous glamour was outdone only by the arrival of Montooth Dix, an exceptionally tall Negro made taller by the top hat that matched his tuxedo. Most members of the Tampa elite had never seen a Negro pass through a party without a serving tray on his palm, but Montooth Dix moved through the crowd of white people like he expected them to serve him.

The party was just respectable enough to be attended without regret and just dangerous enough to be worth remarking on for the rest of the season. Joe Coughlin had a gift for bringing the beacons of the city into contact with her demons and making it all seem like a lark. It helped that Coughlin himself, once rumored to have been a gangster and quite a powerful one, had clearly evolved past the street. He was one of the biggest charity supporters in all of West Central Florida, a friend to numerous hospitals, soup kitchens, libraries, and shelters. And if the other rumors were true—that he hadn't fully left his criminal past behind—well, one couldn't fault a man for a bit of loyalty to those he'd known on the way up. Certainly if some of the assembled tycoons, factory owners, and builders wished to settle any labor unrest or unclog their supply routes, they knew who to call. Joe Coughlin was the bridge in this town between what was proclaimed in public and how it was achieved in private. When he threw a party, you came just to see who'd show up.

Joe himself conferred upon the festivities no further significance than that. When a man threw a party where the upper crust mingled with street thugs and judges chatted with capos as if they'd never met before, either in court or in a back room, when the Sacred Heart pastor showed up and blessed the room before imbibing with the same gusto as everyone else, when Vanessa Belgrave, the pretty but icy wife of the mayor raised a glass of thanks in Joe's direction, and a Negro as fearsome as Montooth Dix could regale a group of stuffy old white men with tales of his exploits in the Great War, and not a cross word or drunken faux pas was witnessed by anyone, well, that party was not only a success, it was quite possibly the success of the season.

The only sign of trouble occurred after Joe stepped out on the back lawn to get some air and saw the little boy. He moved in and out of the darkness at the far edge of the back lawn. He zigzagged back and forth, as if he were playing tag with other boys. But there were no other boys. Judging by his height and build, he was about six or seven years old. He spread his arms wide and made the sound of a propeller and then of a plane engine. He made wings of his arms and careened along the fringe of the tree line, shouting, "*Va-rooooom. Va-roooom.*"

Joe couldn't put his finger on what else was odd about the kid, other than being a child alone at an adult party, until he realized his clothes were a good ten years out of date. More like twenty, actually, the kid was wearing knickerbockers, Joe was pretty sure, and one of those oversize golf caps boys wore way back when Joe himself had been a boy.

The kid was too far away for Joe to get a good look at his face, but he had the odd sensation that even if he were closer, it wouldn't have made a difference. Even from this far away he could tell the boy's face was irrevocably indistinct.

Joe walked off the flagstone patio and crossed the lawn. The boy kept making airplane sounds and ran into the darkness beyond the lawn, vanishing into the stand of trees. Joe heard him buzzing, somewhere back in all that darkness.

Joe was halfway across the lawn when someone off to his right whispered, "Psst. Mr. Coughlin, sir? Joe?"

Joe slipped a hand a few inches from the Derringer nestled at the small of his back, not his normal gun of choice but one he'd found suitable for black-tie events.

"It's me," Bobo Frechetti said as he came out from behind the great banyan tree along the side of the lawn.

Joe dropped his hand back in front of himself. "Bobo, how's the kid?"

"I'm okay, Joe. You?"

"Tip-top." Joe looked at the tree line, saw only darkness. He couldn't hear the kid back in there anymore. He said to Bobo, "Who brought a kid?"

"What?"

"The kid." Joe pointed. "The one who was acting like an airplane."

Bobo stared at him.

"You didn't see a kid over there?" Again, Joe pointed.

Bobo shook his head. Bobo, a guy so small no one had much trouble believing he'd once been a jockey, took off his hat and held it in his hands. "You heard about that safe got opened at that rock-crushing place in Lutz?"

Joe shook his head even though he knew Bobo was talking about the safe that had been robbed of six thousand dollars at Bay Palms Aggregate, a subsidiary of one of the Family's transport companies.

"Me and my partner had no idea it was owned by Vincent Imbruglia." Bobo waved his arms like an umpire calling a guy safe at home. "None."

Joe knew the feeling. His entire path in this life had been determined when he and Dion Bartolo, barely out of diapers, unknowingly robbed a gangster's casino.

"So, then, no big deal." Joe lit a cigarette, offered the pack to the little safecracker. "Give the money back."

"We tried." Bobo took a cigarette and a light from Joe, nodded his thanks. "My partner—you know Phil?"

Phil Cantor. Phil the Bill because of the size of his nose. Joe nodded.

"Phil went to Vincent. Told him about our mistake. Said we had the money and were gonna bring it right back. Know what Vincent did?"

Joe shook his head, though he had an idea.

"Chucked Phil into traffic. Right on Lafayette, middle of the fucking day. Phil bounced off the grille of a Chevy like the one ball off a hard break. Hip's shattered, knees all fucked up, jaw's wired shut. Vincent tells him, as he's lying in the middle of Lafayette, 'You owe us double. You got one week.' And spits on him. What kind of animal spits on a man? Any man, Joe? I'm asking. Never mind one lying on the street with parts of him broken?"

Joe shook his head, then held out his hands. "What can I do?"

Bobo handed Joe a paper bag. "It's all there."

"The original amount or the double Vincent asked for?"

Bobo fidgeted, looking around at the trees before he looked back at Joe. "You can talk to these people. You're not some animal. You can tell them we made a mistake and now my partner's in the hospital for, I dunno, a month? And that seems a high price. Could you float that?"

Joe smoked for a bit. "If I get you out of this soup—"

Bobo grabbed Joe's hand and kissed it, most of his lips landing on Joe's watch.

"*If.* " Joe took his hand back. "What'll you do for me?"

"You name it."

Joe looked at the bag. "Every dollar is in here?"

"Every single one."

Joe took a drag and then loosed a slow exhale. He kept waiting for the kid to return or at least the sound of him, but it was clear those trees were empty.

He looked at Bobo and said, "All right."

"All right? Jesus. All right?"

Joe nodded. "Nothing's free, though, Bobo."

"I know it. I know it. Thank you, thank you."

"If I ever ask you for anything"— he stepped in close—"fucking *anything*, you hop right to. We clear?"

"As a bell, Joe. As a bell."

"If you welsh on me?"

"I won't, I won't."

"I'll have a curse put on you. And not any curse. Witch doctor I know in Havana? Motherfucker never misses."

Bobo, like a lot of guys who'd grown up around racetracks, was highly superstitious. He showed Joe his palms. "You won't have to worry about that."

"I'm not talking about some garden-variety hex, kind you get from an Italian grandmother and her mustache in New Jersey."

"You do not have to worry about me. I will honor my debt."

"I'm talking a Cuba-by-way-of-Hispaniola curse. Haunt your descendents."

"I promise." He looked at Joe with a fresh coat of sweat on his forehead and eyelids. "May God strike me dead."

"Well, we wouldn't want that, Bobo." Joe patted his face. "Then you wouldn't be able to pay me back."

VINCENT IMBRUGLIA WAS SET to get bumped up to captain, even though he didn't know it yet and even though Joe didn't think it was a great idea. But times were tough, strong earners were getting rare, some of their best off in the war, so Vincent was getting his promotion next month. Until then, though, he still worked for Enrico "Rico" DiGiacomo, which meant the money that had been stolen from his stone-crushing company front was really Rico's.

Joe found Rico at the bar. He slid him the money and explained the situation.

Rico sipped his drink and frowned when Joe told him what had happened to poor Phil the Bill.

"Tossed him in front of a fucking car?"

"Indeed." Joe took a sip of his own drink.

"There's just no style to a move like that."

"I agree."

"I mean, have a little fucking class."

"No argument."

Rico gave it some thought as he bought them another round. "Seems to me the punishment's already fit the crime and then some. You tell Bobo he's off the hook but not to show his face in any of our bars for a little while. Let everyone cool down. Broke the poor fuck's jaw, huh?"

Joe nodded. "What the man said, yeah."

"Too bad it wasn't his nose. Maybe it could have got, I dunno, restructured, stop looking like God got drunk, put Phil's elbow where his nose was supposed to go." His voice trailed off as he looked around the room. "This is some party, boss."

He told Rico, "Ain't your boss anymore. Ain't anyone's."

Rico acknowledged that with a flick of his eyebrow, looked around the room some more. "Still a hell of a bash, sir. *Salud*."

Joe looked out on the dance floor, at all the swells dancing with all the former debs, everyone polished to a shine. He saw the kid again, or thought he did, the boy appearing between the swirl of gowns and ruffled hoop dresses. The boy's face was turned away, the back of his head sporting a small cowlick, no hat on him anymore but still wearing the knickerbocker pants.

And then he wasn't there anymore.

Joe placed his drink aside and vowed not to have another for the rest of the evening.

In retrospect, he would look back on it as the Last Party, the final free ride before everything slipped toward that heartless March.

But at the time, it was just a great party.

CHAPTER ONE

In the Matter of Mrs. Del Fresco

IN THE SPRING OF 1941, a man named Tony Del Fresco married a woman named Theresa Del Frisco in Tampa, Florida. This was, unfortunately, the only slightly amusing thing anyone could remember about their marriage. He once hit her with a bottle; she once hit him with a croquet mallet. The mallet belonged to Tony, who'd brought it over from Arezzo some years before and had placed wickets and stakes in the Del Frescos' swampy backyard on the west side of Tampa. Tony repaired clocks by day and cracked safes by night. He claimed croquet was the only thing that settled his mind, which, by his own admission, was filled with a permanent rage made all the blacker for being inexplicable. Tony had two good jobs, after all, a pretty wife, time on weekends for croquet.

However black the thoughts in Tony's head may have been, they all leaked out when Theresa caved in the side of his skull with the mallet early in the winter of 1943. Detectives concluded that after delivering the initial, incapacitating blow, Theresa had stepped on her husband's cheekbone, fixed his head to the kitchen floor, and swung the mallet into the back of his skull until it looked like a pie that fell off a window ledge.

By trade, Theresa was a florist, but most of her true income derived from robbery and the occasional murder, both crimes usually committed on behalf of her boss, Lucius Brozjuola, whom everyone called King Lucius. King Lucius paid the necessary tribute to the Bartolo Family but otherwise ran an independent organization with the illicit profits laundered through the phosphate empire he'd amassed along the Peace River and the wholesale flower business he owned in the Port of Tampa. It had been King Lucius who had trained Theresa as a florist in the first place and King Lucius who financed the flower shop she opened downtown on Lafayette. King Lucius ran a crew of thieves, fences, arsonists, and contract killers who operated under only one concrete rule—no jobs performed in their home state. So Theresa, over the years, had killed five men and one woman, all strangers—two in Kansas City, one in Des Moines, another in Dearborn, one in Philadelphia, and finally, the woman in Washington, D.C., Theresa turning to shoot her in the back of the head two steps after passing her on a soft spring evening in George-town, on a tree-lined street that ticked with the remnants of an afternoon shower.

In one way or another, all those killings haunted her. The man in Des Moines had held a picture of his family in front of his face, forcing her to fire the bullet through it to reach his brain; the one in Philly kept saying "Just tell me why"; the woman in Georgetown had let out a plaintive sigh before she'd crumpled to the wet pavement.

The one killing that didn't haunt Theresa was Tony's. She only wished she'd done it sooner, before Peter was old enough to miss his

parents. He'd been staying with her sister in Lutz that fateful weekend because Theresa had wanted him out of the line of fire when
she kicked Tony out of his own house. His drinking, whoring, and
black moods had been spiraling out of control since the summer,
and Theresa had finally reached her limit. Tony hadn't reached his,
though, which is how he came to hit her with a wine bottle and
how she came to crush his fucking head with a mallet.

At the Tampa City jail, she called King Lucius. Half an hour
later, Jimmy Arnold, house counsel to King Lucius and his various corporations, was sitting across from her. Theresa was worried
about two things—going to the chair and finding herself unable to
provide for Peter. Her control over whether she was electrocuted up
in the state penitentiary at Raiford ended with her husband's life.
As for securing Peter's future comfort, however, she'd been waiting
on payment for a job from King Lucius himself, a job that had har-
vested so bountiful a profit margin that her 5 percent stake would
ensure that the stomachs of Peter, Peter's children, and Peter's
grandchildren never rumbled for anything but a second helping.

Jimmy Arnold assured her that on both counts the outlook was
rosier than she presumed. In the first matter, he'd already informed
the Hillsborough County district attorney Archibald Boll of her history of being beaten by her deceased husband, beatings that had been
documented on the two occasions Tony's fury had put her in the hospital. The DA, a very smart and politically conscious man, would not
send an abused wife to the death chamber when there were plenty
of German and Jap spies Old Sparky would be glad to host first. As
for the monies due her from the Savannah job, Jimmy Arnold was
authorized to say that King Lucius was still in the process of finding
a buyer for the merchandise in question but as soon as he'd done
so and the monies had been received, she would be the second par-
ticipant to get her cut, after King Lucius himself, of course.

Three days after the arrest, Archibald Boll dropped by to offer her a deal. A handsome middle-aged man in a coarse linen suit and matching half-fedora, Archibald Boll's eyes carried the playful light of a grade school mischief maker. Theresa concluded fairly quickly that he was attracted to her, but he was all business when it came to discussing her plea. She would agree before the court that she had committed voluntary manslaughter with extenuating circumstances, a plea that would normally ensure someone with a criminal record as extensive as her own twelve years in prison. But today and today only, Archibald Boll assured her, the district attorney's office of the city of Tampa was offering sixty-two months, to be served at the women's wing of the state prison in Raiford. Which was the location, yes, of Old Sparky, but Archibald Boll promised Theresa she'd never see it.

"Five years." Theresa couldn't believe it.

"And two months," Archibald Boll said, his moony gaze gliding up from her waist to her breasts. "You make the plea tomorrow, we'll have you on the bus out the next morning."

So tomorrow night, Theresa knew, you'll pay your visit.

But she didn't care—for five years and a chance to be out in time for Peter's eighth birthday, she'd fuck not only Archibald Boll but every ADA in his office and still consider herself lucky not to have a metal cap placed to her skull and ten thousand volts of electricity sent surging through her veins.

"Do we have a deal?" Archibald Boll asked, eyes on her legs now.

"We have a deal."

In court, when the judge asked how she pled, Theresa answered, "Guilty," and the judge conferred upon her a sentence of "not more than one thousand eight hundred and ninety days, less time served." They took Theresa back to the jail to await the morning bus to Raiford. Early that evening, when her first visitor was announced, she expected to see Archibald Boll enter the gloamy corridor outside her cell, the tent already pitched in his linen trousers.

Instead it was Jimmy Arnold. He brought her a meal of cold fried chicken and potato salad, better than any meal she'd have for the next sixty-two months, and she wolfed down the chicken and sucked the grease off her fingers without any pretense of dignity. Jimmy Arnold took no interest in any of this. When she handed the plate back to him, he handed her the photograph of her and Peter that had sat atop her dresser. He also handed her the drawing Peter had made of her—a featureless and misshapen oval on top of an askew triangle with a single stick arm, no feet. He'd drawn it shortly after his second birthday, however, and by those standards it was a Rembrandt. Theresa looked down at Jimmy Arnold's two gifts and tried to keep the emotion from her eyes and her throat.

Jimmy Arnold crossed his legs at the ankles and stretched in his chair. He let out a loud yawn and dry-coughed into his fist. He said, "We'll miss you, Theresa."

She ate the last of the potato salad. "Back before you know it."

"There're just so few with your talents."

"In floral arrangement?"

He watched her carefully as his chuckle died. "No, the other thing."

"That just takes a gray heart."

"There's more to it." He waved a finger at her. "Don't sell yourself short."

She shrugged and looked back at the picture her son had drawn.

"Now that you're on the shelf for a while," he said, "who would you say is the best?"

She looked up at the ceiling and out at the other cells. "At floral arrangements."

He smiled. "Yeah, let's call it that. Who's the best florist in Tampa now that you're no longer in the running for the title?"

She didn't have to think long on the subject. "Billy."

"Kovich?"

She nodded.

Jimmy Arnold took that into consideration. "You consider him better than Mank?"

She nodded. "You see Mank coming."

"And on whose shift should this happen?"

She didn't follow the question. "Shift?"

"Detectives," he said.

"You mean locally?"

He nodded.

"You . . ." She looked around the cell, as if to assure herself she was still in it and of this earth. "You want a local contractor to handle a local contract?"

"I'm afraid so," he said.

That went against two decades of King Lucius policy.

"Why?" she asked.

"It must be someone the target knows. No one else could get close enough." He uncrossed his ankles and fanned himself with his hat. "If you think Kovich is the man for the job, I'll make inquiries."

She said, "Does the target have reason to suspect his life could be in danger?"

Jimmy Arnold thought about it and eventually nodded. "He works in our business. Don't we all sleep with one eye open?"

Theresa nodded. "Then, yeah, Kovich is your man. Everybody likes him, even if no one can understand why."

"Let's next consider the question of police jurisdiction and the character of the detectives who are working on the day in question."

16

"What day?"

"A Wednesday."

She ratcheted through a series of names, shifts, and scenarios.

"Ideally," she said, "you would want Kovich to do it between noon and eight in either Ybor, Port Tampa, or Hyde Park. That would ensure a high likelihood that Detectives Feeney and Boatman respond to the call."

His lips moved silently over the names as he fussed with the crease in his trouser leg, his brow furrowing a bit. "Do policemen observe holy days?"

"If they're Catholic, I suppose. Which holy day?"

"Ash Wednesday."

"There's not much to observing Ash Wednesday."

"No?" He seemed genuinely perplexed. "It's been so long since I've practiced the faith myself."

She said, "You go to mass, the priest makes the sign of the cross on your forehead with damp ash, you leave. That's it."

"That's it," he repeated in a soft whisper. He gave his surroundings a kind of distracted smile, like he was a bit surprised to find himself here. He stood. "Good luck, Mrs. Del Fresco. We'll be seeing you."

She watched Jimmy Arnold lift his briefcase off the floor, and she knew she shouldn't ask the question but she couldn't help it.

"Who's the target?" she said.

He looked through the bars at her. Just as she'd known she shouldn't ask the question, he knew he shouldn't answer it. But Jimmy Arnold was famous in their circles for an interesting paradox at his center—ask him the most innocuous question about any of his clients and he wouldn't answer if you set fire to his scrotum. Ask him the most salacious details about anything else, however, and he was all hen.

"Are you sure you want to know?" he asked.

She nodded.

He gave the dark green hallway a glance both ways before he leaned back into the bars, put his lips between them, and said the name.

"Joe Coughlin."

IN THE MORNING SHE BOARDED the bus and it carried her northeast for two hundred miles. Inland Florida was not the Florida of blue ocean, white sand, and crushed-white-shell parking lots. It was a land sun bleached and sickened after too many droughts and wildfires. For six and a half hours they bumped along back roads and bad roads, and most of the people they saw, white or colored or Indian, looked too thin.

The woman chained to Theresa's left wrist didn't talk for fifty miles and then introduced herself as Mrs. Sarah Nez of Zephyrhills. She shook Theresa's hand, assured her she was innocent of all the crimes for which she'd been convicted, and went another twenty-five miles before she moved again. Theresa rested her forehead against the window and looked out at the broiled land through the dust the tires kicked up. Beyond fields so dry the grass resembled paper, she could identify swampland by the smell and the green fog that rose from the far edges of the blanched fields. She thought about her son and the money she was owed to provide for his future, and she hoped King Lucius would make good on his debt because she had no one who could collect if he didn't.

Speaking of debt, she'd been stunned last night when District Attorney Archibald Boll failed to show up at her cell. She'd lain awake with a grateful body but a racing mind. If he hadn't expected her to repay him sexually, why had he offered such a sweetheart deal in the first place? There were no acts of kindness in her business, only acts of cunning; no gifts, only delayed bills. So if Archibald Boll hadn't wanted money from her—and he certainly hadn't given any indication he expected any—then that left sex or information.

Maybe, she told herself, he'd softened her up with the light sentence and now he'd let her stew on it a bit, let her sense of obligation grow. Then he'd come visit her at Raiford sometime this summer to collect on the debt. Except that DAs didn't work that way—they dangled the easy sentence in front of your eyes, but didn't give it to you *until* you'd done their bidding. They never gave you the easy sentence up front. Made no sense.

What made even less sense was the contract on Joe Coughlin. No matter how hard she tried—and she'd been trying all night—Theresa couldn't wrap her head around it. Since he'd stepped down as boss ten years ago, Joe Coughlin had proved a bigger asset to the Bartolo Family and all the other families and crews in town than he'd been when he'd run things. He embodied the highest ideal of a man in their business—he made money for his friends. Therefore, he had a lot of friends.

But enemies?

Theresa knew he'd once had a few, but that was ten years ago, and they'd all been erased in a single day. The police and the public knew about the bullet through the throat that had ended the hopes, dreams, and eating habits of Maso Pescatore, a bullet Coughlin was rumored to have personally fired. But no one but people like Theresa and her associates, people in the Life, knew about the dozen men who'd gone out on a boat to throw Joe Coughlin overboard only to never return, mown down by machine guns and close-range .45s. They'd then been tossed overboard into the Gulf of Mexico, turned into shark chum on a day already hot and uncharitable.

Those victims, and a long dead policeman, were the last enemies anyone knew Coughlin to have had. Since stepping down as boss, he'd stayed away from the heavy stuff, taking cues from Meyer Lansky, with whom he owned several concerns in Cuba. Rarely photographed and, if so, never with others in the Life, he apparently spent his days dreaming up new ways to make everyone even more money than he'd made them the year before.

Long before the Japs attacked Pearl Harbor and war broke out, Joe Coughlin had advised all the major players in the Florida and Cuban liquor concerns to begin stockpiling industrial alcohol to convert to rubber. No one knew what the fuck he was talking about—what did alcohol have to do with rubber and, even if it did, what did that have to do with them? But because he'd made them so much money in the '30s, they listened to him. And by the time the Japs had taken over half the world's rubber-producing regions in the spring of '42, Uncle Sam came running to pay top dollar for anything the government could use to make boots, tires, and bumpers, hell, even asphalt, Theresa had heard. The crews who'd listened to Coughlin—including King Lucius's—made so much money they didn't know what to do with it. One of the few men who didn't listen, Philly Carmona in Miami, took such an ill view of the guy who'd advised him against the deal that he shot him in the stomach.

Everyone in their business had enemies, yes, but as she drifted in and out of a lazy doze on the bus, Theresa couldn't put a face to any of Joe Coughlin's. Talk about killing a golden goose.

A snake slid through the dry gully outside her window. The snake was black and as long as Theresa. It slithered out of the gully and into the brush and Theresa drifted into a near-dream in which it slithered across the floor of her bedroom in the Brooklyn tenement where she'd lived upon first arriving in this country when she was ten. She thought it might be a good thing to have a snake in that room because rats had always been the real problem in those

tenements, and snakes ate rats. But then the snake vanished from
the floor and she could feel it sliding up the bed toward her. She
could feel it but she couldn't see it and she couldn't move because
the dream wouldn't allow it. The snake's scales were rough and cold
against her neck. It knotted itself around her throat and its metal
links dug into her windpipe.

Theresa reached behind her and gripped Sarah Nez's ear,
gripped it so hard she could have pulled it from the woman's head
if she'd had enough time. But she was already running out of oxygen. Sarah had used the chain that united their wrists. She made
small grunting noises as she twisted it tighter, working that chain
like a winch.

"If you accept Christ," she whispered, "if you accept Christ as
your Savior, He will welcome you home. He will love you. Accept
Him and fear not."

Theresa turned her body in toward the window and managed
to get her feet pressed to the wall. When she snapped her head
back, she heard Sarah's nose break and she pushed off the wall at
the same time. They ended up in the aisle and Sarah's grip loosened
long enough for Theresa to croak out something approximating a
scream, more like a yelp really, and she thought she might have seen
one of the guards moving toward them but everything was fading.
Everything was fading and then faded and then black.

TWO WEEKS LATER, she still couldn't speak properly; all that
came out was a gnarled and clogged-up whisper. The bruises that
ringed her neck had turned from purple to yellow recently. It hurt
to eat, and a cough could bring her close to tears.

The second woman who tried to kill her used a metal tray stolen from the infirmary. She hit Theresa on the back of the head

with it while Theresa was taking a shower, and the blow felt far too reminiscent of some of Tony's. The weakness of most people in a fight—men and women—was that they paused. This woman was no different. The force of her first blow knocked Theresa to the floor, and the sound of it seemed to surprise the woman. She stared down at Theresa too long before she dropped to her knees and raised the tray again. If she'd been any good—if she'd been Theresa, for example—she would have followed her victim to the floor immediately, tossed the tray aside, and bludgeoned her against the tile. By the time the woman got to her knees and raised her arms, Theresa had made a fist and turned the knuckle of her middle finger into a point. She drove that point into the center of the woman's throat. Not once, not twice, but four times. The tray fell and Theresa used the woman's body to stand as the woman gasped for oxygen that wouldn't come in the middle of the shower room.

When the guards arrived, they found the woman turning blue on the floor. The doctor was called. A nurse showed up first, and by that point the woman had begun taking gasping, desperate breaths. Theresa watched all this calmly from the edge of the room. She'd dried off and changed into her prison blues. She'd bummed a cigarette off one of the girls; in exchange, she promised to teach the girl how to do to someone what she'd just done to Thelma, which, she'd learned, was the failed killer's name.

When the guards came to Theresa and asked her what happened, she told them.

One of them said, "You know you could have killed her?"

"Apparently," she said, "I've slowed a step."

The other guards walked away and she was left with the one who'd asked the question, the youngest of them.

She said, "Henry, right?"

"Yes, ma'am."

"Henry, do you think you could get me a little of that gauze the nurse has in her satchel? My head's cut."

"How do you know there's gauze in there?"

"What else would be in there, Henry? Comic books?"

He smiled and nodded at the same time and went and got her the gauze.

Later that evening, after lights out, Henry came to her cell. She'd been in prison before so she'd been expecting it sooner or later. At least he was young and nearly handsome and clean.

Afterward, she told him she needed to get a message to someone on the outside.

"Oh, now," Henry Ames said.

"A message," Theresa said, "nothing more."

"I don't know." Henry Ames, less than two minutes removed from the end of his virginity, now had cause to wish he'd held on to it a little longer.

"Henry," Theresa said, "someone with a lot of power is trying to have me killed."

"I can protect you."

She smiled at him. She caressed the side of his neck with her right hand and Henry felt taller, stronger, and more alive than he'd ever felt in his twenty-three years on this earth.

She placed the razor blade to his ear with her left hand. It was double-edged, the kind Henry placed in the brass razor his father had given him when he graduated high school. These days, with the restrictions on metal, Henry used a blade until it was as dull as a spoon, but Theresa's appeared to have never been used until she flicked it lightly under his earlobe. Before he could react, she pulled the handkerchief from his shirt pocket and dabbed at the cut.

"Henry," she whispered, "you can't even protect yourself."

He never saw where she hid the blade; it just wasn't in her hand anymore. He stared into her eyes. They were wide and dark and warm.

"Now," she said gently, "if I don't get word to someone about my predicament, Henry, I won't last a month in here. And my son will grow up an orphan. And that I cannot fucking abide. You hear me?"

He nodded. Theresa continued to dab at his earlobe. Much to his surprise and shame, he felt himself growing hard again. Henry Ames of Ocala, Florida, a farmer's son, asked Female Prisoner 4773 who she wanted the message to go to.

"Go to the home office of Suarez Sugar on Howard Avenue in Tampa and tell the vice president, Joseph Coughlin, that I need to see him. Impress upon him that it's a matter of life and death. His and mine."

"I *can* protect you in here." Henry heard the desperation in his own voice, but even so, he wanted her to believe it.

Theresa handed his handkerchief back. She stared at him for a while.

"That's sweet," she said. "Now remember—Suarez Sugar. Howard Avenue in Tampa. Joe Coughlin."

CHAPTER TWO

The Runner

HENRY AMES WAS OFF FRIDAYS, so as soon as his Thursday shift ended, he left Raiford and drove through the night to Tampa. During the drive, he had plenty of time to think on his transgressions. His father and mother, as morally upright as two people without wings could get, would seize up and die if they knew their eldest son was fornicating with a convicted murderess who'd been left in his charge. And while the other guards turned a blind, if smirking, eye to his relationship with Female Prisoner 4773, it was only because they were all doing the same thing, if not worse, which did little to change the fact that they were all breaking the law. And not just man's law, Henry Ames feared, but the good Lord's as well.

And yet . . .

And yet . . .

What a joy it had been to slip into her cell near the end of every shift this week and be received by her.

Henry was currently courting Rebecca Holinshed, daughter of the local doctor in Lake Butler, where Henry lived, twelve miles west of the prison. The courtship had been arranged by Henry's aunt, who also lived in Lake Butler and had been charged with keeping an eye on him by her sister, Henry's mother. Rebecca Holinshed was a very pretty blond girl with skin so white it appeared to have been boiled. She had told Henry in her very soft voice that she expected the man she married to have ambition beyond just guarding a pack of filthy women with no more moral center than that of a filthy chimpanzee. Rebecca Holinshed used the word *filthy* a lot, always in the softest of tones, as if hesitant for the word to leave her mouth. She'd also never met Henry's eyes, not once in their whole courtship. If someone were to witness their early evening strolls, that witness could be forgiven for believing Rebecca conversed not with Henry but with the road, the porch, the trunks of trees.

Even so, to prove that he did, in fact, have ambition, Henry had enrolled in criminal law courses at night, all the way over in Gainesville. On his free nights, instead of having a few beers with the other guards at Dickie's Roadhouse, or catching up on laundry, or, God forbid, just relaxing, Henry drove ninety minutes each way to sit in a sweltering box of a room near the rear of the University of Florida campus and listen to Professor Blix, a drunk, disbarred lawyer, slur his way through lectures on fraud in the inducement and motions to compel.

Henry knew it was good for him, though. Knew Rebecca was good for him. She'd make a fine mother. One day soon, he hoped, she might even let him kiss her.

Female Prisoner 4773, however, had already kissed Henry Ames pretty much anyplace he had skin. She'd told him about her son, Peter, and her hopes to reunite with him in five years, maybe move back to Italy with the boy if this war ever ended and Mussolini and his Black Shirts were driven from power. Henry knew she was using him—just because he was small town didn't make him an idiot—but she was using him to achieve safety for her and her son, which seemed a worthy cause. She certainly wasn't asking him to become something he didn't want to become—a lawyer—she was just asking him to help save her life.

So he was making a mistake sleeping with her, yes. Maybe the biggest mistake of his life. One he'd never recover from were it exposed. He'd lose his family over it. He'd lose Rebecca. Lose his job. Probably be shipped off immediately to fight the Nazis, flat feet be damned. Die in some bombed-out village along a stagnant river that no one had ever heard of. Leave behind no offspring, no evidence he'd ever existed. A waste of a life.

So why couldn't he stop smiling?

JOE COUGHLIN, the Tampa businessman with the dubious past and a history of great benevolence toward his adopted home of Ybor City, met that morning with Lieutenant Matthew Biel of Naval Intelligence in his office at Suarez Sugar.

Biel was a young man with blond hair cut so tight to his scalp one could see the pink beneath the bristles. He wore sharply pressed khakis and a black sport coat with contrasting gray plaid sleeves over a white shirt. He smelled of starch.

"If you're trying to look like a civilian," Joe told him, "you might want to study a few more J. C. Penney catalogues."

"That where you shop?"

Joe thought of telling this yahoo what he thought of J. C. Penney—he was wearing a suit that had been hand-tailored in fucking Lisbon, for Christ's sake—but he refrained and poured Biel a cup of coffee instead, brought it around the desk to him.

Biel accepted the coffee with a nod of thanks and said, "This is a very unassuming office for a man of your stature."

Joe sat behind his desk. "Seems appropriate for a vice president of a sugar company."

"You also run three import companies, don't you?"

Joe sipped his coffee.

Biel smiled. "Two distilleries, a phosphate mining concern, and pieces of several businesses back home in Boston, including a bank." He looked around the office again. "That's why your attempts at humility here are so fascinating."

Joe put his coffee cup down on the desk. "How about you tell me why you're here, Lieutenant."

Biel leaned forward. "A guy got beaten on the docks in Port Tampa the other night. You hear about it?"

"A guy gets beaten every night in Port Tampa. It's the docks."

"Yeah, well, this guy was one of ours."

"Whose?"

"Naval Intelligence. Apparently he asked one question too many of some of your guys and—"

"My guys?"

Biel closed his eyes for a second, took a breath, opened them. "Fine. Your friend, Dion Bartolo's guys. Longshoremen's Local 126. That ring a bell?"

Those were Dion's guys all right.

"So some swabbie of yours got the snot kicked out of him. You want me to pay for his dry cleaning?"

"No. He'll recover, thank you."

"Help me sleep, knowing that."

"Thing is," Lieutenant Biel said, "we've got stories like that all over the country—Portland, Boston, New York, Miami, Tampa, New Orleans. Hell, our guy in New Orleans almost died. As it was, he lost an eye."

"Yeah, well," Joe said, "I wouldn't fuck with New Orleans. You tell your guy he's lucky he's not blind *and* dead."

"We can't infiltrate the docks," Biel said. "Every time we get a guy in, he gets his head beat in and sent back to us. We understand now—you own the docks, you rule the waterfront. We're not arguing. But we're not after you. Any of you."

"Who am I?" Joe said. "Who are *we*? I'm a legitimate businessman."

Biel grimaced. "You're the consigliere—did I pronounce that right?—for the Bartolo Family, Mr. Coughlin. You're the fixer for the entire Florida criminal syndicate. On top of that, you and Meyer Lansky control Cuba and the narcotics pipeline that begins somewhere in South America and ends somewhere in Maine. So do we really have to play this game where you're 'retired' and I'm a fucking dunce?"

Joe stared across the desk at him until the silence grew uncomfortable. At the moment when Biel couldn't take it any longer, when he'd opened his mouth to speak, Joe said, "Who're you after then?"

"Nazi saboteurs, Jap saboteurs, anybody who could infiltrate the waterfront and commit violence against the government."

"Well, I'd say you can stop worrying about any Jap infiltration. They tend to stick out, even in San Francisco."

"Fair enough."

"I'd worry about a homegrown Kraut," Joe said, "one who could pass himself off as having mick parents or Swede parents. He'd be a problem."

"Could he infiltrate you?"

"I just said he could. Didn't say it was likely, but it could happen."

"Well, then Uncle Sam needs your help."

"And what's Uncle Sam giving in return?"

"The thanks of a grateful nation and a lack of harassment."

"That's what you call harassment—your men getting their heads handed to them on a regular basis? Well, feel free to harass me any day of the week."

"Your legitimate businesses survive on government contracts right now, Mr. Coughlin."

"Some of them do, yeah."

"We could make that relationship a bit more unwieldy."

"Half an hour after you leave this office, Lieutenant, I'm meeting with a gentleman from the War Department, which wants to increase its orders with me, not decrease them. So, if you're going to play a bluff, son, do it from a more informed place, would you?"

Biel said, "Fine. Tell us what you want."

"You know what we want."

"No," Biel said, "I'm not sure we do."

"We want Charlie Luciano released. Simple as that."

Biel's apple-pie face darkened. "It's out of the question. Lucky Luciano's going to rot in Dannemora for the rest of his natural life."

"Okay. He prefers 'Charlie,' by the way. Only his closest friends call him Lucky."

"Whatever he calls himself, we're not giving him amnesty."

"We're not asking for amnesty," Joe said. "After the war—if, that is, you guys don't fuck it up and we actually win—you deport him. He never steps foot on these shores again."

"But."

"But," Joe said, "he's otherwise free to go where he wants and earn a living however he wants."

Biel shook his head. "FDR'll never go for it."

"It's not *his* decision, is it?"

"At a public relations level? Sure it is. Luciano ran the most violent criminal syndicate this country's ever seen." Biel gave it a little more thought and then shook his head emphatically. "Ask for something else. Anything."

Just like the government. So used to paying for what it wanted with free money that it had no idea how to forge a real business deal. *We'd like something for nothing, please; so give it to us, fuck off, and thank us for the privilege.*

Joe studied Lieutenant Biel's open, all-American face. A quarterback in high school to be sure. All the girls had wanted to wear his letter sweater.

"There's nothing else we want," Joe said.

"So that's *it*?" Biel seemed authentically dumbfounded.

"That's it." Joe leaned back in his chair and lit a cigarette.

Biel stood. "You won't like what we do next then."

"You're the government. Liking what you do has never been one of my weaknesses."

"Don't say you weren't warned."

"You've heard our price," Joe said.

Biel stopped at the door, his head down. "We have a file on you, Mr. Coughlin."

"I would have assumed."

"It's not as thick as most because you are very, very good at hiding in plain sight. Never came across anyone who does it as slickly as you. Around the office, know what they call you?"

Joe shrugged.

"The Runner. Because you've been running the table for longer than anyone can remember. But you own a casino in Havana, don't you?"

Joe nodded.

"So you know that luck ends."

Joe smiled. "Message received, Lieutenant."

"Was it?" Biel asked and let himself out.

TEN MINUTES AFTER BIEL LEFT, Joe's intercom buzzed.

He depressed the send button. "Yes, Margaret."

Margaret Toomey, his secretary, said, "There's a gentleman out here to see you. He says he's a guard at the prison in Raiford. He claims it's urgent you speak to him."

Joe lifted the receiver off the cradle. "Tell him to fuck off," he said kindly.

"I tried," Margaret said, "in so many words."

"Then use the exact ones."

"He said to tell you 'Theresa Del Fresco asks for an audience.'"

"Shit, really?" Joe said.

"Shit really," Margaret said.

Joe gave it some thought for a bit and eventually sighed. "Send him in. He a yokel or an operator?"

"The former, sir. He's on his way."

The boy who came through the door looked like he'd climbed out of a playpen. His hair was so blond it was almost white and a sprig of it rose like a crooked finger from the crown. His skin was so unblemished it appeared he'd put it on for the first time this afternoon. His eyes were green and clear as a baby's, and his teeth were as white as his hair.

This child was a *guard*? In the women's wing?

Theresa Del Fresco would have zeroed in on this kid like a town cat on a country mouse.

Joe shook the boy's hand and gestured toward a chair. The boy took it, hitching his trousers at the knees.

The boy explained that he was, in fact, a guard at the Wom-

en's Correctional Wing of the State Prison at Raiford and that
Female Prisoner 4773, or Theresa Del Fresco as she'd been known
in free society, had asked him to visit Mr. Coughlin, sir, because
she believed his life—and her own—was in danger.

"Your life?" Joe asked.

The boy was befuddled. "No, no, sir. Yours."

Joe laughed.

The boy said, "Sir?"

Joe laughed harder. The idea became funnier the more he
thought about it.

"That's her play?" he said as the chuckles began to die away.

"Her play, sir? I'm not following."

Joe wiped his eye with the heel of his hand. "Ah, Jesus. So, yes,
yes, Mrs. Del Fresco thinks my life is in grave danger?"

"And her own."

"Well, at least she's not trying to sell it as a selfless act."

"I'm confused, Mr. Coughlin, and I'm not afraid to say so.
Mrs. Del Fresco has asked me to drive a great distance to tell you
your life is in danger and hers as well, and you act like it's all some
kind of big joke. Well, it's not a very funny one, sir, I'll tell you
what."

Joe looked across the desk at the kid. "You through?"

The boy moved his hat from one knee to the other and tugged
nervously on his right earlobe. "Well, I don't rightly know, sir."

Joe came around his desk and stood in front of the kid and
offered him a cigarette. The boy took one, his hand shaking slightly,
and Joe lit it for him and then lit his own. He placed an ashtray on
the desk beside his hip and took a long drag before he addressed
Henry Ames again.

"Son, I have no doubt that Mrs. Del Fresco has, in her befriend-
ing of you, shown you a banquet of lascivious delights. And I—"

"Sir, I will not allow you to suggest impropriety in the character of either myself or Mrs. Del Fresco."

"Oh, shut the fuck up, kid," Joe said kindly and patted the boy's shoulder. "Where was I? Right. I'm sure fucking Mrs. Del Fresco and being fucked by her has been the high point of your life thus far and, judging strictly on appearance, will remain the high point until you die."

The boy had, if possible, turned whiter. He stared back at Joe like he'd been stricken by an embolism.

"And you should consider that far from trying to aid Mrs. Del Fresco in her plan to get out of prison, you should be doing everything in your power to make sure she stays there and takes you into her bunk and squeaks the springs for as long as she decides to do so." He smiled and patted the boy once more on the shoulder and headed back around his desk. "Now go home, son. Go on." Joe sat back down and flicked his fingers at the boy.

Henry Ames blinked several times and stood. He played with the inside of his hat as he walked to the door and fiddled with the brim as he stood there. "They've already tried to kill her twice. Once on the bus over, the second time in the shower. My uncle worked in Raiford his whole life; he said once they start trying to kill you, they finish the job eventually. So they'll . . ." He looked at the doorknob and then back at the floor, his jaw working. "They'll kill her. She told me she knows they will. And then they'll kill you."

"Who's they, son?" Joe tapped his cigarette ash into the tray.

"Only she knows." The boy stared across the office at Joe, more grit in him than Joe had originally suspected. "But she told me to give you one name."

"The name of the person coming to kill me? Or the man who hired him?"

"I have no idea, sir. She just said to give you the name."

Joe stubbed out his cigarette. He could tell the kid was thinking about walking out, now that he had Joe on a hook, however small. There was a defiance in him that most of his friends and neighbors probably never saw. You might be able to push this boy around, but pushing him into a corner could be a mistake.

"Well?" Joe said.

"And you'll help her? If I give you the name?"

Joe shook his head. "Didn't say that. Your girlfriend started out as a bunco artist who turned into a grifter and then a damn good thief and then a contract killer. She doesn't have any friends because they're too afraid that at some point she'll con them, rob them, or kill them. Or all three. So sorry, son, you can shoo right the fuck out that door and take the name with you and I won't lose a wink of sleep over it. But if you feel like telling me, then—"

The kid nodded and walked out the door.

Joe couldn't believe it. Boy had some *sand*.

He picked up the phone and called down to Richie Cavelli, who manned the back door, through which the majority of their business entered the building. He told him to get up to the front and stop the blond kid on his way out the main door.

Joe took his suit coat off the back of his chair and put it on and headed out of the office.

But Henry Ames was waiting for him in the reception area, hat still in hand.

"Will you agree to see her?"

Joe looked around reception—Margaret clacking away on her Corona, squinting through her own cigarette smoke; a salesman from a grain wholesaler down in Naples; a flunky from the War Department. Joe gave them all a friendly nod—*Go back to your magazines; nothing to see here*—and met the boy's eyes.

"Sure, kid," he said. Just to get him out of the office.

The boy nodded and fiddled with the brim of his hat again. He looked up at Joe. "Gil Valentine."

Joe kept the light smile on his face even as the splash of ice water found his heart and testicles at the same time.

"That's the name she gave you, huh?"

"Gil Valentine," the kid said again and put on his hat. "Good day to you, sir."

"And to you, son."

"I'll expect to see you soon, sir."

Joe said nothing and the boy tipped his hat to Margaret and let himself out. Joe said, "Margaret, call down to Richie. Tell him to forget the order I just gave him and go back to what he was doing. He's at the front door phone."

"Yes, Mr. Coughlin."

Joe smiled at the flunky from the War Department. "David, right?"

The man stood. "Yes, Mr. Coughlin."

"Come on in," Joe said. "I understand Uncle Sam needs some more alcohol."

ALL THROUGH THE MEETING with the fella from the War Department and the subsequent one with Wylie Wholesale, Joe couldn't get his mind off Gil Valentine. Gil Valentine had been something of an exemplar in their thing. He'd come up, like most of them, during the glory days of Prohibition and was both a hell of a distiller and a bootlegger. But what he really had was an ear. Gil could sit in the back row of a revue and single out the one singer-dancer out of twenty who was going to be a star. He wandered nightclubs and juke joints all over the country—St. Louis, St. Paul, Cicero, Chicago, down into Helena, Greenwood and Memphis,

and out into the glitter of New York and the sparkle of Miami—
and he came back with some of the greatest recording artists the
mob ever owned. By the time alcohol was legal again, he was one of
the few guys, like Joe, who'd prepared for a seamless transition into
mostly legitimate business.

Gil Valentine took his whole operation west. When he arrived
in L.A., he paid proper tribute to Mickey Cohen and Jack Dragna,
even though he wasn't doing much of anything illegal anymore. He
created Cupid's Arrow Records and unfurled a seemingly endless
ribbon of hits. He continued paying a cut to the men in Kansas
City who'd given him his start and kicked back to any of the families who'd been in charge of any of the clubs where he'd found his
acts. In the spring of '39, he packaged a tour that combined the
Hart Sisters with the Johnny Stark Orchestra, the Negro singers
Elmore Richards and Toots McGeeks, and the two biggest heart-
throb crooners in the country, Vic Boyer and Frankie Blake. Every
city they scheduled, they had to add two more dates to deal with
the demand. It was the biggest music tour in the history of North
America, and the boys in KC and all the other boys across the
country who owned a piece, however big or small, took their cut.

Gil Valentine was the U.S. Mint with a revolving door instead
of a vault; he made money, hand over fist, for his friends. And they
didn't have to do anything but spend it. Gil made no enemies. He
lived a quiet life in the Holmby Hills with his wife, Masie; two
daughters in braces; and a son who ran track for Beverly Hills High
School. He had no mistress, no addictions, no enemies.

In the summer of 1940, someone disappeared Gil Valentine
from a parking lot in West Los Angeles. For six months, Cohen's
men, Dragna's men, and wiseguys from all over the country scoured
L.A. for the mob's golden boy. Hands were broken, heads were
dented, knees were caved in, but no one knew shit.

And one day, while most of the searchers were chasing a rumor of indeterminate origin that Gil Valentine had been sighted sipping cervezas in the Mexican fishing village of Puerto Nuevo, just south of Tijuana, his son came home from an early morning errand and found his father in canvas bags all over the backyard of the house in Holmby Hills. There was a bag for each arm, a bag for each hand. A big bag that contained his chest, a smaller one that contained his head. Thirteen bags in all.

And no one—not the bosses in KC or the bosses in L.A. or all the hundreds of men who'd searched for him, nor any of his associates in legitimate or illegitimate enterprises—knew why he was dead.

Three years later, few spoke his name. To speak it meant you acknowledged that there were some things beyond the reach of the most powerful business syndicate in the Western Hemisphere. Because the message of Gil Valentine's death grew clearer as time passed, and it was a simple message: Anyone can be killed. At any time. For any reason.

After the salesman from Wylie Wholesale left, Joe sat in his office and looked out the window at the collection of warehouses and factories that spilled all the way down to the port. Then he picked up the phone and told Margaret to look for spaces in his schedule in the next week when he might have time to take a quick trip to Raiford.

CHAPTER THREE

Father and Son

JOE COUGHLIN'S SON, Tomas, was almost ten years old and didn't lie. It was an embarrassing trait he certainly hadn't inherited from his father. Joe came from a family tree whose branches had bent over the centuries with the weight of troubadours, publicans, writers, revolutionaries, magistrates, and policemen—liars all—and now here was his son getting them both in trouble with Miss Narcisa because she'd asked him what he thought of her hair, and Tomas told her it looked fake.

Miss Narcisa Rusen was the governess of their house in Ybor. She stocked the icebox, laundered the sheets twice a week, cooked their meals, and looked after Tomas whenever Joe had to go away on business, which was often. She was fifty, at least, but dyed her hair every few months. Many women her age did, but most made some concession to their actual age. Miss Narcisa, on the other hand, instructed the colorist at Continental Beauty Shop to dye her hair the black of wet road on a moonless night. Which made her chalk-white skin stand out all the more.

"It looks fake," Tomas said as they drove to Sacred Heart in downtown Tampa on Sunday morning.

"But you don't *tell* her that."

"She asked."

"So you tell her what she wants to hear."

"But that's lying."

"Well," Joe tried to keep the frustration from his voice, "it's a white lie. There's a difference."

"What's the difference?"

"White lies are harmless and small. Regular lies are big and hurtful."

Tomas looked at his father, eyes narrowing.

Even Joe didn't understand his own explanation. He tried again. "If you do something bad, and me or one of the nuns or priests or Miss Narcisa asks if you did that thing, then you say yes or otherwise you're lying and that's not good."

"It's a sin."

"It's a sin," Joe agreed, already feeling like his nine-year-old son was setting him up. "But if you tell a woman she looks nice in that dress, even though you don't think so, or you tell a friend—" Joe snapped his fingers. "What's the name of that friend of yours wears the huge glasses?"

"Matthew?"

"Matthew Rigert, right. So if you tell Matthew he's an okay ballplayer, that's being nice, right?"

"But I wouldn't tell him that. He can't hit. He can't catch. He throws six feet over my head."

"But if he asked you if he might get better someday?"

"I'd say I doubted it."

Joe looked over at his son and wondered how it was they were related. "You take after your mother."

"You say that a lot lately."

"Do I? Well, must be true then."

Tomas was dark-haired like his mother but had thin features like his father—thin nose and lips, pronounced jawline and cheekbones. He had his mother's dark eyes but unfortunately her vision too; he'd worn glasses since he was six. He was, for the most part, a quiet boy, but that quiet masked a passion and flair for the dramatic that Joe attributed to his mother. It also hid a sly sense of humor and appreciation for the absurd that had defined Joe when he was that age.

Joe turned onto Twiggs, the spire of Sacred Heart coming into view as the traffic slowed to a bumper-to-bumper crawl, the church three blocks away, its parking lots filling and the lines backing out onto the streets. You couldn't get near the lots on a Sunday unless you arrived half an hour before mass began. And even then you were cutting it close. Joe looked at his watch—forty-five minutes early.

In the spring of '43, everyone prayed. The church could hold eight hundred, and every pew would be packed tighter than a roll of nickels. Some mothers prayed for sons overseas. Others for the souls of those recently returned in coffins. Wives and girlfriends did the same. Undrafted men prayed for a second shot with the draft board or, secretly, that their number would never be called. Fathers prayed for their sons to come home or, barring that, that the lad comport himself well on the field of battle; whatever becomes of him, Lord, please don't let him show cowardice. People of all stripes knelt and prayed that the war stayed There and never reached Here again. Some, sensing End Days,

asked God to take note of them, to see them for what they were—
members of His team, pious and supplicant.

Joe craned his head to see how many cars idled between him
and the nearest parking lot entrance. The lot just past Morgan
Street was still a good twenty cars away. Brake lights flared ahead
of him and he came to another lurching stop. The chief of police
and his wife passed on the sidewalk chatting with Rance Tuckston,
the president of First National Bank. Just behind them was Hayley
Gramercy, the owner of the All American food store chain, and his
wife, Trudy.

"Hey," Tomas said, "there's Uncle D," and waved his hand.

"He can't see us," Joe said.

Dion Bartolo, head of the crime family that bore his name,
exited a lot ahead on the right that had a FULL sign propped by the
entrance. He was flanked by two of his bodyguards, Mike Aubrey
and Geoff the Finn. Dion was a big man and usually a fat one, but
his clothes had begun to hang on him lately, and his cheeks had
grown long. There were rumors floating through their circles of
associates and partners that he was sick. Joe, who knew him better than anyone, knew that wasn't the case. Not that anybody else
needed to know the truth.

Dion buttoned his suit jacket and indicated his men should
do the same, the three of them the picture of brute power as they
strode toward the church. Joe had known that kind of power; he'd
had bodyguards with him day and night. And he didn't miss it.
Not for an instant. What they didn't tell you about absolute power
was that it was never absolute; the instant you had it, someone had
already lined up to try to take it away. Princes could sleep soundly,
but never kings. The ear was always tuned for the creak on the
floorboard, the whine of a hinge.

Joe checked the cars ahead of him—ten, maybe nine.

All the front-pew celebrities were on the streets or milling in front of the church now. The handsome young mayor, Jonathan Belgrave, and his pretty, even younger wife, Vanessa, exchanged pleasantries with Allison Picott and Deborah Minshew, both young wives who had husbands serving overseas. If Allison's and Deborah's husbands didn't make it back, the society scuttlebutt went, they'd survive the blows better than most; both were daughters of two of Tampa's original families, those with streets and hospital wings named after them. Both husbands, on the other hand, had married up.

Tomas turned a page of his history book—he was always reading, this kid—and said, "I told you we'd be late."

"We're not late," Joe said. "We're still early. Other people are just, you know, early-early."

His son gave him a cocked eyebrow.

Joe watched the traffic light at the next intersection go from red to green. As they sat there, without a single car moving, it turned yellow and then red again. To distract himself he turned on the radio, expecting the war news that was a constant, as if there were no other news, as if people didn't need weather reports or stock reports anymore. He was unpleasantly surprised, however, with a breathless account of last night's mass narcotics arrest on the outskirts of Ybor City.

"Here in the Negro section of the city just south of Eleventh Avenue," the reporter said in a tone that intimated he was speaking of a neighborhood where only the fearless or foolish dared tread, "police confiscated an estimated fourteen pounds of narcotics and exchanged gunfire with brutal gangsters, both Negroes and Italian nationals. Captain Edson Miller, of the Tampa PD, reports that his men are looking into the background of all arrested Italians to ensure that none were saboteurs sent to these shores by Mussolini himself. Four suspects were killed by police, while a fifth, Walter Grimes, committed suicide in custody. Captain Miller also stated that police had been watching the narcotics warehouse for some months before they swooped in yesterday eve—"

Joe shut off the radio before he could hear another lie. Wally Grimes had been about as suicidal as the sun, all of the "Italian nationals" had been born here, and the narcotics "warehouse" hadn't been anything of the sort. It had been a cooking facility and it had gone into operation for the first time Friday night, so it was impossible for anyone to have been watching it for a week, never mind a month.

Worse than all the lies, however, were the bodies that had been lost, including a master cook and several excellent street soldiers in a time when brave, able-bodied men were increasingly hard to come by.

"Am I a nigger?" Tomas asked.

Joe's head snapped on its neck. *"What?"*

Tomas chin-gestured at the radio. "Am I?"

"Who called you that?"

"Martha Comstock. Some kids were calling me a spic, but Martha said, 'No, he's a nigger.'"

"She's that triple-chinned little troll never shuts the fuck up?"

A smile found Tomas's face for a moment. "That's her."

"And she called you that?"

"It doesn't bother me," he said.

"I know it bothers you. Question is how much."

"Well, how nigger am I?"

"Hey," Joe said, "you ever heard me use that word?"

"No."

"You know why?"

"No."

"Because *I* got no problem with it, but your mother hated it."

"Well, then, how colored am I?"

Joe shrugged. "I know some of her ancestors came from the slave class. So the bloodline probably started in Africa, got mixed with Spanish and maybe even a white guy or two in the woodpile." His father applied the brake as the car ahead of them lurched to a stop. He laid his head back against the seat for a moment. "Something I loved about your mother's face was that the whole world was in it. I'd look at her sometimes and I'd see some *condesa* walking through her vineyard in Spain. Other times, I'd see a tribeswoman carrying water from the river. I'd see your ancestors crossing deserts and oceans or walking the streets of the Old City with puffy sleeves and swords in their scabbards." The car ahead moved and he eased off the brake and popped the gearshift into first and his head came off the seat. He sighed so softly Tomas doubted he heard it himself. "Your mother had a hell of a beautiful face."

"And you saw all that in it?"

"Not every day. Most days I just saw your mom." He looked over at his son. "But after a few drinks, you never knew."

Tomas chuckled and Joe gave his neck a firm pat.

"Did people call my mother a nigger?"

That cold thing entered his father's eyes—a grayness that could freeze boiling water. "Not around me."

"But you knew they thought it."

His father's face became mild again, benign. "Never cared much what strangers thought, kid."

"Dad," Tomas said, "do you care what *anyone* thinks?"

"Care what you think," Joe said. "And your mom."

"She's dead."

"Yeah, but I like to think she sees us." His father rolled down his window and lit a cigarette. He held the cigarette in his left hand

and dropped his arm along the outside of the door. "I care what your uncle Dion thinks."

"Even though he's not your brother."

"In a lotta ways he's more a brother to me than my real brothers." His father brought his hand into the car to smoke, draped it back down the door as he exhaled. "I cared about what my father thought, but that would have been news to him. That's pretty much the end of the list." He shot his son a sad smile. "I don't have room in my heart for most people. Got nothing against them, but I got nothing for them, either. "

"Even the people in the war?"

"I don't know those people." His father stared out the window. "Frankly, I could give a shit whether they live or die."

Tomas thought of all the dead in Europe and Russia and the Pacific. Sometimes he dreamed of thousands of them spread bloody and broken in dark fields or stone piazzas, limbs turned in the wrong direction, mouths open and frozen. He wished he could pick up a rifle and fight for them, save just one of them.

His father, on the other hand, looked at the war like he looked at most things—as an opportunity to make more money.

"So I shouldn't let it bother me?" Tomas said after a while.

"No," his father said. "Sticks and stones and all that."

"Okay. I'll try."

"Good man."

His father looked over at him and gave him a confident smile, as if that could fix things, and they finally turned into the lot.

They passed Rico DiGiacomo as he was exiting the lot. Rico had been Joe's bodyguard until Joe realized, about six years ago, that he didn't need a bodyguard anymore, and even if he did, Rico was too smart and talented to be mired in the position. Rico rapped his knuckles on Joe's hood and shot him the smile he was famous for, the kind of smile that could light a football field at night long enough to call a few final plays. He was flanked by his mother, Olivia, and his brother, Freddy, the old lady like something out of a Karloff movie, a malignant vision dressed all in black who'd floated in off the moors while everyone was sleeping.

As the DiGiacomos moved on, Tomas asked, "What if there are no spots left?"

"We're one car away," Joe said.

"But what if his is the last car to get in?"

"How does it help me to think about that?"

"I just thought you should consider the possibility."

Joe stared at his son. "Are you sure we're related?"

"You tell me," Tomas said and went back to his book.

CHAPTER FOUR

Absence

JOE AND TOMAS SAT IN THE BACK OF THE CHURCH, not just because they were later in arriving than most of the parishioners, but because Joe preferred the back of any room he found himself in.

In addition to Dion (front pew on the left) and Rico DiGiacomo (fifth pew back on the right), Joe picked up a few more of his associates in the room—killers to a man—and wondered what Jesus would feel if He were, in fact, looking down and had access to their thoughts.

Wait, Jesus would be thinking, *you've missed the point.*

Up on the altar, Father Ruttle's sermon was about hell. He hit all the notes about fire and demons with pitchforks, birds plucking at your liver, but then he took it to a place Joe hadn't been expecting.

"But what is worse than all those punishments? Genesis tells us that our Lord looked down on Adam and said, 'It is not good that man should be alone.' And so the Lord created Eve. Now Eve brought turmoil and betrayal into Paradise, it is true, and condemned us all to suffer the consequences of Original Sin. That is true and the Lord would have known this would happen because He knows all. But yet He created her for Adam? Why? Ask yourselves that—why?"

Joe glanced around the church, tried to find someone besides Tomas who genuinely appeared to be contemplating the question. Most parishioners looked like they were contemplating grocery lists or the evening meal.

"He made Eve," Father Ruttle said, "because seeing Adam alone was more than He could bear. Being alone, you see, is the worst of hell's punishments." He hit the pulpit with the side of his fist and the congregation woke up. "Hell is the absence of God." Again the side of his fist found the ornate wood. "It is the absence of light. It is the absence of love." His neck strained as he looked out on the eight hundred souls arrayed before him. "Do you understand?"

They weren't Baptists; they weren't supposed to answer. But murmurs rolled through the throng.

"Believe in the Lord," the priest said.

"Honor Him, and repent your sins," he said, "and you shall know Him in heaven."

"But repent not?" He looked out at them again. "And you shall be cast from His sight."

It was his voice, Joe realized, that had gripped them. Normally it was dry and benign, but the morning's sermon had altered it, had altered him. He'd spoken with an air of desperation and loss, as if what he'd preached—hell as an infinite and impregnable void—was almost too despairing for the aging priest to contemplate.

"All rise."

Joe and Tomas stood with the rest of the congregation. Joe had never had trouble repenting. In so far as a man with his sins could repent, he had poured tens of thousands of dollars into hospitals, schools, shelters, roads, and plumbing, not just in Boston, where he'd grown up and owned several interests, or in Ybor City, his adopted hometown, but in Cuba, where he lived much of the year in the western tobacco country.

But for the next few minutes, he did think the old priest might have a point. One of Joe's deepest secrets was how completely he feared loneliness. He didn't fear being alone—in fact he liked it— but the solitude he constructed was one that could always be broken with the snap of his fingers. He surrounded his solitude with work, philanthropy, parenting. He controlled it.

As a child, he'd had no control over it. It was foisted upon him, along with the irony that those who seemed most adamant that he grow up a lonely child slept in the next room.

He looked down at his son and ran his hand down the back of his head. Tomas gave him a slightly startled, curious look but followed it with a soft smile. Then he turned his head back toward the altar.

You will have a lot of doubts about me as you grow older, Joe thought as he put his hand on the back of his son's neck and left it there, but you will never feel unloved, unwanted, or alone.

CHAPTER FIVE

Negotiations

THE MILLING ABOUT after mass often lasted as long as the mass itself.

In the fresh morning light outside the church, Mayor Belgrave and his wife paused at the top of the steps, and the crowd swarmed them. Dion acknowledged Joe with a tilt of his head and Joe returned the nod. He and Tomas worked their way through the crowd, turned the corner of the church, and headed for the back. Behind the church was the parochial school with a fenced-in school yard where The Boys met every Sunday to discuss business. There was a second school yard attached to the first, a smaller one for the kids in the early grades, and that's where the wives and the children gathered.

As Joe stopped outside the first school yard, Tomas headed for the second to join the other children. A feeling of helplessness, even minor grief, passed through Joe as he watched his son walk away.

Life was loss; Joe understood this. But lately he'd felt it more acutely than ever before. His son was eight years away from entering college, and every time he walked away toward anything—anything at all—Joe felt as if he were walking right out of his life.

Joe had worried that a boy growing up without a mother would become too hard, too tough. Tomas had grown up with nothing but masculine influences around him—even Miss Narcisa with her brusque ways, stern face, and icy revulsion toward sentiment was, as Dion had noted on numerous occasions, more male than most of them. The boy had also grown up in a soldier's culture, where the men around him wore guns somewhere on their person—he'd have to have been blind not to notice a few of them over the years—and a couple of those men had disappeared. Where they went, Tomas couldn't know because no one ever mentioned them again. It surprised Joe to watch his son, with no softness in his life, develop into a quiet, gentle boy. If he found a heat-sick lizard on the gallery (and that's where you usually found them in the summer, already calcifying), he would slide a matchbook under it and carry it down to the garden, release it into the moist earth beneath dark leaves. When he was younger, he'd always befriended the boys who were bullied at home or bullied at school. He wasn't athletic, or maybe he just wasn't interested. His grades were only so-so, yet all his teachers agreed he was smart for his age. He liked to paint. And sketch in thick pencil. The paintings were usually cityscapes, the buildings always slanted for some reason, as if all cities were built on crumbling land. The sketches were all of his mother. There was only one photograph of her in the house and half of her face was in shadow, but the sketches he drew over the years picked up an uncanny resemblance for a nine-year-old boy who'd just reached his second birthday when she died.

Joe asked him about it once. "How do you know what she looks like off one picture? Do you remember her?"

"No," the boy said. There was no loss in his voice. It was as if Joe had asked him about anything else from that time period—Do you remember your crib? Your teddy bear? That dog we had in Cuba that ran into the path of a tobacco truck? No.

"So how is it you draw her face so well?"

"You."

"Me?"

Tomas nodded. "You compared things to her a lot. You'd say, 'Your mother's hair was that color but thicker," or 'Your mother had those beauty marks, but they were along her collarbone.'"

Joe said, "I did, huh?"

Another nod. "I don't think you realize how much you used to talk about her."

"Used to?"

His son looked at him. "You don't anymore. Not much anyway."

Joe knew the reason why, even if his son didn't, and he sent a silently apology to Graciela. Yes, honey, you—even you—fade.

DION SHOOED HIS BODYGUARDS off to the side and he and Joe exchanged handshakes, then stood in the long shadows of the church and waited for the brothers DiGiacomo.

Dion and Joe had been friends since they were kids running the streets of South Boston. They'd been outlaws, then criminals, then gangsters together. Dion had once worked for Joe. Now Joe worked for Dion. Kind of. The specifics could get cloudy. Joe was no longer a boss and Dion was. But Joe was an active member of the Commission. A boss had more power than any single member of the Commission, but the Commission had more power than any one boss. It complicated things at times.

Rico and Freddy didn't keep them waiting, though Rico and his matinee-idol looks and charm pressed a lot of flesh on his way over. Freddy, on the other hand, looked as sullen and confused as ever. He was the older of the two, but his younger brother had received all the proceeds from the genetic jackpot. Rico got the looks, the charm, and the intelligence. Freddy just got the itch for thinking the world owed him something. Everyone admitted Freddy was a good earner—though, not surprisingly, not nearly as good as his brother—but given his taste for needless violence and some question regarding his sexual appetites, it was common knowledge that if Rico weren't his brother, he'd still be a foot soldier.

They all shook hands, Rico adding a slug to Joe's shoulder and a pinch of Dion's jowl before they got down to it.

The first order of business was what they should do for Shel Gold's family now that Shel had caught some kind of muscle disease that confined him to a wheelchair. Shel was a Jew and so not part of the Family, but they'd made a lot of money with him over the years and he was funny as all hell. At first, when he'd begun falling for no discernible reasons and one of his eyelids had started to droop, they thought he was just having everyone on. But now he was in the wheelchair and he couldn't speak too well and he twitched a lot. He was only forty-five, had three kids with the wife, Esther, and another three scattered around the darker parts of town. They decided to slip Esther five hundred bucks and a fruit basket.

The next item for consideration was whether to ask the Commission to open the books for Paul Battalia, who'd turned things around with the sanitation locals and had doubled the book he'd inherited from Salvy LaPretto in six months, which confirmed most people's opinion that Salvy, six months dead after three strokes in one week, had been the laziest gangster since Ralph Capone.

Rico DiGiacomo wondered if Paul was too young to be made. Six years ago, Joe had encouraged Rico—back then, just a kid, maybe nineteen, Jesus—to think bigger. Now Rico owned several bookmaking joints, two whorehouses, and a phosphate transport company. Plus, most lucratively, he owned a piece of just about every man who worked the docks. And, much like Joe, he'd seemed to have managed it without making many enemies. A miracle in their business far more impressive than turning water into wine or parting a parched sea at low tide. When Dion pointed out that Paul was a year older than Rico himself had been when he'd been welcomed into the Outfit, they both looked to Joe. Joe, an Irishman, could never be a made guy, but as a member of the Commission, he best knew what Battalia's chances would be.

"I'm not saying exceptions can't be made," Joe said, "but the book is pretty much closed for the duration of the thing in Europe. Question is whether Paul is that exception." He looked at Dion. "Is he?"

"He can ride the bench another year," Dion said.

Over in the other school yard, Mrs. DiGiacomo swatted at a kid who ran too close to her. Freddy, the more dutiful of the sons, kept his eyes on her. Or, Joe wondered not for the first time, was that all his eyes fell on over there? Sometimes Freddy found reason to retrieve his mother before she exited on her own, and he would always come out of there with sweat on his upper lip, a sodden, distracted look in his eyes.

This morning, though, he looked away from his mother and the school yard full of kids quickly enough, and held the morning paper to his chest. "Anybody want to talk about it?"

Taking up the lower-right-hand corner of the front page was an article on the bust at the cook house in Brown Town.

"How much this cost us?" Dion asked, looking at Joe and Rico.

"In the right now?" Joe said. "About two hundred thousand."

"What?"

Joe nodded. "That was two months' supply that got wiped out in there."

Rico chimed in. "But that's not including what happens when our competitors fill the void and build some customer loyalty. It also doesn't include the loss of personnel—one of Montooth's is dead, one of ours, plus nine in jail. Half the guys in jail ran book, the other half ran policy. We gotta cover their routes, we gotta find replacements, bump guys up, find guys to replace *those guys*. It's a mess."

Dion said what no one wanted to. "How'd they know?"

Rico threw his hands softly in the air. Joe let out a long breath.

Freddy stated the obvious. "We got a fucking rat in our crew. Or the niggers got one in theirs. I'm betting the niggers."

"Why?" Joe said.

Freddy couldn't follow. "'Cause they're niggers, Joe."

"You don't think they know they'd be the first people we'd blame if we lost nearly a quarter million dollars' worth of product? Montooth Dix is a smart guy. A fucking legend. And he's gonna rat us out? For what?"

"Who knows?" Freddy said. "He took a pinch we don't know about. They caught one of his wives without a green card. Who knows what it takes to turn a nigger into a rat?"

Joe looked at Dion, who was holding out his hands, as if to say Freddy had a point.

"The only two people outside of us who knew where the cook house was going to be," Dion said, "was Montooth Dix and Wally Grimes."

"And Wally Grimes," Rico said, "is no longer with us."

"Which is convenient," Joe said, looking over at Freddy, "if someone, say, wanted to push Montooth Dix out of the policy and narcotics businesses in Brown Town."

"You saying someone *framed* Montooth Dix for being a rat?" Freddy said, a curious smile on his face.

"No," Joe said. "I'm just noting that if Montooth *is* the rat, that works out real well for anyone who covets the coin he's making down there."

"I'm here to make money. Why the good Lord"—Freddy blessed himself quickly—"put us on this earth." He shrugged. "I don't apologize for it. Montooth Dix is earning so much, he's a threat to all of us."

"Or just you?" Joe asked. "I hear your crew's been tuning up some of the coloreds down there, Freddy."

"We get pushed, Joe, we're gonna push back."

"And you don't think they feel the same way?"

"But, Joe," Freddy said reasonably, "they're niggers."

Besides being vain, arrogant, and secretly convinced that he'd never met a man as smart as himself, Joe Coughlin had also killed, stolen, maimed, and assaulted his way through his thirty-seven years on the planet. So he rarely felt like he held the moral high ground over anyone. But he could live a hundred lives and never understand the bigots in his midst. Seemed every race had been the niggers of someplace at some point in their history. And as soon as the black niggers got respectable, the next scapegoat race would be duly designated, maybe by the very niggers who'd just escaped into respectability.

He wondered, and not for the first time, how any of them had allowed a guy like Freddy to head up his own crew. But it was the same problem everyone was having during this war—you just couldn't find good help. Plus, he was Rico's brother, and sometimes you just had to take the bad with the good.

Joe said to Dion, "So what about it?"

Dion stoked his cigar, one eye clenched shut. "We figure out a way to find this rat. Until then, no one does anything. No one causes any trouble." He opened the eye and fixed it on Freddy and Rico. "Clear?"

"Crystal," Rico said.

TOMAS FOUND HIS FATHER in the outer school yard and they walked back around to the front of the church. They were heading for Twiggs when the mayor and his wife crossed their path. The mayor gave Joe a tip of the hat. His young wife gave Joe and Tomas a bright, if distant, smile.

"Mr. Mayor," the mayor said to Joe with a hearty laugh and a firm handshake.

Back when Joe had run things in the 1920s and early 1930s, the Cubans and Spaniards had dubbed him "Mayor of Ybor." Even now, the nickname showed up as a parenthetical in some newspaper articles when he was mentioned.

Joe could tell by the pinched look on Vanessa Belgrave's face that she wasn't a fan of the nickname.

Joe shook the man's hand. "You're the leader of this city, sir. Of that there's no doubt. You know my son, Tomas?"

Jonathan Belgrave hitched his pants and bent to shake Tomas's hand. "How are you, Tomas?"

"Fine, sir. Thank you."

"I understand you're fluent in Spanish."

"Yes, sir."

"You'll have to sit at my side next time I negotiate with Circulo Cubano and the cigar workers' unions."

"Yes, sir."

"Very good, son. Very good." The mayor chuckled, clapped Tomas's shoulder, and straightened. "And you know Vanessa, of course."

"Mrs. Mayor," Joe said.

"Mr. Coughlin."

Even in the elite circles of Tampa where snobbery and an ice-cold demeanor were considered de rigueur, the chill Vanessa Belgrave reserved for people she deemed not up to snuff was legendary.

And she didn't like Joe at all. He'd turned down a request from her once because she'd presented herself as someone due a favor, not someone asking for one. Her husband had just been elected mayor and wasn't nearly as powerful as he was now, but Joe had smoothed it over with him anyway, as a matter of good form, granting him the loan of a crane to place a statue of Major Francis Dade in front of the new waterworks building. These days, the mayor and Joe met for a drink and a steak at Bern's every now and again, but Vanessa Belgrave made it clear her feelings would not be smoothed over, her opinion would not change. She'd been overheard referring to Joe as "the Yankee gangster with the Yankee lack of manners and the Yankee lack of tact."

The mayor beamed an expectant smile at his wife. "Ask him."

Joe cocked his head slightly and squared himself to the young woman. Her reputation was so intimidating he often forgot how pretty she was, her lips the same color as her hair—a red as dark as dried blood.

"Ask me?"

She could tell he was enjoying this and it brought a slight curl to the left side of her mouth before she fixed her electric blue eyes on him. "You're aware of my foundation?"

"Of course," Joe said.

"Like most charitable foundations during a war, it's fallen on hard times, I don't mind telling you."

"I'm sorry to hear that."

"Yours seem to flourish, however."

"I'm sorry?"

"Come, Mr. Coughlin, your charities here in Tampa. I see you just built a new Corrales Shelter for Women in Lutz."

"That's a direct result *of* the war," Joe said. "Even more women are finding themselves without husbands or means to support their children. Even more children are losing their fathers."

"Well, sure," Jonathan Belgrave said, "there's a lot of truth to that theory, Joe. But even so, any charity not benefiting the war effort has taken a massive hit to its coffers. Yet yours seem to keep chugging along. Why, that party you threw just before Christmas, I bet that raised a pretty penny."

Joe chuckled as he lit a cigarette. "So what do you want—my donor lists?"

"Actually," Vanessa said, "that's exactly what I'd like."

Joe coughed as he exhaled. "You're serious?"

"Well, it's hardly as gauche as asking you to hand me the list right here. I'd like to offer you a position on the board of the Sloane Benevolence Foundation."

Vanessa Belgrave was born Vanessa Sloane, and grew up the only child of Arthur and Eleanor Sloane of Atlanta. The Sloane family—of lumber, of banking, of textiles, of summers on Jekyll Island, of two semiannual galas that set the high-water mark for all other gatherings in southern society each season—could claim generals in both the Revolutionary War and the Civil War. The Sloanes were as close to royalty as Georgia got.

"There's an open spot?"

The mayor nodded. "Jeb Toschen passed away."

"I'm sorry to hear that."

"He was ninety-two," the mayor said.

Joe looked into Vanessa's bright eyes. This was clearly killing her. But it was true that all the other local charities were drowning, while Joe's organizations were, if not thriving, certainly solid. This was partially due to Joe's gifts as a fund-raiser, but mostly to how much lower a fella could keep his overhead if he'd fleeced half his supplies and building materials.

"Have someone contact my girl," he said eventually.

"Is that a yes?" Vanessa asked.

"It's close enough, dear." Her husband smiled at Joe. "We're still working on the part where she realizes the absence of a negative is always a positive."

Vanessa smiled. "Actually, we're just working on the part where I like to hear 'yes.'"

Joe held out his hand. She shook it.

"Have someone call my girl in the morning. We'll give it our due attention."

Her grip tightened around his and he wouldn't have been surprised if his bones or her teeth cracked with a loud splintering.

"I will," she said. "And thank you for your consideration."

"My pleasure, Mrs. Belgrave."

CHAPTER SIX

Names on the Wind

FREDDY DiGIACOMO caught up with Wyatt Pettigrue in the maternity ward of St. Joseph's Hospital, Wyatt holding his newborn daughter in both hands while his cigarette smoldered in the ashtray by his knee. His daughter's name was still undecided, although his wife, Mae, was leaning toward Velma, which had been her grandmother's name. Wyatt had lobbied for Greta, but Mae had cooled to it ever since she'd found Wyatt leafing too slowly through a copy of *Photoplay* that had Greta Garbo on the cover.

When Sister Mary Theodore came and took his daughter back from him, Wyatt watched them go, his pride at having brought life into the world doing battle with his relief that he didn't have to hold her anymore while she squealed like a piglet that had fallen down a well. The whole time she'd been in his hands he'd been sure he'd drop her. He also got the feeling she didn't like him; she didn't look at him—she didn't look at anything really—but he sensed she could smell him and wasn't fond of his odor. He had no idea what he was supposed to do now, how he was supposed to reorder his life and his expectations to accommodate this tiny, unreasonable creature's existence. Her arrival, he was certain, meant Mae would have even less room in her heart for him.

Christ, he thought, and she wants three more.

Freddy DiGiacomo said, "She's a beautiful girl, Wyatt. A heartbreaker, that one. You can see it."

"Thanks."

"You must be very proud."

"I am."

Freddy clapped his back. "Where are the cigars? Huh?"

Wyatt found them in the pocket of his sport coat. He snipped off the end of one and lit it for Freddy, who puffed until the coal glowed red.

"I need you to do that thing for me now, Wyatt."

"*Now?*"

"By tonight'll be fine."

Mae's entire family was either crammed into the hospital room with her or waiting for him back home. The ones back home would expect him to fill the icebox they'd cleaned out last night. The ones in the hospital room would expect him to tend to his wife, who'd had a difficult labor, or at least stand around while they tended to her. There was no winning to it. The whole family—five brothers, four sisters, the angry-silent mother, and the angry-loud father—had judged Wyatt inferior a long time ago. Now, on the rare occasions they did pay him attention, they did so only long enough to reconfirm their initial impression.

Wyatt said to Freddy, "I have no idea how I'd tell her I've got to go to work."

Freddy smiled, his eyes kind. "Know what I've discovered? It's a lot easier to ask a woman's forgiveness than her permission." He took his raincoat off the back of his chair. "You coming?"

WYATT PETTIGRUE HAD SPENT the last few weeks shadowing Montooth Dix around the Negro section of Ybor City. Most days, this would have been an impossible task for a white man, but Wyatt's only distinguishing characteristic, since he was a child, was his ability to go unnoticed. In school, teachers had not only never called on him, on two occasions they'd forgotten to give him grades. Team buses left without him, coworkers usually called him by the wrong name ("William," "Wesley," or, for some reason, "Lloyd"), even his own father had been known to snap his fingers several times before he dredged up his son's name. For the past three weeks, Wyatt Pettigrue had driven into Ybor City every day, crossed the white/colored border at Eleventh Avenue, and driven down streets where the only pale men the inhabitants had seen in five years were milkmen, icemen, firemen, policemen, and the occasional landlord.

He'd tailed Montooth Dix from the series of apartments the big Negro occupied above a pool hall to the coffee shop on Tenth Street, the laundry on Eighth Avenue, the drugstore on Nebraska, the chicken joint on Meridian, and the tiny but tidy cemetery on Ninth Street. Except for the cemetery, where, Wyatt had learned, Montooth Dix's father, mother, two aunts, and an uncle were buried, all the other establishments either paid Montooth for protection, collected bets on policy numbers for him, or fronted for his illegal distilleries, which were still big business for anyone who sold liquor to people who didn't give a shit whether their booze came bearing a federal tax stamp or not. Montooth Dix's customers did not. Montooth Dix's customers were the only people more invisible than Wyatt Pettigrue. In Ybor City, an already amputated community, the Afro-Cubans and Afro-Americans were further cut off by that extra shade of darkness that separated black skin from toffee.

Montooth Dix was their mayor, their governor, their king. He exacted a tax for his services, but he provided those services. When they went on strike, he protected them from the goon squads, left food on their back stoops when they were sick, even wrote off a few debts when, during the last decade's years of strife and starvation, the men took off and never came back. Most of his people loved him, even the ones who owed him money.

Which, of late, was more people than had owed him in some time, at least since the Turnaround had begun in '38. For the second time this month, several of the debtors on the weekly payment program had cried poor, so Montooth decided to personally see to the accounts. Kincaid, the fruit man on Ninth, gave it up as soon as Montooth walked through his door. Montooth, at six foot two and in the habit of wearing hats that made him appear three inches taller, cut an imposing figure, and Kincaid was the first of three debtors who miraculously found the money they owed and right quick.

Which allowed Montooth, who'd been feeling tired lately— and not sick-tired, but sick-of-all-this-shit-tired, sick of what it took to keep a firm hand on a shifting pulse—to duck the responsibility of asking *why* the debtors had been so remiss in forking over the cash the previous two weeks. Montooth was exactly as old as the century, but he felt older lately. Growing older seemed only to teach you that new crops of people kept coming up behind you doing the same stupid shit the previous crop had done. Nobody learned nothing. Nobody evolved.

Christ. Montooth missed the days when everything just

hummed along, everyone happy to make their money, spend their money, and get up the next day and do it the fuck over again. Those days when Joe Coughlin had run everything, Montooth had long since realized, had been the golden age. Now, at least until this war stopped scooping up their best muscle and their best customers, they were in a holding pattern. Nothing wrong with holding patterns, at least not on the surface, but they did tend to make everyone antsy, braid them up tighter than barbed wire.

It was only at the end of his night, when he dropped in on Pearl Eyes Milton, the haberdasher on Tenth Street, and Pearl Eyes told him he couldn't pay him, "least not this week and probably not the next," that Montooth asked the question he didn't want to know the answer to.

"Why you doing me like this, Pearl?"

"Ain't trying to do you any which way, Mr. Dix, you know that."

"I don't."

"But I ain't got it."

Montooth pulled a silk tie from the rack beside him, let that imported silk slide across the palm of his hand. Lord. Since the war started, he'd forgotten how soft silk felt. "Why ain't you got it?"

Pearl Eyes, a kindly old man and grandfather to nine, said, "I just ain't. Times been tough."

Montooth looked down at the floor on his side of the counter. "But you leave a ten-dollar bill just lying around on the floor."

"A what?"

"A ten-dollar bill, Negro." Montooth pointed down and stepped back.

Pearl Eyes put his elbows on the counter and craned his head over the edge. Montooth looped the silk tie around his neck and set to strangling the old coot. He got in close and spoke into Pearl Eyes's bushy, pink ear.

"Who you paying if you not paying me? Who?"

"No one. I just—"

Montooth pulled hard on both ends of the tie and yanked Pearl Eyes over the counter and onto the floor. He let go of the tie. The old man bounced off the floor and lay there groaning and moaning for a spell.

Montooth dusted the floor with a handkerchief he found in another rack. He sat across from Pearl Eyes.

"What you sell here, old man?"

"What?" This between a lot of coughs and sputtering. "What?"

"Tell me what you sell."

Pearl Eyes pulled at the tie around his throat like it was alive. Yanked it off and threw it to the floor. "Clothes."

"Clothes is what you stock." Montooth shook his head and clucked. "What you sell is class. Brothers come through this door they expect elegance. They expect the refined touch. I mean, look at that suit you wearing. How much that cost retail?"

Another cough, but dryer. "'Bout eighty dollars."

"Eighty dollars. Whoo." Montooth whistled. "Most brothers I know don't make that in a month, but you wearing it and telling me you can't pay your debt."

"I . . ." Pearl Eyes looked down at the floor.

Montooth said, "Who's taking my money out your pocket before you can give it to me?"

Pearl Eyes said, "No one."

"Okay." Montooth stood. "Okay."

He headed for the door.

"Okay?" Pearl Eyes said.

Montooth stopped by a table covered in white shirts, looked back. "One of my boys will be by, maybe tonight to your house, maybe back here in the morning, but soon. I'd do it myself, but blood gets on the clothes no matter how hard you try avoiding it and I got me a date tonight with my middle wife at the Gin Gin Club."

"Blood?"

Montooth nodded. "Gonna cut up your face, Pearl. Carve it up like a chicken 'fore a picnic. See how much class and elegance you be selling then. Good night."

As he reached for the door, he saw a gray Plymouth heading north on the far side of the street, something about the car that Montooth didn't like, but he couldn't put his finger on what immediately, because Pearl Eyes piped up from back at the counter with:

"Little Lamar."

Montooth watched the man get to his feet.

Pearl Eyes rubbed his throat. "Little Lamar say he taking over. Say your time is done. Say a new boss runs this here town."

Montooth smiled. "When I push him back off this block and into his grave, what you say then?"

"Little Lamar say he got backing."

"I got backing."

"Son," the old man said with a weary pity that shook Montooth to his core, "word going around is the only backing you got anymore is your own damn spine. Whatever you had in the white world is done gone by."

Montooth watched the old man shuffle across the floor to him. Pearl Eyes Milton shot his cuffs as he neared, revealing a pair of antique diamond cuff links he always wore, ones supposedly went back a century or more to some white man in Philadelphia who'd once been deputy mayor. Pearl Eyes removed the cuff links and held them out to Montooth.

"They worth at least a month of what I owe you. Take 'em. They all I got."

Montooth opened his palm and Pearl Eyes dropped them into it.

"I'll deal with Lamar," Montooth said. "What you hearing is just wind."

"Wind of change maybe," Pearl Eyes said softly. "I'm old enough to know it when I feel it in my hair."

Montooth smiled. "You ain't got much hair left."

"That's 'cause the wind took it," Pearl Eyes said and turned his back on Montooth, headed back into his shop.

AS SOON AS MONTOOTH STEPPED OUT of the haberdashery, the gray Plymouth P4 appeared out of the soft night. Heading south this time, right in front of him. The rear window was already rolled down so Montooth didn't wait to see the muzzle of whatever gun was perched there. He just dropped to his knees behind the nearest parked car and started scrabbling.

The steel jackets smacked the other side of the car like someone had hurled a bucketful of lug nuts at it. The shots hit the building behind him too, sent sparks shooting off the brick. The windows popped out of the cars up and down the street, and Montooth stayed low and made his way down the sidewalk toward the alley. He'd been shot at by a machine gun before, back in the war, but that had been near twenty years ago, and this kind of noise, this hail of death, those fucking bullets ricocheting all over the fucking place— *ping ping ping*—could make a man lose his thoughts. Lord, for a moment there, he forgot why he was on this street, forgot his name.

But nothing could keep him from moving. He understood the way a baby knows how to cry to say it's hungry that he needed to keep crawling, keep scrabbling, keep clawing his way across the pavement. He reached the last car before the alley. As he did, it buckled and sagged; the asshole with the tommy gun had blown out its tires on the passenger side.

The shooting stopped.

Possibility #1: Motherfucker was reloading. Possibility #2: Motherfucker knew Montooth's general location and was drawing a bead on the mouth of the alley, waiting for old Montooth to stick his head out. Montooth drew one of his own guns—the long-nosed .44 his uncle Romeo had given him back in '23. Truest gun he owned.

There was a third possibility: The gunner knew exactly where Montooth was hiding and was fixing to get out of the car right now and finish this.

That was the worst of the scenarios. If the gunner got out of that car, he could take three long strides and be standing over Montooth's black ass. With a machine gun. End of fucking discussion. The echoes of the gunfire that had filled his ears subsided and he could hear the engine of the Plymouth idling and then the unmistakable snap of a fresh drum being slapped into the receiver of the Thompson.

Motherfucker had stopped to reload.

Well, Lord, Montooth thought as he looked up at the black sky and its low gray clouds, I guess hindsight *is* twenty-twenty, ain't she?

Montooth pocketed his pistol, placed the heels of his hands to the sidewalk, and shot off the pavement like a runner from his blocks, went straight for the alley and had reached the mouth when he heard the two white boys shouting. He didn't need to hear the words, though, because the gist became clear when the night opened up again with that jackhammer roar.

Montooth ran with the bullets chucking brick chips and dust into his face, ran like he hadn't run since the trenches in France, ran like he was young again, like his lungs could never burn and his heart could never seize. *Where were you, boy,* he wanted to ask the gunner, *in the days when I was young? Live ten lifetimes, you'll never have half the fine pussy as I've had, never know half as much joy, live half as much life. You ain't nothing, hear? I'm Montooth Dix, ruler of Black Ybor, and you ain't shit.*

He'd chosen the alley for its Dumpsters. There were a full dozen of them on either side, and even if you could make it past them—and no car Montooth was aware of could—two-thirds of the way down the alley, Little Bo's flophouse backed its ass another ten feet deeper into the alley than any of its neighbors. Couldn't slide a fart through that end of the alley without cutting it in half first.

Ping ping ping ping ping ping.

And then nothing but the revving of an engine, the white boys trying to wrap their heads around the fact that there'd be no driving through this alley. Not tonight, not any night.

Montooth was halfway down the alley, behind the Dumpster shared by the eye doctor and the butcher, when the Plymouth peeled out in reverse. He heard it out on Tenth Street, racing around the block, hoping to catch him coming out by the flophouse. Instead, he went back up the alley the way he'd come, took a left at the end and stepped into the first doorway on his left, doorway of a place had gone belly-up like so many others during the prior decade and never found its second wind. The windows had been replaced by dark green metal sheets, and the light socket above the doorway had been empty since 1938. Unless you were standing two feet away with a lighthouse beam on your shoulder, you wouldn't see a man standing in this doorway until he wanted you to, until, perhaps, it was too fucking late to do anything about it.

The Plymouth came around the block for another look. When it was maybe ten feet short of the alley, Montooth stepped out into the street, took a long breath and careful aim, and fired straight through the windshield.

AS THEY CAME BACK around the block and Wyatt, sitting in the backseat with his Thompson, got a good look at all the cars he'd strafed in the first pass, he couldn't connect the damage to himself. It seemed impossible that little Wyatt Pettigrue, of Slausen Avenue, could have grown up to be a man who fired a machine gun at other men. But it was a strange world. If Wyatt was overseas doing this very thing because his government had ordered him to, he'd be a hero. But he was doing it on the streets of Ybor because his boss had ordered him to. Wyatt failed to see any distinction, even if the world probably would.

Kermit, the driver, never even saw Montooth Dix step into the street. The soft rain had returned and Kermit was reaching for the wiper switch when Wyatt saw—actually, just sensed—movement to their left. He only saw Montooth's face in the muzzle flash, it appeared out of the darkness like something disconnected from the man's body, like a death mask in a fun house, and then the windshield spiderwebbed. Kermit grunted and wet pieces of him splashed onto Wyatt's face. Kermit slumped forward, his head spraying itself all over the car, a clogged-drain sound coming from him, but the car actually accelerating. Wyatt pulled Kermit's shoulder to get his foot off the gas, but they hit the curb and then a pole. Wyatt's nose broke against the back of the seat, and he was thrown into the back of the car again, where he rattled around for a bit.

His hair caught fire. It felt like that anyway. But when he slapped at his head he found a hand there instead of flame. A big hand, its fingers sunk deep in his hair as it settled into its grip and pulled. Wyatt was lifted off the backseat of the Plymouth and pulled through the window, his spine bump-bump-bumping off the sill. As his feet cleared the window, Montooth Dix twisted his body and dropped him. Wyatt found himself on his knees in the middle of Tenth Street, looking up at the barrel of a .44 Smith.

"My uncle gave me this gun," Montooth Dix said. "Said it'd never fail me, and it never has. What I'm telling you, white boy, is I don't need a hundred rounds to hit my target and every fucking car on the street. Who sent you?"

Wyatt knew the moment he answered the question he was a dead man. But if he could keep Montooth talking, maybe the police—fuck, *somebody*—would come. He'd made an awful racket on these streets in the last few minutes.

"Ain't gonna ask you twice," Montooth Dix said.

"Your uncle gave you that gun?" Wyatt said.

Dix nodded, the impatience in his eyes as clear as day.

"How old were you?"

"Fourteen."

"I saw you visit his grave a couple times," Wyatt said. "Your parents' too. Family's important."

"That so?" Montooth said.

Wyatt nodded solemnly. He could feel the wet street soaking into his knees. He was pretty sure his left forearm was fractured. Was that a siren in the distance?

"I became a father today," Wyatt told the man.

"Yeah?" Montooth shot Wyatt twice in the chest. He put another round in the man's forehead to be sure, then looked into the dead man's eyes and spit on the street. "Who's to say you would've been any good at it?"

CHAPTER SEVEN

Room 107

THE SUNDOWNER MOTOR LODGE in St. Petersburg had closed to the public in the mid-1930s. Its two low-slung, white stucco main buildings and small front office formed a horseshoe around a flat oval of dirt where grass declined to grow or palms to take root. The buildings had remained sitting behind a bait and tackle shop on Gandy Boulevard for seven or eight years now, the weeds allowed to grow tall around the edges of the property. The owners of the bait shop, two brothers, Patrick and Andrew Cantillon, also owned the sandwich shop next door and the boatyard behind the motel. The Cantillon brothers owned most of the small piers that jutted off the edge of the shoreline into Tampa Bay and made a comfortable profit selling blocks of ice and cold beer to the fishermen who left their spit of shoreline every morning before the light had licked the sky. They'd return around midday, redder than rubies, skin as rough as the rope they used to tie off their boats.

The Cantillons had been in business with Joe back when they all were running rum across the Florida Straits. Joe was responsible for the lion's share of their personal fortune. As a small token of their gratitude, Patrick and Andrew blocked off the best room in the former Sundowner for Joe's use and Joe's use only. The rest of the rooms were kept just as clean and fresh and were mostly used by old friends of the brothers who'd hit a patch of trouble—anything from a failed marriage to a trip on the lam.

Room 107, though, which faced the bay, was Joe's. It was there that he made love to Vanessa Belgrave late Monday morning on sheets that smelled of bleach and starch and sea salt. Outside, the gulls fought over shrimp tails and fish bones. Inside, a black iron table fan squeaked and clacked.

Sometimes when he and Vanessa made love it felt like being wrapped in an undertow, spinning softly in a warm dark world with no guarantee he'd resurface. And in those moments, as long as he didn't think of his son, he'd find himself happy at the prospect of never seeing this world again.

The Vanessa Belgrave the public saw—cool, imperious, so well bred that anything interesting or spontaneous had been bred out of her—was far from the truth of the woman. Behind closed doors, she was an explosion of carnal curiosity and goofy observations, hands down the funniest woman Joe had ever met. Sometimes she laughed so hard she snorted, a loud, wet, honking sound that was even more delightful because it emanated from such an otherwise graceful source.

Her parents didn't approve of that laugh or an adolescent affinity for trousers, but they were never able to produce another child. Seven miscarriages, no sons, no more daughters. So once they passed on, Sloane Amalgamated Industries—a one-hundred-and-fifty-year-old company—would pass to their daughter.

She'd told Joe, "If the southern-gentlemen shareholders see a ditzy woman who would rather read Emily Dickinson than a trade confirmation summary, the war to steal the company from me will be declared immediately. And it'll be over before it begins. But if they think I'm my father with slightly different appendages, and if they're as afraid of me as they are of him, then the business runs another hundred years, as long as I have a son at some point."

"And that's what you want, to run the family business?"

"No. God, no. But what's my choice—to let a multimillion-dollar corporation fade into insignificance on my watch? Only a child thinks life is about her wants."

"But what *do* you want? If you could have it."

"Gosh, Joe," she'd said, batting her eyelashes, "just you, you big lug." And then she'd jumped on him and covered his face in a pillow. "Admit it—that's what you wanted to hear."

He'd shaken his head, tried to let loose a very muffled "No."

She'd given his head a few more rough shakes and then removed the pillow. Straddling him, slightly out of breath, she'd taken a drink of wine. "I want an end to irreconcilable wants." She'd widened her eyes and mouth at him. "Drive that around the block, smarty-pants." And then she'd poured the rest of her wine on his chest and licked it up.

That had been three months ago on a cool and rainy afternoon.

Now, on a warm, bright day with humidity in the air but not yet stultifying, Vanessa stood at the window with the sheet wrapped around her lower half and peeked outside through the crack in the curtains.

Joe joined her and looked out at the boatyard with its forlorn engine blocks blackening in the sun, its peeling iceboxes and flaking diesel pumps. And beyond, the wobbly dock and the ever-present swarm of dark insects that hovered over this fetid end of the bay in shimmering fists.

Joe dropped his hand from the curtain and ran both palms along the sides of Vanessa's torso, reintoxicated with her already, just minutes after he'd spent himself. He grew harder, if not hard, as he removed the sheet from around her waist and pressed himself to her. That's as far as he went for the moment, content to feel her back against his chest, her ass against his thigh as he ran his palms lightly over her abdomen and buried his nose in her hair.

"Do you think we overdid it yesterday?" Vanessa asked.

"Overdid what?"

"Our alleged distaste for each other?"

"No." Joe shook his head. "This is the beginning of our 'thaw' period. Next step— a 'grudging respect' will surely crop up between us. We'll never be each other's cup of tea, but people will admire our professionalism when we lay aside our clear distaste for each other to make a success of your foundation." He slid one hand down over her pubic bone and ran his fingers through the hair there.

She leaned her head back and groaned into his neck. "I'm getting so tired of this."

"Of this?" He removed his hand.

She grabbed the hand and placed it back in position. She let loose a small gasp as he found the magic spot with his middle finger. "No. Definitely not this. I'm sick of playing the role. The stuck-up bitch, the rich daddy's girl." Another small gasp. "Yes. Right there would be great."

"Right there?"

"Mmm-hmm."

Her rib cage expanded as she sucked the air in through her nostrils. She exhaled through her mouth in one long slow breath.

"If you're sick of the role," he whispered in her ear, "stop playing it."

"Can't."

"Why not?"

"Oh, my lug, you know why."

"Ah, yes, the family business."

She spun in his arms. She gripped his wrist and put his hand right back where it had been, her eyes on his as she sat back on the windowsill and thrust against his fingers. A challenge rose in her blue eyes now. He'd tripped one of her wires, which reminded him that you couldn't be as good at faking a persona as Vanessa was unless some of that persona wasn't faked.

"Would *you* walk away from *your* career?" Her breath came quicker now, eyes still flashing with a complicated mix of indignation and desire.

"Depends."

She dug her fingernails into his ass. "Bullshit."

"For the right reason, I'd walk away."

"Bull*shit*," she repeated. She winced and bit her lip, and her fingernails, up by his hip now, dug deeper into his flesh. "You . . ." She puffed her cheeks and exhaled. "Never assume I'd give up something you wouldn't give up yourself."

She threw her head to the side and clutched his shoulder at the same time. When he entered her, her eyes widened and she bit his lips softly as he lifted her off the windowsill. At no point in the seven years since Graciela had died would he have imagined it possible, but he had no desire to ever shed himself of this woman. He had no desire to ever leave this room.

They fell back to the bed. Her orgasm took the form of a series of small shudders and one long low groan. Her eyes cleared and she smiled and looked down at him as she continued to move up and down on him.

"Smile," she said.

"I thought I was smiling."

"Give me all thousand watts."

He did.

"God," she said, "you put that smile together with your eyes and it's a marvel you were ever convicted of anything. I bet it got you out of a hundred jams when you were a kid."

"Ah, no," Joe said.

"Bullshit."

Joe shook his head. "Didn't have it then. When I was a kid one of my brother's called me the Cumberland Gap."

She laughed. "Whatever for?"

"My two front teeth were gone. Seriously. I knocked 'em out when I was, like, not even three? I don't remember doing it, but my brother said I took a spill and went face-first into a curb. So, yeah, Cumberland Gap."

Vanessa said, "I truly cannot imagine you hideous."

"Oh, I was hideous. And here's the kicker—most kids' real teeth come in at six, right? 'Round then? My others did. Not the front ones. They didn't show up till I was almost eight."

"No!"

"Yeah. Fucking embarrassing, I tell ya. I didn't smile with an open mouth till I was about twenty."

"Are we in love?" she asked him.

"*What*?" He went to move her off him.

She ground herself into him. "Or just very good at this part?"

"The latter," he said.

"Even if we were in love—"

"Are you in love?"

"With you?" Her eyes widened. "Heavens, no."

"Well, all right then."

"But even if I were—"

"Which you're not—"

"And neither are you."

"Correct."

"But if we *were*"—she took his hands and placed them on her hips and her smile was soft and sad—"it wouldn't save us, would it?"

"From what?"

"From what the world out there wants of us."

He said nothing. She lowered her chest to his.

"There was another shooting." Vanessa's fingers crept back and forth along his clavicle, her breath warm on his neck.

"What do you mean, another?"

"Well, those men the night before last. Those drug dealers shot by police. The man who committed suicide in his cell."

"Uh-huh . . ."

"And then this morning, I heard it on the radio as I was pulling in, some Negro shot two white men in Ybor."

Montooth Dix, Joe thought. Shit. Freddy Fucking DiGiacomo probably left the powwow at the church and went right into Brown Town to stir shit up.

Mother. Fucker.

"When was this?" he asked.

"Jonathan was called to the scene around . . ." She gave it some thought. "Two in the morning?"

"In Brown Town?"

She nodded. "He wants to be known as a hands-on mayor."

And now Joe had his hands on his wife. He went to remove them but changed his mind and ran them over her hips in slow circles. Whatever was going on in the black section of Ybor right now, there wasn't a damn thing Joe could do about it at the moment.

"When you sit for a haircut," Vanessa asked, "which door do you watch? Front or back?"

Shit. The old fight. The one that had started five minutes after the first time they'd made love.

"I'm not the kind of guy who gets shot," Joe said.

"No?" Her voice was bright and curious. "What are you?"

"I'm a businessman who's slightly more corrupt than average." He ran his palms over her rib cage.

"The newspapers keep calling you a gangster."

"That's because they lack imagination. You really want to talk about this?"

She rolled off him. "Yes."

"I've never lied to you."

"As far as I know."

"Hey," he said softly.

She closed her eyes, opened them. "Okay, you've never lied to me."

"So *was* I a gangster?" He nodded. "Yes. Now I'm an advisor to people."

"Criminals."

He shrugged. "A friend of mine was Public Enemy Number Three about six years ago—"

She sat up quickly. "See, that's what I'm saying. Who could begin a sentence, 'A friend of mine was Public Enemy' anything?"

Joe spoke evenly. "Guy who lived in the mansion next door? Threw people out of their homes for a living because they couldn't pay their mortgages. The reason they couldn't is because all the banks played fast and loose with their money on margin in '29 and lost it all. So these people had no savings and no jobs because either their employers or the banks pissed away their savings and their houses. The people who threw other people out of their houses, though, they thrived. As for my friend? He fixed horse races and sold narcotics. The FBI shot him to death as he was off-loading a boat down by Pass-a-Grille. His next-door neighbor? Bought his house. Also got his picture in the paper last week when your husband gave him a good citizen award. So, about the only difference I see between a thief and a banker most times is a college degree."

She shook her head. "Bankers don't shoot each other in the streets, Joe."

"Because they don't like wrinkling their suits, Vanessa. Just because they do their dirt with a pen doesn't make them cleaner."

She searched his face, her eyes wide and unsettled. "You really believe this."

"Yes," he said. "I do."

Neither of them said anything for a bit.

She reached over him and lifted her watch off the table. "It's getting late."

He found her bra and then her underwear in the sheets, handed them to her.

"Trade you." She handed him his briefs.

As soon as she'd slipped into her underwear and slid her arms into her bra straps, he wanted to strip her naked. Once again, he felt that irrational urge to never leave this room.

She smiled at him. "Every time we do this, we get in deeper to each other."

"And that's a problem?"

"Oh, *no*. Whatever would put that thought in your pretty little head?" She laughed and looked around the bed. "You see my blouse, sweetness?"

He found it behind a chair. "And we are, as you said, very good at this."

She took her blouse from him. "We are, aren't we? But you know that fades."

"The regard or the sex?"

"That's what we're calling it—'regard'?"

He nodded.

"Well, in that case, both at times. And what could ever bind us together if those two things went on vacation? Not our shared upbringing."

"Not our shared values."

"Not our shared professions."

"Well, shit." He chuckled and shook his head. "Why are we even together?"

"I know!" She threw a pillow at him and knocked over a lamp. "Joseph Coughlin, we are *fucked*." She finished buttoning her blouse. "You're paying for that lamp, by the way."

They found her skirt and his trousers and worked their way into their shoes, exchanging idiotic grins and slightly embarrassed, slightly lustful glances. They never risked lingering in the parking lot, so their last kiss always took place at the door. This kiss was almost as hungry as the first one they'd exchanged this morning, and when they broke it, she kept her eyes closed and her hand on the doorjamb.

She opened her eyes and looked at the bed, the old chair that sat by the old radio, the white curtains, the porcelain washbasin, the overturned lamp.

"I love this room."

"I love it too," he said.

"This is probably the happiest—no, actually, it *is* the happiest—I've ever been." She took his hand and kissed his palm. She ran it along her jaw and the side of her neck. She let go of it and went back to looking at the room. "But don't think that when the day comes that Daddy says 'Sugarplum, it's time for you to take over and carry the Sloane name into the next age, breed yourself some chillun to take over after you've gone,' that I won't do exactly what's expected of me." She looked up at him with eyes so blue they could cut bronze. "Because, son, I assure you I will."

SHE LEFT THE ROOM FIRST. Joe gave her a ten-minute head start. He sat by the window and listened to the news reports on the radio. The dock outside the window creaked from nothing at all, just a slight breeze perhaps and age. The wood had been violated beyond fairness by termites and water and the incessant rot-march of humidity. The next strong wind would cripple it, the next tropical storm would wipe it from memory.

A boy stood at the end of it.

A second or two ago, the dock had been empty. Until it wasn't.

The boy. The same one he'd seen running along the tree line at the party back in December. Somehow, Joe had always known he'd make another appearance.

He had his back to Joe. He was hatless. The cowlick Joe had noticed previously was tamped in place, though a small nub of it peeked up like an arched knuckle. His hair was so blond it was almost white.

Joe raised the window and said, "Hey."

A warm and lazy breeze rippled the water but not the boy's hair.

"Hey," Joe said again, a little louder.

No reaction from the boy.

Joe lowered his head and stared at the cracks in the windowsill for a count of five. When he looked back up, the boy stood in the same spot, his face in the process of turning away from Joe. As Joe had guessed the first time he'd seen him, what little he glimpsed of the boy's profile was indistinct, as if the features were still forming.

Joe left the room and came around the corner of the building to the dock. The boy was no longer there. The sagging dock creaked some more. Joe imagined it being swept away in churning waters. Someone would put up a new one. Or not.

Men had built this dock. They'd driven in the posts, they'd measured and cut, they'd drilled and hammered. When they were finished, they were the first to ever set foot on it. They'd felt pride. Maybe not a lot, but certainly some. They'd set out to build something and they'd built it. It existed because they had. By now, they'd probably passed on. The dock would follow. Someday, they'd bulldoze this motel. Time is rented, Joe thought, never owned.

Across from the dock, about forty yards away, was a spit of sand and a few trees, the kind of baby key that was usually submerged in all but low tide. The boy stood there. The boy and his blond hair and indistinct features, facing Joe, staring at him with closed eyes.

Until the tall reeds and the thin trees inhaled him.

As if there weren't enough on my plate, Joe thought, now I've got a ghost.

CHAPTER EIGHT

A Resemblance

PLANS FOR DEPARTURE to Raiford hit an immediate snag when
Joe returned home from the Sundowner to discover Tomas had
the chicken pox. Miss Narcisa had ordered the boy upstairs and
was walking around the house with a wet facecloth tied by kitchen
twine over her nose and mouth. Miss Narcisa informed Joe that
she had not contracted the virus as a child and was not going to
catch it now, as an adult.

"No," she said, one hand shooting up into the air, the other throw-
ing items into the canvas bag she carried everywhere. "No, no, no."

"Of course not," Joe said, hoping secretly that she already had
it, a reflexive response to anyone who'd treat his son like a pariah.
And I hope it scabs up.

When she told him she'd cooked three days' worth of meals
and left them in the icebox, pressed four of his suits, and cleaned

the house, though, he did remind himself how handy she was to have around.

At the door, trying to keep the desperation from his voice, he said, "So when will we see you?"

She looked back at him, her flat face as flat as a pan. "When he is no longer sick."

Joe, who'd had the chicken pox as a boy, went up to Tomas's room and sat with him. "I knew you looked under the weather yesterday."

Tomas turned a page of Dumas's *Twenty Years After*. "How bad do I look?"

"You'd have to put the book down, buddy."

Tomas lowered the book and looked at his father with a face that appeared to have been ravaged by bees and then left under a strong sun.

"You look great," Joe said. "Barely noticeable."

Tomas raised the book in front of his face. "Ha-ha."

"Okay, you look awful."

He lowered the book and cocked an eyebrow at his father.

"No," Joe said, "you really do."

Tomas grimaced. "These are times I miss not having a mother."

Joe came out of his chair and hopped on the bed and lay beside his son. "Oh, sweetie, does it hurt? Can I get you some warm milk?"

Tomas slapped at his father, and Joe tickled him hard enough that he dropped the book to the floor. Joe came off the bed to pick it up. He went to hand it to his son, found Tomas giving him a strange, hesitant look.

"What?" Joe said, a smile finding his face.

"Could you read it to me?"

"What?"

"Like you used to all the time. Remember?"

Joe remembered. The Grimm brothers, Aesop, the Greek and Roman myths, Verne, Stevenson, H. Rider Haggard, and, of course, Dumas. He looked down at his son and smoothed the cowlick rising from the back of the boy's head.

"Sure."

He kicked off his shoes, climbed on the bed, and opened the book.

After Tomas fell asleep, Joe sat in the office he kept in the back of the house on the first floor. It was at night, alone, when he most thought about what the yokel from Raiford had told him in his office on Friday. He knew it was ridiculous—*no one* would be stupid enough to try to kill him—and yet he pulled the drapes over the French doors, though the thickness of the glass and the height of the wall out back made it unlikely, if not impossible, that anyone could see him from the street.

But if, say, someone had scaled the wall with a rifle, they could easily make out the shape of his head through the glass.

"Christ," he said as he poured himself a scotch from the decanter, "stop it." He caught his reflection in the bar mirror as he corked the decanter. "Okay? Just stop."

He told himself to reopen the drapes, but he didn't.

Instead, he sat at his desk, with the plan of doing nothing more than reliving his last encounter with Vanessa, when his phone rang.

"Fuck." His feet came off the desk and he lifted the receiver. "Hello."

"It's me."

Dion.

"Hey, you. How's things?"

"Pretty fucking bad at the moment, Joseph."

"Do explain, Dionysius."

"Ah ha." Dion chuckled. "You would prefer I call you 'Joe.'"

"Always, good sir. Always." Joe put his feet back on the desk. He and Dion had been friends since they were thirteen. They'd each saved the other's life more than once. They could read each other's moods and minds better than most married couples. Joe knew that Dion was turning out to be a middling boss at best—the best soldiers often did, and Dion had been an exceptional soldier. He knew that Dion's fits of rage, always fearsome, had only worsened with age and that most men with any wits were terrified of him. He also knew—though few others did—that Dion's taste for the cocaine they brought in from Bolivia once a month seemed to contribute to his mood swings and his violence. He knew all these things about his friend, and yet Dion was, in fact, his friend. His oldest friend. The only man who'd known him before the fine suits and the four-dollar haircuts and the refined taste in food and liquor. Dion had known him when he was someone's son, someone's little brother, when he was callow and impulsive and unformed. And he'd known Dion when he was much jollier, much fatter, so much more playful. He missed that Dion, but he trusted he was still in there somewhere.

"You heard about the thing happened in Brown Town?" Dion asked.

"Yup."

"Your thoughts?"

"Freddy DiGiacomo's a fucking knucklehead."

"Anything you might want to tell me that I don't already know?"

"Montooth has been a great earner for us for fourteen years. Since the day you and I got here, D."

"That is a fact."

"In a sane world, we'd apologize for bothering him. And for our penance, we'd hit Freddy over the fucking head with a rock and throw him in the bay."

"Sure," Dion said, "in a sane world. But two of ours are dead. That has to be addressed. We'll have a sit-down tomorrow."

"What time?"

"Let's say four."

Joe did the math on what kind of time it would take to get to Raiford and back. "Any way you could push it to five?"

"Don't see why not."

"Then I'll be there."

"Good enough." Dion inhaled on one of his ever-present cigars. "How's my pal?"

"He's got chicken pox."

"No shit?"

"No shit. And Narcisa won't watch him until he's over it."

"Who works for who over there?"

"Best governess I ever had."

"She must be, she makes her own hours."

"What about you?"

Dion yawned. "Same muck and shit as every other day."

"Aww. Is the crown too heavy?"

"It was too heavy for you."

"Nah. Charlie pushed me out because I wasn't a wop."

"That's how you remember it."

"How it was."

"Hmm. I recall someone whining about how they just couldn't take it anymore, all the blood, all the responsibility. Wah wah wah."

Joe chuckled. "Good night."

"Good night."

When he hung up, he thought of parting the drapes. Most nights, he opened the French doors to breathe in the mint and bougainvillea, look out at the wading pool, the dark gardens, the stucco wall covered in ivy and Spanish moss.

If someone were perched on that wall with a rifle, though . . .

What would they see? He'd left the lights off behind him. He could take a peek out there at least.

He turned his chair and slipped a finger between the drapes. He looked out through the slit at the stucco wall the color of a new penny and the one orange tree he could see.

The boy stood in front of the tree, wearing a white sailor suit with matching bloomer pants. He cocked his head, as if he hadn't expected to see Joe, and then he skipped away. Didn't walk. Skipped.

Before he knew he was doing it, Joe threw back the drapes and stared out at his still and empty yard.

In the next instant, he pictured a bullet leaving a rifle and pushed his chair back, let the drapes fall over the doors.

He wheeled the chair away from the window and stopped where two of his bookcases met in a V. As he sat there, the boy walked past his office door and headed for the stairs.

The chair spun when Joe left it. He reached the hall and climbed the empty stairs. He checked in on Tomas and found him sleeping. He looked under his bed. Took a look in his closet. Once more, down on his knees, to look under the bed. Nothing.

He moved through the other bedrooms. A vein pulsed under his jaw. The flesh nearest to his spine felt as if ants were crawling under it, and the air in the house was so cold he could feel it in his teeth.

He searched the entire house. When he was done, he entered his bedroom, where he expected to find the boy, but the room was empty.

Joe sat awake well into the night. When the boy had passed by his office door, his features had been more distinct than on previous encounters. This allowed Joe to confirm a clear family resemblance. He had the long Coughlin jaw and small ears. If, in that moment, he'd turned and looked directly at him, Joe wouldn't have been surprised if he'd done so with the face of his father.

But why would his father take the form of a child? Even when his father had been a child, Joe doubted he'd ever seemed childlike.

Joe had never encountered a ghost. Hadn't much expected to, either. After Graciela died, he'd expected—even prayed—that she'd return to him in some form. But most nights she'd even refused to find his dreams. When he did dream of her, the dreams were invariably banal. Most took place on the boat they'd taken from Havana the day she died. Tomas had just turned a rambunctious two. Joe had spent the trip chasing him all over the boat because Graciela had been seasick. She'd vomited once. The rest of the trip, she took shallow breaths and kept a damp towel pressed to her forehead. As the nubs of the Tampa skyline crept above the border where swollen sky met the Florida Straits, Joe brought Graciela another damp towel, but she waved him off. "I changed my mind. Two is enough."

In the dreams, the other damp towels were usually strewn all over the deck, hanging from the rails, strung from the flagpoles. Damp towels and dry ones, white ones and red, some as small as pocket squares, some as large as mattresses.

In reality, to the best of Joe's recollection, he hadn't seen another towel, just the one on her forehead.

Within the hour, Graciela would lie bleeding to death on the pier, her killer crushed under the wheels of a coal truck. Joe couldn't even recall how long he'd remained on his knees by her. Tomas squirmed, and at times, squealed in his arms, and the light took flight from his wife's eyes. He watched her cross whatever transom led to whatever world or void lay beyond this one. In the final thirty seconds of her life, her eyelids fluttered nine times. And then never again.

He was still on his knees when the police arrived. Still there when the ambulance driver placed a stethoscope to his wife's chest and then looked over at the lead detective and shook his head. By the time the coroner arrived, Joe stood a few feet from her corpse and those of Seppe Carbone and Enrico Pozzetta, answering the questions of Detective Poston and his partner.

When it came time to remove her body, the coroner, a disheveled young man with pale, yellowish skin and lank dark hair, approached Joe.

"I'm Dr. Jefferts," he said softly. "I'd like to transport your wife, Mr. Coughlin, but I'm concerned it could be difficult for your son to see that."

Tomas had wrapped himself around Joe's leg and remained there throughout the detectives' questions.

Joe looked at the young man and his wrinkled suit. His shirt and tie were spotted with flecks of dried soup, and Joe thought at first that it was unprofessional for such a messy man to be placed in charge of his wife's autopsy. But another look in the man's eyes, at the compassion that lived there for a small boy he'd never met and that boy's grieving father, and Joe nodded his thanks.

Joe detached his son from his leg and lifted him to his chest, held him there. Tomas propped his chin on Joe's shoulder. He still hadn't wept. He'd simply repeated the word *Mama*, in a kind of breathless mantra. He'd fall silent for a while, and then it would start again. "Ma-ma, Ma-ma, Ma-ma . . ."

Dr. Jefferts said, "We'll treat her with respect, Mr. Coughlin. You have my word."

Joe shook his hand, not trusting himself to speak, and then carried his son off the pier.

And now, seven years removed from that shittiest of shitty days, he rarely dreamed of her at all.

The last time had been four or five months ago. In that dream, instead of bringing her a wet towel, he had brought her a grapefruit. She looked up at him from her deck chair, her face too thin, almost skeletal, and said the same thing. "I changed my mind. Two is enough."

He'd looked around her chair and the deck and couldn't see any grapefruit. "But you don't even have one."

She gave him a look of confusion so total it bordered on contempt. "Some things you shouldn't joke about."

And the blood bloomed on her dress and her eyelids fluttered and then stopped.

After that dream, Joe had taken a glass of scotch out onto the gallery and smoked half a pack of cigarettes.

Tonight he found the scotch and the cigarettes, but he stayed inside and didn't smoke as much. He fell asleep sitting up, waiting for the boy.

CHAPTER NINE

In the Pines, In the Pines

SINCE THE DAY HE'D WALKED OUT of a prison in 1929, Joe had vowed never to step back into one. For three years he'd been incarcerated at Charlestown Penitentiary in Boston, one of the worst prisons in the country. Fourteen years later, the sound the bars had made when they snapped shut at 8:00 P.M. lockdown could poison his dreams. He'd wake in a damp and gummy panic, eyes scurrying around his bedroom until he'd assured himself that it was, in fact, his bedroom. He'd only admitted the source of his night terrors to Graciela. She'd said it made sense—given that he'd never sat still in all the time she'd known him, she could barely imagine him being contained in a house, never mind a cage.

He and Tomas flew on the Suarez Sugar cargo plane to a landing strip in Crystal Springs not far from Jacksonville and then drove south thirty miles to Raiford. His advance man in the region was

Al Butters, a moonshiner and first-class getaway driver with the Bunsford Mob. The Bunsfords ran Duval County and a small swatch of northern Georgia. They gave Joe Al because he'd contracted chicken pox as a child himself. When Tomas dozed off in the heat of the backseat, Al assured Joe that all the necessary people had been paid, all the necessary arrangements made. Sure enough, at Raiford, the deputy warden, man went by the name of Cummings, met him outside the gate and led him alongside the fence that ran the length of the western side of the prison. After about five hundred yards, they reached a small section of yard where Theresa Del Fresco sat waiting, perching her small body on an orange crate she'd turned on its side.

Deputy Warden Cummings said, "Well, I'll leave you to it," and walked back up the small incline a good hundred yards before he stopped and lit his pipe.

Joe had always heard Theresa was small, and he guessed by the look of her she couldn't weigh more than a hundred pounds. But the way she came off the crate and moved to the fence reminded Joe of a panther he'd seen once in the swamplands of unincorporated Tampa. The cat had moved with coiled languor. Theresa moved the same way, as if to give everyone else a sporting chance. He'd bet she could climb the fence between them in the time it took for him to glance at his watch.

"You came," she said.

He nodded. "It was a reasonably compelling message."

"What did he tell you?"

"Your . . . friend?"

"If you like."

"He potty trained yet?"

"Aww, Mr. Coughlin," she said, "that's so below you."

He lit a cigarette, removed a tobacco leaf from his tongue. "He said someone put a contract out on you—"

"He used that word? *Contract?*"

"No," Joe said. "He's a yokel. I can't remember what word he used. But the gist was if you die you'll never be able to tell me who's supposedly trying to kill me."

"There's no 'supposedly' about it."

"Theresa," he said. "Okay if I call you Theresa?"

"Sure. What do I call you?"

"Joe will do. Theresa, why would anyone want to kill me?"

"That's what I was wondering. You're the fair-haired boy."

"I'm the gray-haired boy lately."

She smiled.

"What?"

"Nothing."

"No, what?"

"I'd heard you were vain."

"It's vain to mention I'm going gray in my thirties?"

"It's vain the way you mention it. Hoping I'll correct you. Tell you it's not *that* gray, tell you your baby blues still set the gals' hearts a swooning."

He chuckled. "Heard you had a mouth on you. Guess we both heard right."

She lit her own cigarette and they set to walking, she on her side of the fence, he on his, Deputy Warden Cummings taking up the trail behind them, maintaining a steady distance of a hundred yards.

"So let's start with who's trying to kill you," Joe said.

She nodded. "My guess would be my boss."

"Why would Lucius want you dead?"

"We robbed a German ship three months ago in Key West."

"A what?"

She nodded several times. "It sailed under the Union Jack out of St. Thomas, allegedly to bring supplies to our troops in North Africa. They stopped off in Key West to take on fuel, but really they were transporting diamonds smuggled out of Germany months ago, sent down through Argentina and then on to St. Thomas. They were going to off-load them in Key West, get them to one of their operatives in New York, finance his whole sabotage ring for years to come. But we hit them as they were off-loading. Killed eight of them, all Krauts. So, you might want to say thank you; we helped the war effort."

"Thank you," Joe said. "You're swell."

She gave him a small curtsey.

"Lucius bankroll the job?"

She nodded.

"And how much did he make?"

"It's a scary number."

"Try me."

"Two million."

Jesus. His whole life Joe had never heard of a score that big. And he'd heard of, or been part of, some pretty big scores. But two million dollars? That was the kind of money railroads and oil companies netted in a year. Hell, the entire Bartolo Family operation only made a million and a half last year—*gross*—and they were swimming in green.

Joe asked Theresa, "What was your cut?"

"Five percent."

Enough to live out her days comfortably in a style well beyond any she'd been accustomed to up to now.

"And you're worried he won't pay it."

"I *know* he won't pay it. Two bitches have already tried to kill me in here and I was only sentenced last week. I couldn't figure out why the prosecutor—Archie Boll, you know him?"

Joe nodded.

"Couldn't figure out why he was in such a forgiving mood. I mean, shit, I smashed Tony's head so hard there were pieces of him sticking to cabinets on the other side of the kitchen. And they let me plead to *involuntary manslaughter*? So I just assumed Archie Boll was trying to fuck me; figured he'd drop by the jail the night before they shipped me over here. But when he didn't? I started asking the kind of questions I should have asked when they offered me the deal."

"Why didn't you ask them then?"

"Who's looking a gift horse like that in the mouth? I got a record, I'm Italian, and, oh right, I beat my husband to death with a mallet. They could have given me the chair. Instead they gave me five years. I get out, my son will be eight. Young enough to start fresh with me." She nodded to herself. "But if I *had* asked around, I would have figured out what I bet you already know." She looked through the fence at him.

He nodded and spoke softly. "That Archie Boll is all the way in King Lucius's pocket."

"Yup."

"Which means," Joe said, "the object was always just to get you in here."

Another nod, followed by a bitter exhalation of smoke. "As soon as I killed Tony, King Lucius saw a way to hold on to another hundred grand. And maybe he thinks someone'll come along soon and offer me a deal to turn state's. Either way he looks at it, me breathing is bad for him. Me not breathing? That'll give him clear skies and a full sail."

"So you want me to talk to him?"

She chewed the skin around one of her nails. "I was kind of depending on it, yeah."

"And what are you paying for your life?"

She took a big breath and let it out.

"Ninety percent. He puts ten grand in a bank account for my son, and he lets me live. That's worth ninety thousand dollars to me."

Joe gave it some thought. "That's a big number and it's a smart number. What you have to consider is that Lucius may take it but then spend the next few months second-guessing himself and thinking, 'She's going to come out of prison and be pissed. She doesn't think so, but she's gonna be furious about this deal. Not now, but *then*. And that makes her a liability again.'"

She was nodding. "I thought of that."

"And?"

"If you make the deal with him, you have to bring along a witness. Then it's out there, part of the lore in our thing. Everyone will know."

"But then everyone will know he tried to kill you over the hundred grand."

"Who *wouldn't*, though? If my employee took a pinch when I owed her a hundred grand, I'd put a contract on her too. That's just smart business."

Christ, Joe thought, Lucius's people are a hard fucking breed.

Theresa said, "But if word gets out that I bought my life back and paid a pretty hefty sum to do so and Lucius killed me anyway, well, even in our thing, Joe, there are ethics."

"There are?" Joe thought about it. "I guess you got as good a point as any. So let's say I find somebody with the balls to step on Lucius's boat with me and I proffer him your deal. And let's say he takes it. What's it worth to me, though?"

"You wouldn't save a life out of the goodness of your heart?"

"Depends on the life. You've put a lot of people in the ground, including a couple of my acquaintances. I'm not sure your death is the tragedy you think it is."

"What about my son?"

"Someone who didn't murder his father will raise him."

"So why come see me?"

"Curiosity. I couldn't for the life of me figure out why you'd ask for me."

"Well, that's just it—for the life of you." She allowed herself a small, haughty smile. "And for your son, Joe, so *he* doesn't grow up in an orphanage any more than mine."

Joe matched her smile with his own. "You want me to believe *my* life's in danger. I make money, not waves. My death would do serious damage to the profit margin of our thing in Tampa, in Havana, in Boston, and in Portland, Maine. So who would want me dead?"

"Anyone who wants to do serious damage to the profit margin of our thing in Tampa, Havana, Boston, and Portland."

Joe had to give her that one. "So the threat's from without? Not normally the way it works in this business."

"I honestly don't know where it's from—within, without, the German high command, I have no idea. All I have is a name and a date."

Joe laughed. "When I'm supposed to be killed? Someone picked a fucking *day*?"

She nodded. "Ash Wednesday."

"So my killers are religious? Or just from New Orleans?"

"You can joke your way right into the cemetery, Joseph. Be my guest."

They turned another corner of the fence. The parking lot was now just off to their left. Joe could see Al and Tomas in the car, Al with his hat over his eyes, Tomas watching his father. Joe gave him a small wave and his son returned it.

"So you really don't know much," Joe said, "about this alleged hit."

"I know who's gonna carry it out and I'm pretty sure I know who subcontracted the job in the first place."

Tomas went back to reading his book.

Joe said, "Well, if *you* heard about it, then Lucius is holding the paper on it. That's an easy one. And you want me to go into the lion's den—no, fuck the den, into his jaws—and buy your freedom."

"Lucius doesn't kill anymore."

"Tell that to the last two guys who got on his boat and didn't get back off."

"Then bring someone unassailable with you, someone no one would dare touch."

Joe gave that a tight grin. "Until two days ago, I would have said that person was me."

"Gil Valentine would have said the same thing back in 1940."

"So who *did* kill Gil?"

"I have no idea. I don't know anyone who does. I mentioned his name so you'd realize—actually, so you'd *remember*—that no one is safe in our thing." She flicked her cigarette off into the grass and smiled through the fence at him. "Not even you."

"So you'll tell me who's taken the contract on me."

A nod. "The second my ten percent shows up in my bank account."

"There aren't too many guys up to the job of killing me. What if I just used my powers of deduction to figure out who it is?"

"And what if you were wrong?"

Behind Theresa, on the other side of the yard and the other side of the next fence, the boy watched them from a bright green knoll.

"Theresa."

"Yes, Joseph."

"Can you do me a favor and turn around? Tell me what you see at twelve o'clock?"

She gave him a curious arch of an eyebrow, but then she swiveled, looked straight through the fence at the knoll.

The boy was dressed in dark blue suspender shorts and a large-collar white shirt today. He didn't vanish when Theresa turned to look at him. Instead, he sat down on the grass and hugged his knees to his chest.

"I see a fence," Theresa said.

"Beyond the fence."

Theresa pointed. "Right there?"

Joe nodded. "Straight ahead. You see anything on that little hill?"

Theresa looked back at him with a tiny smile. "Sure."

"What is it?"

"Your vision that bad?"

"What is it?" he repeated.

"A fawn," she said. "Cute. There he goes."

The boy climbed the knoll and disappeared over the other side.

"A fawn."

Theresa nodded. "Baby deer, you know? Like Bambi?"

"Like Bambi," Joe said.

"Yeah." She shrugged. "You got a pen to take down my bank account number?"

TOMAS SAT IN THE BACK OF THE PACKARD and tried not to scratch his face or arms. It took so much effort, it actually made him sleepy again.

He watched his father talk to the small, slender woman in the orange prison clothes, and he wondered, not for the first time, exactly what it was his father did for a living. He knew he was a businessman and that he had a sugar company and a rum company with Uncle Esteban, who, like Uncle Dion, wasn't really an uncle. A lot of things in their life that seemed to be one thing could also be something else.

He watched his father turn and walk back the way he'd come along the fence line. The woman walked parallel to him on the other side of the chain-link. She had very dark hair, which often set Tomas to brooding about his mother; it was the only memory he was certain he had of her. His face had been pressed to her neck and her abundant hair fell around him like a cowl. She'd smelled of soap and had been humming a song. He never forgot the tune either. When he was five, he hummed it for his father, who was so shocked, his eyes filled.

"Do you know the song, Daddy?"

"I know the song."

"Is it Cuban?"

His father shook his head. "American. Your mother was very fond of it, even though it's a very sad song."

There were only a couple of lyrics and Tomas learned them before he turned six, even though, to this day, he didn't fully understand them:

Black girl, black girl, don't lie to me
Tell me where did you sleep last night
In the pines, in the pines
Where the sun don't ever shine
I shivered the whole night through

There was another verse about a man who may or may not have been the girl's husband who died when he was hit by a train. Tomas's father told him the song was known as either "In the Pines" or "Black Girl," though some people called it "Where Did You Sleep Last Night?"

It was a scary song, Tomas had always felt, a threatening one when the singer sang, "Don't lie to me." Tomas's fascination didn't stem from it giving him pleasure, because it gave him no pleasure at all. It broke his heart every time he played it on the Victrola. But in that sadness, he felt he touched his mother. Because his mother, he believed, was now the girl in the pines, in the pines, and she was alone and shivering the whole night through.

Other days, he believed his mother was not in the pines, she was not shivering the whole night through. She was in a world beyond the night and the cold. She was someplace very warm, where the sun baked the brick streets below her feet. She was strolling through a piazza on market day and selecting items she'd have ready for the day he and his father joined her.

She handed Tomas a red silk scarf and said, "Hold that for me, my little man," and hummed "In the Pines" as she selected another scarf, a light blue one this time. She turned to him with it trailing from her hand and was about to hand it to him when the car door opened and he snapped awake as his father hopped in the backseat with him.

They pulled away from the prison and onto the main road and the sun was low and hot and all around them. His father rolled down his window, removed his hat, and let the wind muss his hair.

"You were thinking about your mother, weren't you?"

"How'd you know?"

"Just a look you get."

"What kind of look?"

"An inward one," his father said.

"I think she's happy."

"Okay. Last time you said she was alone in the dark."

"It changes."

"Fair enough."

"Do you think she's happy? Wherever she is?"

His father turned on the seat and faced him. "Matter of fact, I do."

"But she must be lonely."

"Depends. If you believe time works like it does down here, then, yeah, she's only got her father for company and she didn't much like him." He patted Tomas's knee. "But what if there's no such thing as time after this life?"

"I don't understand."

"No minutes, no hours, no clocks. No night turning into day. I like to think your mother's not alone, because she's not waiting for us. We're already there."

Tomas looked into his father's kind face and was struck, as he sometimes was, by how much *belief* his father had. He couldn't define all the beliefs and they didn't necessarily share anything in common, but when Joe Coughlin decided upon something, he never second-guessed himself. Tomas was just old enough to suspect that kind of conviction could lead to its own problems, but to be around his father for any length of time was to feel a security unlike he'd encountered anywhere else in his life. His father, wry and glamorous and occasionally prickly, was a man who infected others with his unwavering self-assurance.

"So we're already with her?" Tomas said.

His father leaned across the seat and kissed the top of his head. "Yup."

Tomas smiled, still sleepy. He blinked a few times and his father began to blur before him, and he fell asleep feeling that kiss on his head like the foot of a very small bird.

SOMEONE IS TRYING TO KILL YOU.

It was a hard thought to shake. The rational side of Joe knew it

made zero sense. If there was such a thing as an irreplaceable asset
in the Bartolo Family, it was him. And not just to the Bartolo
Family; he was integral to Lansky's operations so, by extension,
he was integral to Luciano's. He was tight with Marcello in New
Orleans, Moe Dietz in Cleveland, Frank Costello in New York,
and Little Augie in Miami.

Not me.

People had tried to kill him in the past, of course, but back then
it had made sense—a mentor who decided Joe had gotten too big
for his britches; before that, members of the Klan who didn't much
cotton to a pasty Yankee coming down to their turf and showing
them how real money got made; and before that, a gangster whose
girlfriend he'd fallen in love with.

But those hatreds had made sense.

Why me?

Joe couldn't remember the last time he'd angered anyone of
note. Dion pissed people off. Dion made enemies and then usually killed them so their existence wouldn't disturb his sleep. Since
taking over the Tampa operation from Joe back in '35, Dion had
spilled a lot of blood. Far less than he would have had he not had
Joe as his consigliere, but even so, it was a notable amount. Maybe
the hit was on Dion and they just figured they had to take out his
brain trust while they were at it. But, no, the killing of a boss like
Dion always had to be approved; and the only people who could
confer that approval were all close associates of Joe's, and all people
who lined their pockets because of him and expected to do so well
into the future.

Besides, Theresa had sworn that Lucius's attorney specifically
named Joe as the target. Not one of the targets. *The* target.

But Theresa was a killer and a con woman and had a lot more
motive than most to lay the con at Joe's doorstep. If Joe was suit-

ably motivated, he was one of a very select few who might be able to approach King Lucius and change his mind. It would be a smart play, if one were Theresa, to approach Joe with news of a plot to kill him that was vague yet just specific enough to put a clock in the back of his mind: Ash Wednesday was eight days away. He could assure himself that there was no earthly reason anyone would want him dead and that if there were, he had enough friends in this business that one of them would have heard of the plot and informed him of it by now. He could tell himself that with the exception of one bit of jailhouse gossip exchanged between a shyster and a killer there was no more substance to this rumor than there was to the smoke uncoiling off the end of his cigarette. And if the intended victim were anyone but himself he would have laughed off the ruse for what it was—a desperate woman's attempt to curry favor with a man she believed could save her life.

But the rumor, however vague, insubstantial, and unsubstantiated, *was* about him.

He looked across the seat and smiled at his son, who was blinking, futilely it seemed, at sleep. Tomas gave him a quizzical smile back and narrowed his eyes. Joe shook his head to say, *It's nothing. All is A-OK.* And Tomas's eyes closed and his head drooped. Joe sat with the back of his head to the open window and smoked.

Up front, Al Butters told Joe he needed to pull over to relieve himself.

Joe said fine, just be careful of the gators and the snakes.

"Ain't nobody interested in this old carcass, no." Al pulled to the side of the road, the passenger-side tires sinking into the soft green shoulder.

Al exited the car and walked a few feet before unzipping his fly. Joe had to assume he was unzipping his fly since, with his back to them, Joe didn't exactly know what his hands were touching. Could be a gun.

The road was a bright white strip cut between oceans of green saw grass and scrub oak and sickly thin pines. The sky was as white as the road.

The Bunsford Mob could have subcontracted for the job. If so, Al Butters could turn with a pistol in his hand and take Joe out first, put the next bullet through his son's forehead. Nothing to do then but stand around and wait for the getaway car, which could be idling on the side of the road around the next bend.

Al Butters turned from the grass and headed back toward the car, zipping his fly.

Joe waited for him to get in the car and pull off the shoulder before he placed his hat down his forehead and closed his eyes. He could feel shadows of the trees play across his face and pat his eyelids.

Then it was Graciela patting his face, gently at first but growing a little less gentle, the method she'd used to wake him the day of Tomas's birth. Joe had just returned from a business trip that had taken him and Esteban to the northern tip of South America, and he hadn't slept well in days. He opened his eyes and saw the truth in his wife's face—they were about to become parents.

"It's time?"

"It's time." She pulled back the sheets. "Time for the first one."

He'd slept in his clothes. He sat up, rubbing his face, and then placed the hand to her belly.

A contraction hit and she winced. "Come, come."

He climbed out of bed and followed her to the stairs. "The first one, uh?"

She looked back at him and winced again. "Of course, *mi amor.*" She gripped the banister with her left hand.

"Yeah?" He took her free arm. "How many we gonna have?"

"At least three."

JOE OPENED HIS EYES and felt the heat on his face.

That last day of her life, she hadn't been talking about towels. Or grapefruit.

She'd been talking about children.

CHAPTER TEN

A Verdict

THE BARTOLO FAMILY EMPIRE was headquartered on the top floor of the American Cigarette Machines Service Company, a dark brown building with beige leaded windows caked gray with dust at the end of Pier 6 in Port Tampa. When he arrived, Joe found Rico DiGiacomo already sitting in the waiting room.

The waiting room was almost as nice as the office beyond it. The floor was composed of wide planks of honey-colored pine. The leather armchairs and couches had been imported from Burma before the war. Large full-color photographs of Manganaro, the tiny Sicilian town where Dion Bartolo had been born, adorned the brick walls. Two years after he'd taken over as boss of the family, Dion had paid a *Life* photographer an obscene amount of money to travel to Manganaro to take those pictures. They were shot in amber hues on Polaroid stock, the images as rich and warm as the leather chairs and honey floors. In one, a man and his donkey trudged up a hill, the sun pancaking into the field to their right. In another, three old women laughed about something in front of a butcher. The porticos of a narrow church dwarfed a dog sleeping in their shadows. A child rode his bicycle past a stand of olive trees.

Joe, never stricken with the disorder of nostalgia, always felt the photos spoke to Dion's desire to recapture a world he barely remembered, a world gone by before he'd tasted it or fully smelled it. He'd left Italy when he was four; so he'd gotten, at best, a whiff of the world the photos portrayed, but that scent stayed with him the rest of his life. It became the home he almost knew, the boy he almost was.

Joe exchanged a handshake with Rico and took a seat on the couch beside him. Rico pointed at one of the photos. "Think that old geezer and his donkey do that every day, just walk up that hill?"

"I don't know about these days, with the war and all."

Rico stared at the photo. "I bet he does, even now. He's like my old man—it's all about putting in the day's work. Even if—no, no, *particularly if*—someone's dropping bombs on you. Him and that donkey, Joe, they've probably been blown up by now. But he went out doing what he committed his life to."

"Which was?"

"By the looks of it, walking that fucking donkey up a hill every day."

Joe chuckled. He'd forgotten how much fun it was to hang around Rico. Probably the hardest part of promoting him from his personal bodyguard to a much more rewarding career track in their thing was that Joe missed the guy's company.

They both looked at the oak door that led to Dion's office. "Anyone in there with him now?"

Rico nodded. "My brother."

Joe exhaled slowly. "So what happened?"

Rico shrugged and moved his hat from one knee to the other. "Couple of Freddy's guys ran into Montooth on Tenth Street—"

"These are white guys?"

"Yeah. Kermit—"

"We use guys named Kermit these days?"

Rico shrugged. "It is what it is. Half our ginzos are overseas, you know that."

Joe closed his eyes and pinched the top of his nose, exhaled. "So, uh, Kermit and a friend are just two white guys strolling around Brown Town at ten o'clock at night?"

Rico gave that a soft smile and another shrug. "Anyway, they started beefing right there on the street. Big nigger pulls a gun, starts pop-pop-popping away. Next thing you know, he's put a round through Wyatt Pettigrue's squash."

"Pettigrue? That little kid from Third Avenue, by the Mongolian grocer?"

"He ain't a kid no more, Joe. Well, shit, he ain't nothing anymore. But, yeah, he was maybe twenty-one? Just became a father."

"Jesus." Joe remembered getting shines from the kid on the corner of Third and Sixth. The kid wasn't that good at shining, but he had a fun patter, and he could rattle off all the important stories from the morning papers for you.

"So, yeah, he's down at Blake's Funeral Parlor right now," Rico said, "two in the chest, one in the face. Daughter's three days old. Fucking tragedy, I don't mind saying."

They both looked at the clock above the door at the same time: ten past the hour. Another hallmark of the Dion Bartolo regime—meetings never started on time.

Joe said, "So Montooth put two of ours down. And what happened to him?"

"Oh, he's still with the human race. Can't say for how long, though, hot as Freddy is."

"And you're on board with that?" Joe asked.

Rico squirmed a bit and sighed loudly. "What am I going to do? It's like having a kid who fucks up—do you disown him? Look, Freddy is a fuckhead. We know this. He stepped into Montooth's territory, told him he was taking it, and Montooth, man that he is, said, 'The fuck you are.' I mean, I blame myself."

"Why?"

"I let it get to this. If I'd stepped in months ago, before the water started to really bubble, I could have kept it from reaching a boil. But I didn't. And now Montooth killed two of Freddy's guys, which means he killed two of our guys. He's supposed to get a pass?"

Joe nodded and then shook his head and then nodded again. "I dunno, I dunno. I mean, Freddy moved on *him*. What else was Montooth supposed to do?"

Rico held out his hands, reasonable and plaintive at the same time. "Not kill two white guys."

Joe shook his head again at the waste of it.

Rico appraised Joe's suit. "You been traveling?"

Joe nodded. "It's obvious?"

"Never known you to have a wrinkle, but that suit looks slept in."

"Thanks. How's the hair?"

"Hair's all right. Tie could use a straightening. Where were you?"

Joe worked on his tie as he told Rico about traveling to Raiford, told him what Theresa claimed about his imminent demise.

"A hit? On *you*?" Rico chuckled hard. "Joe, that's fucking ridiculous."

"That's what I said."

"And all you got is the word of this vicious fucking dame who's sucked up in her own paranoia?"

"Yeah. Though, in her case, the paranoia's pretty justified."

"Well, sure, you go to work for King Lucius, you go to work for Beelzebub. That's the foundation block of that relationship." Rico stroked his smooth, pointed chin. "It's in your head, though, isn't it? The *idea* that someone could be out there gunning for you."

Joe said, "It's not rational, but yeah."

"How you supposed to be rational you hear someone may have thrown your name in the hat?" Rico looked at him, his eyes widening. "But it makes no sense, Joe. You can see that much, right?"

Joe nodded.

"I mean, none," Rico said. "Shit, just your list of judges is worth more than every whorehouse in Tampa combined." He laughed. "You're the golden goose."

Joe said, "So why don't I feel safe?"

"Because whoever did this got in your head. Which is probably the point."

"Fine. But why?"

Rico opened his mouth, then closed it. He stared into the middle distance of the room for a bit, then gave Joe a sheepish smile. "Fuck if I know." He shook his head. "It just sounds like bullshit."

Joe said, "But you try and put your head to a pillow thinking somebody's coming for you."

Rico said, "Remember when Claudio Frechetti thought I was fucking his wife?"

"You were fucking his wife."

"But he couldn't prove it. But then he thought he could? And he said he was going to kill me? And they hadn't opened the books for me yet, so I was just a nobody and he was a big earner back then. Christ, I didn't sleep in the same place two nights running for six weeks. I had my back on more couches than a bad actress. Then I run into Claudio himself coming out of the Rexall downtown and *he's* got bags under his eyes and twitchy shoulders because he heard someone had put out a contract on him. The whole time, he couldn't have given a shit about me. Six weeks I lost hiding out and he's worried about the bullet with his own name on it."

"Which arrived about a week later, right?"

Rico nodded. "He had his hand in the till. Wasn't that it?"

Joe shook his head. "Snitch."

"Claudio?"

Joe nodded. "That's how we lost all those loads on Forty-one that time. Fifty K of product ends up getting burned behind the Bureau of Narcotics Building, somebody's gonna get found out and somebody's gonna pay."

They sat looking at the clock for a bit more until Rico said, "Why not take off for a couple weeks? Go to Cuba? You won't have to sleep on a couch."

Joe looked over at him. "What if that's the play, though? The hitter's waiting there for me. I run right into his arms."

"That'd be a smart play," Rico agreed. "Who do we know who's that smart, though?"

"King Lucius's name keeps coming up."

"So go talk to him."

"On my way tomorrow. You got plans?"

Rico smiled big. "Like old times?"

"Like old times."

"That'd be a kick."

"Yeah?"

"Hell, yeah."

The thick oak door to Dion's office opened and they were ushered in by Mike Aubrey. Geoff the Finn was waiting just inside the door, suit jacket off, his shoulder holster and pistol exposed. Both Mike and Geoff the Finn wore their stone faces for the guests today, but Joe had his doubts either of them would stand tall if they ever faced the kind of shit Dion and Joe had back in the 1930s.

Joe and Rico made themselves drinks and Captain Dale Byner of the Fifth Precinct showed up, made his own drink. Byner had been in their pocket since he was a detective sergeant. One day he'd be commissioner. He wasn't exceptionally corrupt—you could never place a bet on those guys—he just wanted to keep the peace, by whatever means necessary. He was also people-smart but money-dumb, a perfect combination.

Joe sat on the couch across from Dion's desk and Freddy sat down beside him, sat so close their knees touched. It immediately got on Joe's nerves. Fucking Freddy sitting there like both the injured party and the puppy who'd had another accident on the rug. Wanted everyone to believe it was beyond his control, wanted everyone to believe he meant well.

Dion lit his cigar, looked through the smoke at Freddy, and said, "All right, make your case."

Freddy couldn't believe what he'd been asked. "My *case*? My case is Montooth Dix killed two of my guys, so he's gotta go. That's it. Plain and simple."

The police captain, Dale Byner, said, "There's been rumblings for months, Freddy, that you were pushing the guy off his racket."

"The *guy*?" Freddy said. "Like you drink with him down the Elks, Byner? He ever showed up in your neighborhood, you'd shoot him on sight."

Joe said, "Montooth Dix has been running the numbers in Brown Town since I got here in '29. He's always been a business-man, always been fair in his dealings, even hid the Sukulowski brothers after that clusterfuck in Oldsmar two years ago. Every cop in the city looking for them, and Montooth was a tall glass of ice on our behalf."

"That's how the Sukulowskis got out?" Captain Byner asked.

"Yup." Joe lit a cigarette.

"Where'd they end up?"

Joe tossed his match in the ashtray. "You don't really want to know."

Rico said, "Gentlemen, I agree with you. Freddy was a fucking asshole going after Montooth in the first place."

Freddy, already aggrieved, looked even more dismayed.

"You were." Rico looked Freddy in the eye and formed a circle with the thumb and index of his right hand. "Huge asshole. Size of a fucking paint can." He turned to the other men in the room. "But, gents, we can't let a nigger kill a white man. Even if it's a nigger we like, and I like Montooth Dix. I've broken bread with the man. But still. And we can't let a guy who's not in our thing kill someone who is. No matter what. Dion? Joe? You two taught *me* that. Anyone hits our family gets hits back *by* our family. That's gospel."

Dion looked at Joe for a long moment. "What do you think? Business-wise, not emotional."

"You ever known me to let emotion rule the day?"

Dion started to open his mouth.

Joe cut him off. "This decade?"

Dion eventually nodded. "Fair enough."

"From a business standpoint," Joe said, "there's a lot of potential for disaster. All Montooth's people turn against us? They can fuck us on heroin, our *bolita* cut, our control of some of the cigar factories. In terms of hookers, they control the Jamaican and Haitian pipelines, which is almost half the business down here. We always act like they're a separate thing, but they are not. Anyone who's come at Montooth's throne in the past twenty years has died bloody. And there's no appointed successor. Which means, whichever way the wind blows, there's gonna be a nightmare of a power vacuum left in his wake. And all our profits down there will get sucked up into it."

"He's got sons," Freddy said.

Joe turned to Freddy and hid his contempt. He appeared logical, reasonable, and respectful. "But only one of them—Breezy—is strong. And I can think of at least three guys down there who would come at Breezy if he got the throne."

Dion said, "But would any have a shot?"

They looked at Rico because it was his territory at the end of the day.

"Nah." He shook his head, then paused, then shook his head again. "No, I don't think so."

"Who?" Dion said.

Rico looked at Joe for confirmation.

Joe said, "You thinking who I'm thinking?"

Rico nodded, and they turned to Dion and said it together. "Little Lamar."

Dion said, "The guy deals in Chinks?"

Joe nodded.

Rico said, "He's the only one who's got a shot at uniting the tribe if he takes the throne fast enough."

"They trust him that much?" Dion asked.

Joe shook his head. "They fear him that much."

Dion said, "So can anyone deal with him?"

Now it was Freddy and Rico who looked at each other.

Rico said, "I think he can be reasoned with you put enough green in front of him."

Freddy nodded. "He's a businessman. He—"

"He's a fucking snake."

They all looked over at Captain Byner.

"Slaughter his own young if there was ten dollars in it. Fuck their corpses for twenty." Byner leaned forward and refilled his drink. "That 'Chink business' he's into? We found a shipping container of them last year—nine men, seven women, seven children—at the bottom of the ocean. Best we pieced it together, one of the men in the container had been the father of a girl Lamar pimped out on Fifteenth Street. She ran off with another Chink, lit out for San Francisco. He heard her father was coming over on a Chink freighter that he'd bought into? He had them dump the container overboard. Killed twenty-three people because a whore ran off on him. That's who you're thinking of putting in power."

"You know," Freddy said to Byner, "shut the fuck up." He grimaced like he'd bit into a lemon. "All right? Just shut the fuck up, you."

Byner said, "Hey, Freddy, anytime you want to meet off the clock, we'll see if you can make me shut up. We'll give that a try. Okay?"

"Enough," Dion said. "Christ." He took a pull from his own drink. He pointed the glass at Joe and Rico. "This comes down to you two. What do I know from the streets of Brown Town anymore?"

Joe knew the retort in everyone's mind: What do you know from the streets anywhere in Tampa anymore?

But the last guy who'd publicly suggested Dion was too hands-off as a boss encountered Dion's hands around his throat until his windpipe snapped.

Joe ceded the floor to Rico with a glance.

The younger man slapped some peanut dust off his palms and leaned forward. "I wish I could see another solution, but I can't. Dix has gotta go. And to keep reprisals to a minimum, his son's gotta go next. We put Lamar behind the big desk, and if he proves too crazy to handle it, by that time we'll have found his replacement. Or we'll be close. And the temporary loss in profits during the transition stage will be more than compensated for by the fact we'll own Montooth's book. All those numbers they play down there? It's a religion." He reached for some more peanuts. "I wish there was another way, like I said. But there ain't."

Everyone looked at Joe.

Joe stubbed out his cigarette. "I don't think Lamar can be dealt with. He's too off the beam. But I know Breezy Dix isn't strong enough to take over for his father *and* fight off Little Lamar. So I think the hit to our profits is going to be a lot bigger than Rico does. Montooth runs a tight shop, and everyone respects him down there. So there's been peace in Black Ybor now since 1920. Because of Montooth Dix. So I suggest we let Freddy have what he came for—he takes over Montooth's book, cuts the man in as a junior partner, but Montooth will take the hit willingly because he knows the alternative to it is death."

Joe sat back against the couch and Dion looked around the room for a bit and no one said anything. Dion rose and took his drink and his cigar to the enormous full-circle window that looked out on the ship cranes and grain silos and the sluggish channel. He turned back from the window and Joe saw the answer in his face.

"Shine's gotta go." He shrugged. "Sends the wrong message we let him kill two of ours."

"It won't be an easy hit," Captain Byner said. "He's holed up in that fortress of his. He's got provisions. He's got soldiers manning all the doors and windows. Got a few on the roof. It's impregnable right now."

"Burn him out," Freddy said.

"Christ." Rico shook his head. "Fuck is *wrong* with you?"

"What?"

"He's got his three wives in there," Rico said.

"And six kids," Joe said.

"So?"

Even Dion, who'd spilled more blood than any boss in recent memory, looked aghast.

Freddy said, "So, yeah, a wife or kid may burn up, but it's war. Bad things happen in war. Where am I wrong on this?"

"You see baboons in this room? Fucking jackals?" Dion asked. "We're not animals."

"All I'm saying is—"

"I hear you suggest killing kids again," Joe said quietly, "and, Freddy? I'll kill you myself." He turned so Freddy could look in his eyes when he smiled at him.

"Ho!" Rico threw up his hands. "Let's all bring the temperature back down, shall we, gents? Freddy, no one's killing kids, and, Joe, no one's killing Freddy. *Capice?*" He turned to Dion. "Just tell us what to do, boss."

"Put some guns on the building. If he pops his head up, blow it off. If he doesn't, he won't last more than a few weeks until cabin fever gets to him. And we'll kill him then. In the meantime, start getting your ducks aligned down there, so the transition will be smooth once he is gone. Make sense?"

"Why you're the boss." Rico nodded, a bright smile on his boyish face.

CHAPTER ELEVEN

Infinite Capacity

DUNCAN JEFFERTS WAS LOCKING UP the back door of the Hillsborough County medical examiner's office when a man he'd never expected to see again strolled out from behind the nearest meat wagon and said, "Hello."

Jefferts was on top of a loading bay as Joe Coughlin ambled up the ramp toward him. The gangster, allegedly retired, wore a cream-colored suit, matching Panama hat, crisp white shirt, perfectly knotted tie, and polished shoes that reflected the lights above the loading bay. His face was a bit more weathered than it had been seven years ago, but the eyes were just as boyish, almost innocent. Light burned bright in the irises, light that promised great things for you the closer you got to it. Jefferts had watched that light turn dead the day he'd met Joe Coughlin, though, the day Coughlin's wife had died and Jefferts had first introduced himself. For the longest moment of his life, Coughlin had stared at him with no life, no light, and Duncan remembered the irrational conviction that Coughlin would, in the next second, cut his throat. Instead, the death had left the man's eyes, to be replaced with gratitude that Duncan Jefferts was showing concern for Tomas Coughlin. Joe Coughlin had squeezed his shoulder, shook his hand, and led his son off the pier.

Jefferts rarely spoke of meeting the infamous "retired" gangster, Joe Coughlin. He tried telling his wife once but only flailed about, trying to articulate something that, he suspected, was too messy for words. In their brief encounter, he'd felt emanating from the man more grief, love, power, charisma, and potential for evil than he'd come across before or since.

What seemed to define Joe Coughlin, he tried explaining to his wife, was an infinite capacity.

"Capacity for what?" his wife had asked.

"Anything," he'd said.

When he reached the top of the loading dock, Joe held out his hand. "Remember me?"

Jefferts shook his hand. "I do, yes. Mr. Coughlin, the importer."

"Dr. Jefferts, the coroner."

They stood under the harsh light above the door and smiled awkwardly at each other.

"Uh . . ."

"What's that?"

"Can I help you with something?"

"I dunno. Can you?"

"I'm not sure—"

"How's that?"

"—why you're here at this time of night."

"What time of night is it?"

"Two in the morning."

"My wife."

Jefferts found the man looking at him suddenly as he tipped his hat back off his forehead a bit. "What about your wife?"

"You did the autopsy on her, correct?"

"You knew that."

"No, I didn't know that. I just knew you picked up her body. I gotta figure there are other coroners here. But you yourself performed the autopsy."

"Yes."

Joe perched himself on the iron rail that fringed the sides of the loading dock. He lit a cigarette and offered the pack to Jefferts, who took one. When he leaned in for a light, Coughlin said, "You're married now yourself."

Jefferts never wore his ring to work because he'd once lost it in a body. It had taken him half an hour to retrieve it and four more hours to repair the damage he'd done.

"How would you know that?"

"Your appearance is tidier. Slobby guys don't get tidier if they stay single."

"I'll mention that to my wife. She'll be pleased."

Joe nodded and spit a piece of tobacco off his tongue. "Was she pregnant?"

"Excuse me?"

"My wife. Graciela Corrales Coughlin, died September twenty-ninth, 1935." He smiled at Jefferts, but the blue eyes were gray. "Was she pregnant?"

Jefferts looked out into the parking lot for a moment. He tried to gauge if he had any ethical quandary here, but if he did, he couldn't find it.

"Yes," he told Joe.

"Gender?"

Jefferts shook his head.

"It was seven years ago," Joe said. "You seem awfully sure."

"It . . ." Jefferts exhaled and dropped his cigarette off the dock.

"What?"

"It was my first autopsy." He turned and met Joe's gaze. "I remember everything about it. The fetus was quite small. It had been gestating for no more than six weeks. The genital tubercle? The thing that turns into the penis or the clitoris? That was still far too underdeveloped to make a gender determination."

Joe finished his cigarette and flicked it off into the night. He hopped down off the rail and stuck out his hand again. "Thank you, Doctor."

Jefferts nodded and returned the handshake.

Joe had reached the parking lot when Jefferts asked, "Why do you care about the gender of an unborn fetus?"

Coughlin, hands in his pockets, looked back up at him for a long time. Then he shrugged and walked off into the night.

CHAPTER TWELVE

Bone Valley

TO REACH KING LUCIUS, they drove south on Route 5 until they reached Route 32, then headed east through damp country under a sky so purple it was nearly black. Farther east, rain clouds spilled and sprayed—smaller bruises bleeding within the bigger one. Once the rain found them—and it would, it was only a matter of when—it would be warm, Joe guessed. Warm and oily, like the gods were sweating. It was ten in the morning and they had their lights on. Weather in Florida was numbingly predictable until it wasn't. And then it became something vengeful—lightning that cleaved the sky, wind that shrieked like the ghosts of a dead army, a sun so white and cruel it set autumn fields ablaze. The weather here reminded him that he was just a man. For all his delusions of power, he was just that.

About thirty minutes out of Tampa, Rico asked Joe if he wanted him to take the wheel.

"No," Joe said, "I'm fine for now."

Rico settled low into his seat, dropped his fedora halfway down his forehead. "It's good we got time to talk."

"Yeah?"

"Yeah. I mean, I know that clipping Montooth sits bad with you, and I never forgot that about working with you—you're the most moral motherfucking gangster I ever met."

Joe frowned. "It's not morality, it's ethics. Montooth did right by us until Freddy pushed into his territory. And now Montooth's gotta take a dirt nap because, well, no offense, Freddy's a shithead."

Rico sighed. "I know it. I know it. He's my brother and he's a shithead and he's an asshole and still, Joe, what am I gonna do?"

Neither said anything for a bit.

"But I'm of the mind," Rico said eventually, "that Montooth is the least of our problems right now."

"What're the bigger ones?"

"We got a rat in the organization for starters. Our loads are getting hit at twice the rate of any other crews. And they ain't getting hit by other gangsters; they're getting hit by Feds and local law. I think we can survive it for a while longer because we're a family of earners. I mean, we get after it. *And* we got you."

Joe glanced over at him. "And you."

Rico started to protest but then shrugged. "Okay. Fair enough. I do earn."

"Rico, you earn about twenty percent of the Family's nut."

Rico pushed the hat back up his forehead and sat straighter in his seat. "There's a lot of scary talk around campfires right now, Joe. Lot of it."

"About the rat?"

"About the whole organization. We look weak. We look ripe for takeover."

"To who?"

"Where you want to start? Santo's guys."

Joe didn't argue that one. Santo worked out of the Italian Social Club on Seventh Avenue, and was looking very hungry of late. Hungry and humorless, always a bad combination.

"Who else?"

Rico lit a smoke, tossed the match out the window. "Fucking whatshisname, uh, from Miami." He snapped his fingers.

"Anthony Crowe?"

Rico pointed an affirmative finger at him. "Nick Pisano knows he has to give him some big territory right fucking soon or Anthony's gonna come for Nick Pisano. He might-could tell Anthony to help himself to ours."

"Crowe's not full-blooded Italian. He can't take over."

"Sorry to break the news, but he is. Parents changed the name from Crochetti or something when they came over, but that fucker can trace his roots right back to Sicily. He's smart, he's mean, and he's not satisfied with his spot at the table anymore. Wants his own dining hall."

Joe gave it some thought. "We're not *that* weak. We're a little shaky right now, okay. Everybody is. Revenue's down all over because of that Kraut midget and his mustache and the fucking war. But we still control one of the richest ports in this country, we control narcotics for half the state, gambling for a quarter of it, and trucking for damn near all of it."

Rico said, "But our house is out of order. And everyone knows it."

Joe took his time lighting his own cigarette. Took his time cracking his window to let the smoke out. "You talking treason, Rico?"

"What?"

"You talking about removing the boss?"

Rico stared across the seat at Joe for a long moment and then held up his hands. "Fuck no. Dion's the boss and that's all there is to it."

"That is all there is to it."

"I know."

"But?"

"But somebody's gotta talk to him, Joe. Somebody he listens to. Somebody has to . . ."

"What?"

"Get him to take the reins again. He took over? Everyone loved him. They still do, but he doesn't seem to be watching the store the same way. You know? There's a lot of bad talk going around, is all I'm saying."

"Let me hear it."

Rico took a moment. "Everyone knows the boss has a problem with the cards. And the horses. And the wheel."

"Noted," Joe said.

"The big weight loss over the last few years? People think he's sick. You know, dying."

"He's not dying. It's something else."

"I *know* that." Rico tapped the side of his nose a few times. "But it's not common knowledge outside the Family. And what do you say to people—he ain't dying, he's just getting tight on the powder?" Rico held up his hands again. "Joe, this is said just between us and with all respect."

Joe drove for a bit in silence, let Rico twist for a while.

"I'll agree you might have a point," he said eventually. He glanced across the seat. "Don't give you the right to talk about it, though."

"You don't think I know that?" Rico flicked his cigarette out the window and took a long slow exhale. "I love our thing. You know? I fucking love it. We wake up every day and find new ways to screw the system. Don't take a knee for anyone, don't line up in rows of two for anyone. We"—he drove his index finger into the dashboard—"make our lives, make our rules, make our way like men." He hunched forward. "I fucking *love* being a gangster."

Joe chuckled softly.

"What?"

"Nothing," Joe said.

"No, what?"

Joe looked over at him. "I like it a whole hell of a lot too."

"So, so . . ." Rico took a breath. "I risked talking about, you know, problems with—"

"*Perceived* problems."

"Right. I risked talking about perceived problems with the boss because I don't want to lose this thing. I don't want to end up with two in the dome or doing time, come out nobody knows me anymore, I gotta fucking get a straight job or something. I never made an honest buck in my life, and I don't want to learn how."

Joe nodded and said nothing until they were just outside Sarasota.

"I'll talk to Dion," he said eventually. "I'll impress upon him that we need to find this rat and get our house in order."

"He'll go for it."

Joe shrugged. "He might."

"He will," Rico said, "because it comes from you. He still looks up to you, I think."

"Get the fuck out of this car."

"No, really."

"Let me tell you something about Dion—he was the boss of our crew when we were kids. He was the toughest and scariest of all of us. Only reason he ended up taking orders from me was because of a bank job that went bad. He ended up on the run; I ended up making powerful friends. Except for that little . . . run of time, he's always been my boss, not the other way around."

"Might be so," Rico said, "but you're still the only guy he looks at like he cares what you think."

Joe said nothing and they drove on along a ghostly strip of road under the ruined plum sky.

"Tomas." Rico said, "Kid's growing like a weed. I couldn't believe it when I saw him the other day."

"Tell me about it. His mother was tall. His uncles are tall."

"You're not a midget."

"But I might look like one standing next to him someday."

"How do you like it?" Rico said, his voice a bit more serious.

"Being a father?"

"Yeah."

"I like it a lot. I mean, I'm terrible at it most days. Lose my temper more than I ever thought I would."

"I've never even heard you raise your voice."

"I know, I know." Joe shook his head. "Most people haven't. My son, though? Seen it so many times, he rolls his eyes if I do it now. They get to you. I mean, he's a great kid, but he still does shit like climb up on a barn roof when he knows the roof is weak and needs repairs. That's how he broke his arm last year at our farm in Cuba. When he was a toddler, he was always trying to swallow small, sharp rocks. Or I'd be giving him a bath, I'd look away for a second, he'd be standing up trying to dance. And, *boom,* down he goes. And all you're thinking is, My *job* is to keep you alive. Keep you from getting another broken arm or losing an eye. So, you know, stop fucking dancing in the fucking tub."

Rico cracked up and Joe laughed along with him.

"You can't believe it now," Joe said, "but once you have one, buckle up, partner."

"I will be having one."

Joe looked over at him.

Rico raised his eyebrows up and down and Joe punched him in the shoulder.

"Damn." Rico rubbed the shoulder.

"Who's the girl?"

"Kathryn Contarino. Everyone calls her Kat?"

"From South Tampa?"

A proud, boyish smile. "Yeah."

"Beautiful girl," Joe said. "Congratulations."

"Thanks," Rico said. "Yeah, I . . . yeah." He looked out the window. "I'm lucky."

"What're you," Joe asked, "smitten?"

Rico rolled his eyes and then nodded. "Matter of fact. Gonna marry her."

"What?" Joe swerved the car slightly.

"What's the big deal? People get married."

"I never took you for the type."

"Not 'the type,'" Rico said, smoothing his shirt into his pants where it had bunched up from the car ride. "The fucking nerve of ya. What about you?"

Joe laughed.

"No, really. No one's seen you with a steady filly in seven years. You got something secret stashed away?"

"Nope."

"Sure?"

"You know I'd tell *you* if I did," Joe said with a straight face.

Rico gave him the finger. "You hardly ever go to whores, Joe. And the ones you do see say you take them to dinner and buy 'em nice dresses and earrings and half the time you don't even fuck them."

"I got someone regular in Cuba," Joe said to get him off his back. "Not Havana. A village girl in the west, near my farm. She cooks well, she's real pretty, lets me come and go as I please. Ain't true love, but it ain't bad."

"Well, good for you," Rico said. "Now we just gotta find a girl for my brother."

She'd have to be a young one, Joe thought. Or a boy.

"Yeah, I'll get thinking on that," Joe told him.

About a half an hour west of Zolfo Springs, Rico said, "Are we ready for this?"

Joe said, "Lucius?"

Rico nodded, lips parted, his eyes a little wider than usual.

"We've both dealt with the man before."

"Not on his boat, though. You ever been on his boat?"

Joe shook his head.

"People get on, sometimes they don't come off. You heard about those Adrocalese, or whatever they call them?"

"*Androphagi,*" Joe said. Lucius's Palace Guard, a group of twenty men you had to pass through before you got to him.

"I heard the reason nobody ever finds the bodies Lucius drops is because they eat them."

Joe forced a chuckle. "That's what *Androphagi* means, yeah."

Rico looked over at him. "Means what?"

"A tribe of cannibals."

"Fuck." Rico exhaled the word, turning one syllable into three or four. "How do you know this shit?"

"Jesuit high school," Joe said. "You study a lot of Greek mythology."

"The Greeks had cannibals?"

Joe shook his head. "This was a private army. Some say they were out of Africa, others say they were Finns or Russians. Either way, they helped Darius the Great invade Southern Russia. And supposedly they, uh, ate a few people." He tried to lighten his tone, had to work at it. "So Lucius names his guys *Androphagi* to scare the shit out of everyone."

Rico said, "Succeeded."

After another mile, Joe said, "You don't have to board with me. Just drop me off. As long as you're seen."

Rico shook his head with a wry smile. "I talk to calm my nerves. Don't mean I'm some fucking moke would leave a pal in his hour of need. Fuck, Joe, the two of us? Take a battalion of these fucking Androcalese—"

"*Androphagi.*"

"*Andro-fuck-them.* Okay? Take a battalion of them to get the better of a couple tough monkeys like us." He took out his flask and handed it to Joe. "Drink to that."

Joe raised the flask. "Glad to have you with me, Rico." He drank and handed the flask back.

"Glad to be here, Joe." Rico took a powerful snort. "If they try to fuck with a couple of downtown fellas like us, we'll show these country assholes a thing or two."

THE RAIN FOUND THEM a few miles short of Zolfo Springs. It lashed the car and floated across the road in great sheets. They'd rolled down their windows to smoke but now they rolled them back up and the rain clattered on the roof and the road hissed under their tires and the frame of the Pontiac shuddered in gusts that came and went at random.

They reached Zolfo Springs and left the main road and from there Rico had to read from the directions Joe had placed on the seat between them. Right here, next left, no second left, sorry. The low sky and the bending palm trees formed a cowl around the car, and the rain slowed but the drops thickened. It was like driving through broth.

Charlie Luciano himself had once said he never wanted to get any closer to the devil on this earth than he already had to his gate-keeper, King Lucius. Meyer wouldn't deal with Lucius face-to-face, and even Joe had avoided the man whenever humanly possible over the past fifteen years.

King Lucius had appeared on the scene during the Florida land boom back in '23, coming, some said, from Russia by way of New Orleans. It was impossible to pinpoint his accent because it was so maddeningly faint. It could have been Russian or Montenegron or even Albanian. It was definitely aristocratic, as was the care Lucius took with his eyebrows and nails.

Over the years, he and his crew had pulled down more high-end scores in more parts of the country than any other. And yet no matter where he hit—from as far away as Santa Barbara, California, to as close as Key West—he always paid tribute to the men within whose boundaries his base of operations lay. He paid the Bartolos in Tampa, the Pisanos in Miami, and the Nicolo brothers in Jacksonville. Not *every* job, of course—they would have lost respect for anyone that honest—but a solid 90 percent of them. He made the three Florida families so much money that he could pretty much live with impunity. Which he did. When someone mentioned back in '36 that Eliot Fergs had advanced an opinion on Lucius's taste in women, Lucius personally beat Eliot to death in the back room of Eliot's service station. In the late fall of '38, he fed Jeremy Kay to the gators. When Jeremy's brother came looking less than a month later, a few people saw him board King Lucius's boat, but no one ever saw him disembark.

If anyone else had clipped three employees of the Family, they

would have been clipped themselves. It was a testament to King
Lucius's power that he wasn't even called before the Commission,
though Joe himself had taken a trip to Central Florida back in '39,
shortly after Jeremy Kay's brother vanished, to tell King Lucius
that as far as they were concerned, he'd gotten three freebies; there
wouldn't be a fourth.

King Lucius was, first and foremost, a phosphate king, his
kingdom stretching for seventy miles down the Peace River from
Fort Meade to Port Charlotte. For years, he'd invested his ill-gotten
gains into dredging and mining the waters of the Bone Valley of
Central Florida. He owned a majority share in the Bone Valley Fertilizer Company, and had even used shell companies to buy small
pieces of the other twelve mining concerns that operated along the
Peace, all of them involved in the procurement of phosphates to
make fertilizer or, since the war had broken out, munitions.

Joe was a partial owner in BVFC, as was Dion Bartolo and Rico
DiGiacomo. They weren't majority shareholders, but they didn't have
to be; when it came to phosphates in Florida, half the job was mining
it, but the rest lay in transporting it. When Prohibition wound down
in the early 1930s, Joe and men like him were left with an unfortu-
nate surplus of trucks, boats, and the occasional seaplane with no
one to sell them to and nothing illegal left to transport. In 1935, Joe,
Esteban Suarez, Dion Bartolo, and Rico joined up, when Rico was
nothing but a smart, baby-faced kid who'd grown up in the bosom
of Port Tampa, to form Bay Area Transport Company. And after ten
years under Joe's guidance and Rico DiGiacomo's stewardship, nothing moved off the Peace River—not so much as a pebble—if it wasn't
transported by Bay Area Transport.

King Lucius's cut—however sizable it may have been—was
limited to Bone Valley Fertilizer Company. He didn't own a single
share of Bay Area Transport, and that forced parity into the rela-

tionship. He could mine all the phosphate he wanted, but if he couldn't get it to a rail line or across to the ocean, he couldn't do dick with it.

King Lucius kept a suite at the Commodore Hotel in Naples and another at the Vinoy in St. Petersburg, but most nights he could be found on his houseboat, which motored up and down the Peace River. The houseboat was two-tiered and had been imported from India. It had been constructed over a hundred years ago in the Kerala region of *anjili* wood planks as smooth and dark as frozen toffee and was held together by not a single screw or nail, but by coir knots coated in boiled cashew resin. With a curved roof of bamboo and palm leaves, six bedrooms, and a second-floor dining room that could seat fourteen, the boat cut an impressive figure on the silver-thread surface of the Peace River. To behold it, one could easily imagine he'd been transported to the banks of the Ganges.

Joe and Rico pulled into a crushed-shell parking lot and looked through the rain at the boat until Al Butters pulled down the small incline into the mine site from what remained of the jungle behind them. They'd chopped down so much of it and burned so much more, felled cypress and banyan trees that had stood for centuries, since before men had possessed the words to name them or the tools to kill them. Al pulled alongside them in the same faded green Packard he'd driven Joe around in the last time they'd met. He pointed the nose of his car at the trunk of theirs, so his window ended up parallel to Joe's.

The rain stopped. As if someone had turned it off with a switch.

Al Butters rolled down his window, and Joe rolled down his own.

Joe looked out at the houseboat as Ogden Semple, King Lucius's longtime aide, stepped onto the rear deck and stared back at the cars.

"I should come with you guys." Al didn't sound excited by the prospect.

"Nah." Joe moved his tongue around, tried to get some liquid going in there. "There's a Thompson in the trunk in case we don't come back off the boat."

"What do I do with it? Come find you?"

"No." Something ticked at the base of Joe's throat. Felt like a beetle. "You just strafe the boat until whoever killed us is dead too. There's a can of gas back there with the gun. You light that fucking thing up and watch till it sinks." He looked over at him. "You do that for us, Al?"

"He's got an army on there."

Rico leaned across the seat. "And you'll have a Thompson. If we die, you respond. Clear?"

Al eventually nodded, his lips moving, his eyes too big.

"What?" Joe said. "Just say it."

"You can't kill the devil."

"He's not the devil," Joe said. "The devil's charming."

He and Rico got out of the car. Joe straightened his tie and the line of his suit in the same motion. He removed his hat, a straw half-fedora with a black silk band, and raised it to the satin sky, which gave off a glare from a sun he couldn't see; it hid behind the pewter clouds. Across the river, past the ravaged shore, and back through the burned and spoiled land, a small flash of light glittered once, twice, and then no more. Rico saw it too.

"How many guys?"

"Six," Joe said. "All pros with long-range rifles. If I remove my tie on the boat, get ready to duck."

"Won't be enough." Rico adjusted his own hat.

"Won't even be close. But we'll take a few with us if it goes wrong. Fuck. Let's do this."

"You said it."

Joe put the hat back on and he and Rico walked up the gang-plank.

Ogden Semple met them up top. Ogden had lost an eye in a knife fight a dozen years back, so his right eyelids were permanently sewn together. The remaining eye was milky, pale, and intensely focused. He looked at everything like a man squinting to peer through a microscope. Joe handed Ogden his Savage .32 automatic and a switchblade from his front pocket. Rico handed over a Smith & Wesson .38.

Ogden said, "I hope you catch it."

They stared back at him. "Catch what?"

"The King's cold. He should be in bed resting, but instead he's attending a meeting you insisted upon. It could make him sicker." He dropped their weapons into a leather pouch he'd brought for the occasion. "I hope you get what he has but you get it worse."

Joe knew many assumed Ogden was King Lucius's lover, but Joe knew he loved a whore at one of Joe's brothels in Tampa. Her name was Matilda, and Ogden liked to read her bedtime stories and scrub her clean during long baths. Matilda reported to Joe that Ogden was a gentle, considerate lover and hung like a White House chandelier. His only kink was that he insisted on calling her Ruth. Matilda had no proof, but she believed Ruth was a dead sister or dead daughter from very long ago. Matilda's eyes had picked up a sheen when she told this to Joe, and just before he left her room, she said to him, "Is everyone we know broken?"

Joe had looked back at her and told the truth. "Pretty much."

On the boat, Ogden gestured for them to climb the ladder to the second deck. He stayed below, however, their guns in the pouch at his feet and looked out at Al Butters in the parking lot as the boat pulled away from the dock and headed downriver.

CHAPTER THIRTEEN

An Absence of Illness

ON THE UPPER DECK, twenty men formed a wall between Joe, Rico, and the rest of the boat. Two of them stepped from the pack to frisk the guests. The rest stood motionless under a pale brown canopy, all light missing from their eyes. Most were tall. None wore shirts, which exposed the track marks in their arms, as black as worms burned into asphalt. Their rib cages protruded.

They represented a multitude of races—Turks, Russians, two Orientals, three or four who looked like garden-variety American white trash. The one who frisked Joe had toffee skin, straw-yellow hair cut close to his scalp, and a harelip. He wore a long curved knife on his hip with an ivory handle sheathed in a leather scabbard. The one who frisked Rico had sharp Slavic features and hair as dark as the sky. Both sported long nails. Joe looked at the other eighteen men and saw that all grew their nails long. A few had pared them to points. Most brandished knives in the waistbands of their tattered trousers. The ones who didn't tucked pistols there. When the two had finished frisking Joe and Rico, the wall parted to reveal Lucius on the other side, sitting in a mahogany plantation chair.

Joe had heard a pit boss in Havana describe King Lucius as weighing "three bills easy. Huge head, bald as an egg." Another time, he'd overheard a Tampa bartender tell three drunks that Lucius was "thinner than Death and taller than God."

Joe had known Lucius for almost fifteen years and was often struck by how forgettable he appeared. He was three or four inches shy of six feet, much like Joe himself. His head was shaped like a peach with reddened cheeks and ears. His hair was pale and thinning. His full lips would have been considered sensual on a woman; his tiny teeth were gray. His light green eyes seemed fixed in a state of mild wonder. Even when they were perfectly still, however, they somehow managed to move. Joe had often felt circled by them.

He wore an oversize white Cuban guayabera over loose seersucker trousers with thick sandals on his pink feet. He looked the blandest of fellows.

A girl lay facedown on the chaise beside him and he slapped her ass lightly as he rose from his chair. "Chop-chop, Vidalia, there's business on the day's agenda." As the girl roused herself, he came to Joe and Rico with an outstretched hand. "Gentlemen."

The girl stumbled her way toward them, either half-asleep or half-bombed on something.

"Say hi to my friends, Vidalia."

"Hi, friends," the girl mumbled as she reached them. She wore an unbelted white silk bathrobe over her ruffled black bathing suit.

"Shake their hands."

If he hadn't been told her name, Joe might not have placed her. But Joe had only met one other Vidalia in his lifetime—Bobby O's

girlfriend last year—and he realized it was the same girl. The realiza-
tion became a lament. The Vidalia Langston of twelve-to-fourteen
months ago had been, as all Bobby O's girlfriends were back then,
jailbait. Recently transplanted from either Iowa or Idaho, if he
remembered correctly. A high school senior at Hillsborough High,
member of the cheerleading squad, and class treasurer, she'd con-
fided to Joe, because she was a little too wild for anyone to let her
run for class president. That Vidalia Langston had been unbridled
in just about everything she did—the roar of her laugh, the thrusts
of her hips when she broke into impromptu dances in the club, the
abundance of dark hair that fell over one eye in a peek-a-boo cut.

   She'd run so many rings around Bobby O she may have cured
him of his taste for jailbait, though; after Vidalia, he took to dat-
ing middle-aged coffee-shop waitresses. Even Joe, who'd never seen
the attraction in bedding a girl whose brains were still years from
catching up to her body, recalled feeling pleasantly uncomfortable
around Vidalia a few times.

   Now, though, when they shook hands, hers felt like an old
woman's. She smacked her lips, as if her mouth was far too dry, and
wavered slightly from side to side. He couldn't tell if she remembered him. She dropped his hand and crossed to the other deck to
lie on another chaise past the canopy. When she dropped the silk
robe off her shoulders, he could see the bones in her back. Her hair
spilled down her spine, reaching almost to her lowest ribs. Lucius
always picked them that way—young with long, abundant hair. At
the start. At the finish, they were always something else. This, Joe
wished he'd told Vidalia a year ago, is how unbridled dreams often
end—bridled beyond hope.

   Lucius led them back under the canopy. He waved them to
chairs to the right and left of his own. When they all sat, he clapped
once, as if harmony had been achieved. "My partners."

Joe nodded. "Good to see you again."

"And you, Joe."

"How are you feeling?" Rico asked.

"Fit as a fiddle, Enrico. Why?"

"Heard you had a bit of a cold."

"Where'd you hear that?"

Rico, already realizing he'd managed to step in it, tried to deflect. "Just hoping it passes quick. Warm weather ones are the worst."

"I don't have a cold."

On the table beside him—hot tea, a lemon, and a box of tissues. He stared back at them, his face an open book.

"Well, you look great anyway," Rico said.

"You say that with some surprise."

"No."

"Did someone *else* suggest I was ill?"

"No," Rico said.

"Weak or frail or laid low by maladies?"

"Nope. Just mentioning you look good."

"As do you, Rico." He turned and appraised Joe. "You look tired, however."

"Can't imagine why."

"Been sleeping well?"

"Like a champ."

"Well, then, we're all looking good enough to have to buy our way out of the draft." He flashed his gray smile. "What brings you by? You said it was urgent."

As Joe told him about being contacted by Theresa Del Fresco and her fears for her safety, various *Androphagi* placed a large coffee table between them and laid out place mats, followed by plates and silverware. That was followed by stemware, linen napkins, a pitcher of water, and a bottle of white wine in a bucket of ice.

Lucius listened to Joe with one eyebrow softly raised, his mouth occasionally forming an O of surprise. He nodded at one of his men, and the man poured them each a glass of wine.

When Joe finished talking, Lucius said, "I'm confused. Does Theresa think I have anything to do with these attempts on her life? Do you?"

"Absolutely not."

"Absolutely not." Lucius smiled at Rico. "I've noticed people speak most emphatically when they're selling something." He turned back to Joe. "Because why else would you be telling me this unless you believed I had something to do with these inexcusable acts?"

"Because you're the only man with the reach in these parts to make the acts stop."

"You have powerful friends. You're powerful yourself."

"My reach has limits."

"But mine doesn't?"

"Not in Union County."

Lucius reached for his wine and motioned for them to do the same. He raised his glass. "To a continued partnership."

Rico and Joe both nodded and raised their glasses before drinking. The *Androphagi* returned with food—two roasted chickens, boiled potatoes, ears of steamed corn. One of the men carved the chickens at the table, his long knife slicing through the meat like beams of light flashing through a cave. In moments, a pile of meat rose from a platter in the center of the table, and the pillaged carcasses were removed.

"So you've come to purchase protection for Theresa Del Fresco?"

"Yes."

"Why?" Lucius forked some chicken onto his plate. Before Joe could answer, Lucius said, "Go on. Help yourselves. Rico, start with the corn. Joe, the potatoes."

They made themselves plates. As they did, Vidalia stumbled past them, told Lucius she was heading down for a nap. She gave Joe and Rico a distant, disenchanted smile and Lucius a small wave. As she headed for the stairs Joe wondered, not for the first time, if men in their thing soiled all women whose paths they crossed, or if certain women came to them because they preferred to be soiled. That distant smile she'd given them wasn't part of her repertoire a year ago; back then she had a laugh you couldn't have caught with a steel net. He'd remember the sound of it for the rest of his life; he wondered if she remembered it at all.

"Why did I come?" he asked Lucius. "That's your question?"

"Why are you helping a woman you barely know?"

"She asked. It seemed a small favor to reach out to a business associate."

Lucius coughed several times into his fist. They were wet, rattling coughs and he held up a hand until they passed. He sat back for a moment, a hand to his chest. His eyes focused and he cleared his throat. "And she's offering me compensation for this service?"

"Yes."

"And what compensation did she offer you?"

"She claims to have information crucial to my survival."

"How so?"

"She claims there's a contract on me." Joe tried some of the chicken.

Lucius looked at Rico, then back at Joe, then down at his plate. The houseboat moved lazily down the river. Mounds of phosphogypsum rose along the shoreline like hills of damp ash. Beyond the hills lay dead trees and piles of curled and blackened palm fronds. The white sun had returned and beat down on it all.

Lucius sipped his drink and watched Joe over the rim of the glass. "That would strike me as odd."

"Why's that? This is a rough business."

"Not for golden boys like yourself who threaten no one. You have no pretensions to power anymore. You're not known for having a hot temper or a gambling problem. You don't fuck other men's wives, at least not the wives of men in our profession. And the last enemies you did have you dispatched in one day, so no one would take you lightly on that score, either." He sipped some more wine and leaned forward. "Do you think you're an evil man?"

"Never gave it much thought."

"You profit from prostitution, narcotics, loan-sharking, illegal gambling—"

"A lot of which is legal when I do it in Cuba."

"Legal isn't, as a matter of course, moral."

Joe nodded. "And, by the same logic, illegal isn't necessarily immoral."

Lucius smiled. "Didn't you run some illegal Chinese through Havana into Tampa a few years back? Hundreds of them, if not thousands?"

Joe nodded.

Rico chimed in. "We both did. That was a joint venture"

Lucius ignored him, eyes never leaving Joe. "Didn't several of them die?"

For several moments, Joe watched sandpipers scuttle along a damp stretch of shoreline. He looked back at Lucius. "On one trip, yeah."

"Women? Children? A one-year-old, if I remember correctly, boiled like a holiday ham in the cargo hold?"

Joe nodded.

"So we'll add trafficking in human beings to your ledger. And you've killed, of course. Killed your own mentor. Ordered the death of his son and several of his men on the same day."

"After they'd killed some of mine."

A thin smile. Another gaze leveled over the top of his glass. "But you're not evil?"

"I'm having a little trouble following the point of this conversation, Lucius."

Lucius stared at the water. "You think feeling bad about your sins makes you good. Some might find that kind of delusion contemptible." He turned his gaze back on them. "And maybe my initial disbelief on hearing there could be a contract on you—which I presume was your initial reaction, and yours too, Rico?"

"Definitely," Rico said.

"Possibly that disbelief was naïve. You have put a lot of sin out into the world, Joseph. Maybe it's rolling back in on the tide. Maybe men like us, in order to be men like us, sacrifice peace of mind forevermore."

"Maybe we do," Joe said, "which is a theory I'm willing to consider in my leisure next month if I'm still alive."

Lucius clasped his hands together and leaned forward. "Let's start with logic—where did you hear there was a contract on you?"

Joe said, "Theresa."

"Why did she share the information with you? Theresa never did anything in her life unless it benefited Theresa."

"So I'd go to you for her protection."

"And so you did." One of his silent men replaced the bottle of wine with a fresh one. "What's Theresa offering me?"

"Ninety percent of her share of that German boat your crew took off in Key West."

"Ninety."

Joe nodded. "The other ten percent to be handed to me, which I'll put in an account for her son, so Theresa's mother can access it while she's in prison."

"Ninety percent," Lucius said again.

"For full protection her entire stay in prison."

"We have a small problem." King Lucius sat back in his chair and crossed his left ankle onto his right knee.

"What's that?"

"She's offering me money I already have, and you're offering me nothing. I'm unconvinced how continuing this conversation benefits me."

"You and I are partners," Joe said. "You can mine all the phosphate you want, but you can't move it without me."

"That's not entirely so," Lucius said. "If some calamity were to befall you, god forbid, I trust your associates would place their considerable grief aside and carry on. Do you consider our current terms fair?"

"Very," Joe said.

Lucius laughed. "Of course you would! They benefit you. But what if I find your rates usurious?"

"Do you?" Rico asked.

"Let's say that on occasion or two it's troubled my sleep."

Joe said, "You pay far less than the going rate to use our trucks. We're charging you . . ." He looked over at Rico.

"Twenty cents a pound, four dollars a mile."

"Those are loss leaders," Joe said.

"Fifteen cents a pound," Lucius said.

"Seventeen."

"And three dollars a mile."

"You're dreaming."

"Three twenty-five."

"Any idea what gas costs these days?" Joe said. "Three seventy-five."

"Three fifty."

"Three sixty-five."

Lucius looked down at his plate and chewed his food for a bit. Then he turned to Rico and grinned. He indicated Joe with his knife. "Young Rico, you can learn from this one. He's always been a very bright boy."

Lucius dropped his knife and extended his hand across the table.

Joe had to lean forward to shake it.

"I, for one, hope you are among the living, Joe, at least as long as I am."

They broke the handshake.

Along the shoreline, several Negro children fished from a canted pier in waters turned chalky with phosphorous debris. Behind the Negro children, the green and yellow jungle was pocked with small shacks. Back behind the shacks, a white cross rose from the local church, which didn't appear much bigger or much better than the shacks. On the opposite shoreline, the trees had all been cut away and the road ran close to the riverbank and Joe saw Al Butters, clear as day, puttering along in his car.

"What about you?" Lucius said to Rico.

"What about me?"

"Are you your brother's keeper?"

"Not that I'm aware."

"Then why are you here?"

Rico gave Lucius a befuddled smile. "Wanted to get out of the city for a day, see some country. You know how it is."

"Not really." Lucius wasn't smiling. "You're a crew boss, aren't you?"

"Yup."

"Youngest in the organization."

"I guess."

"A prodigy like your mentor here was."

"Just a guy, Lucius, going about his business."

"So this is business? You're here on business."

Rico lit a cigarette, trying hard to look casual. "No. Just came to lend support."

Lucius gestured at Joe. "Support for him?"

"Yeah."

"But why does he need support?"

"He doesn't."

"Then why are you here?"

"I told you."

"Tell me again."

"I felt like taking a ride."

Lucius's face was very still. "Or did you want to bear witness?"

"To what?"

"To whatever occurs here today."

Rico squared himself a bit and his eyes grew smaller. "All that's occurring here today is a few business associates catching up."

"And one associate bribing another to protect a third party."

"And that."

Lucius poured himself a third glass of wine. "I think you came out here to bear witness to my promises, in which case you presume I could renege at a later date. Either that, or you came in the futile hopes of protecting your friend, in which case you take me for the kind of man who would offer his guests food, wine, and shelter and then hurt them. Which would be a disgraceful transgression. In either proposition, Enrico, your presence here is an insult." He turned to Joe. "And you, you're even worse. You think those snipers out in the trees escaped my notice? Those are my trees. This is my water. Avilka."

The yellow-haired *Androphagi* appeared. He knelt by Lucius and

Lucius spoke into his ear. Avilka nodded several times and then stood. He left his boss's side and headed down to the lower deck.

Lucius smiled at Joe. "You send a troll from the fucking Bunsford Mob to keep watch? Where's the respect, Joe? The common courtesy?"

"I wasn't showing disrespect to you, Lucius. I was showing respect to the Bunsfords because I landed my plane in their territory last week."

"And then brought their stink into mine?" Lucius drank more wine, his jaw working, his eyes moving from side to side, out toward the water, in toward himself. "Lucky for you," he said, "I'm not easily offended."

Ogden Semple and Avilka appeared by the bow. Ogden came to their table with a large manila envelope that he handed to Lucius.

Lucius tossed the envelope onto Joe's lap. "Her ten percent. Count it if you want."

"No need," Joe said.

The boat veered toward the shoreline before it angled right and completed its turn in the river. They were headed back, the heavy motors working harder now, growing louder.

"You're not playing me for a fool, are you, Joe?"

"I can't even imagine how a fella would go about that, Lucius."

"People have tried. Would that surprise you to hear?"

"Yes," Joe said.

Lucius opened his cigarette case and before he had the cigarette to his lips, Ogden Semple held a lighter underneath it.

"Would that surprise you to hear, Ogden?"

Ogden snapped the lighter closed. "Very much, sir."

"And why's that?"

"Because no one plays you for a fool."

"Why not?"

"Because you're a king."

Lucius nodded. At first it appeared to Joe as if he were simply nodding in agreement with Ogden, but then two of the *Androphagi* stepped out of the group and one stabbed Ogden in the back while the other stabbed his chest. They worked quickly, putting sixteen or seventeen holes in the man within as many seconds. Sharp yelps left his mouth, then small grunts. When his killers stepped away from him, his blood splattered their bare chests. Ogden fell to his knees on the deck. He looked up at Lucius, confused, one arm trying to hold on to parts of him that kept slithering from the holes in his belly.

Lucius told Ogden, "Don't you ever tell anyone—in this life or the next—that I'm unwell."

Ogden started to respond, but Avilka knelt behind him and used the curved blade to open his throat. It spilled its contents down onto the mess that was the rest of him and he lay on the deck and closed his one good eye.

Out on the river, a white heron flapped its large white wings and glided past the houseboat.

Lucius locked eyes with Joe and gestured at the corpse. "How do you think I *feel* about that? Good or bad?"

"I wouldn't know."

"Guess."

"Bad."

"Why?"

"He worked for you for a long time."

Lucius shrugged. "The truth is, I don't feel anything at all. For him. For any living thing. And I can't remember the last time I did. Yet, under the watchful eyes of God," he said, and squinted up at the sun, "I thrive."

CHAPTER FOURTEEN

Crosshairs

"THINK THEY ATE HIM?" Rico asked as he drove them west on 32.

"I have no opinion on the subject." Joe took a swig from the pint of rye they'd bought at a roadside fruit stand manned by two Indian children and an old woman. He passed it across the seat to Rico, who took a swig of his own.

"What is *wrong* with that guy?"

"Another thing I couldn't begin to guess at."

They drove in silence for a bit and passed the bottle back and forth enough times that the flora around them grew sharper and greener.

"I mean, all right, look, I've killed guys," Rico said. "Never killed a woman or a kid."

Joe looked at him.

"Not intentionally," Rico said. "That Chinese kid was just bad luck. You killed guys, right?"

"Of course."

"But there was a reason."

"I thought so at the time."

"There was no *reason* here. Fucking guy let slip to us that his boss had a cold, and now he's fucking *dead*? What kind of standards are these?"

Joe could feel that boat in his pores, wished he could scrub it from his scalp.

"I recognized the girl from somewhere," Rico said. "Was that the one used to bump uglies with Georgie B?"

Joe shook his head. "Bobby O."

Rico snapped his fingers. "Right, right."

"Used to come into the Calypso Club."

"Yeah, no, now I remember her. Shit. She'd set knees to knocking, that one."

"Not anymore."

"Not anymore."

Rico let loose a low, slow whistle. "Girl had some *power*."

Joe nodded and then they looked at each other and said it together: "Not anymore."

"Girl thinks she has power in her pussy, and maybe sometimes she's right, for a while. We think we have it in our balls and our muscle. And maybe we're right. For a while." Rico shook his head ruefully. "A little, little while."

Joe nodded. Power—most power anyway, certainly Vidalia's brand of it—was the fly that called itself a hawk. It could only govern those who agreed to call it a hawk instead of a fly, a tiger instead of a cat, a king instead of a man.

They drove the steaming white road under the white sun, the cypress spilling, wilting, and surging on either side of them. No one had developed this stretch of the state yet. It teemed with unchecked jungle growth, gators, panthers, and oily swamps that glistened under thin layers of green fog.

Rico said, "You got, what, a week until Ash Wednesday?"

"Yup."

"Christ, Joe. Christ."

"What?"

"Nothing."

"No. Spit it out."

"It'll insult your intelligence."

"Insult away."

Rico chewed on it for a few moments, his eyes hard on the road. "I wasn't a believer until I got a whiff of Lucius again and remembered what a demented fucking twist he is. If he hadn't killed Ogden today, he would have killed Al Butters. Or that girl. Or one of us. Point was, he was going to kill someone today. And just because. No better reason than that. So if he's anywhere near this contract that's out on you, you gotta vamoose until the smoke clears. Shit, just lay low at your farm for a week or two. Let me and my guys find out who's holding the paper on you, find out why, and cancel their fucking check." He looked over at Joe. "Be a pleasure, believe me."

Joe said, "I appreciate the offer."

Rico slapped the wheel. "Don't give me a 'but' here. Don't you do it, Joe."

"But I got things to attend to in town."

"They'll *keep*." He looked over at him. "I don't like the way this feels. That's all I'm saying. Been a thug my whole life. Built up a pretty good instinct in that time, and my instinct says you fucking duck out."

Joe looked out the window.

"There's no shame in it, Joe. You're not running. You're taking a vacation."

"We'll see," Joe said. "See what it takes to tidy up my affairs."

"All right, look, promise me one thing then—let me or Dion, your pick, put some guards on your house."

"On my house," Joe agreed. "Not me. If I feel like moving without them, I'm moving. Deal?"

"Yeah. Fine." He looked over at Joe and smiled.

"What?"

"Now, I *know* you're fucking someone local. Who is she?"

"Just drive."

"Okay, okay." He chuckled softly. "Knew it."

They drove for a bit without saying anything and then Rico exhaled through pursed lips and Joe knew who he was thinking about.

Rico's fingers were white against the wheel. "I mean, again, I've killed people. But that guy? He's a fucking savage."

Joe stared out at all the prehistoric flora and told himself that's exactly what was troubling him, that's what was gnawing at his soul—the difference between him and a savage.

He told himself—and then he pledged to himself—that there was a difference.

There was.

There was.

A couple more snorts of rye, and he almost believed it.

AT RAIFORD, Rico waited in the car while Joe and the warden again shook hands on the dirt path that ringed the prison. The warden stood watch while Joe walked up the hill to the fence line. Theresa approached the chain-link and Joe opened the envelope so she could see inside.

"There's your ten. I'll bank it in the morning."

She nodded and looked through the fence at him. "You drunk?"

"What gives you that impression?"

"The careful way you walked up here."

"I've had a few." Joe lit a cigarette. "All right, let's get to it."

She laced her fingers through the fence. "Billy Kovich. And the hit's going to happen in Ybor, so I presume while you're at home."

"I'd never let Billy Kovich enter my house."

"He'll use a rifle then. He's a hell of a sniper. What he did in the Great War is what I heard."

Gone were the days Joe would be sitting by the window in his study.

"Or," Theresa said, "he'll take you on the street, maybe near that coffee shop you like or anyplace you do something on a regular basis. And if you stop your routines, he'll know you're onto him."

"And go away?"

She let loose a cold, sharp laugh and shook her head. "He'll accelerate the timetable. I would, anyway."

Joe nodded. He looked down and noticed his shoes were heavily scuffed from his day in the boonies.

"Why don't you take a vacation?" Theresa asked.

Joe stared back at her for a bit. "Because I think someone wants me out of town. All these pieces just fell into place too neatly."

"So you don't think anyone's trying to kill you?"

"Rationally speaking, I think the odds are about two-to-one."

"And you're comfy with those odds?"

"You kidding?" he said. "I'm scared shitless."

"Then run."

He shrugged. "Lived my whole life on the theory that my brains are more helpful than my balls. But this is the first time I can't tell which of them is making the decisions."

"So you're gonna stick around."

He nodded.

"Well, it's been nice knowing you." She indicated the bag in his hand. "If you don't mind, make that deposit sooner rather than later."

He smiled. "First thing in the morning."

"Good-bye, Joe."

"'Bye, Theresa."

He walked back down the hill, imagining crosshairs on his spine, on his chest, on the center of his forehead.

VANESSA WASN'T IN ROOM 107 WHEN HE ARRIVED, she was down on the dock. It creaked when he stepped onto it, and he flashed on the boy waiting for him here the last time, but he kept his stride even and a smile on his face and sat down across from her.

"If I said I didn't feel like it today," she said, "would you be offended?"

"No," he said and was surprised to realize he was telling the truth.

"You could sit beside me, though." She patted the wood by her hip.

He crab-walked over and sat so that their hips touched and he took her hand in his and they sat looking out at the water.

"Something bothering you?" he asked.

"Oh," she said, "everything and nothing."

"Want to talk about it?"

She shook her head. "Not particularly, no. You?"

"Hmm?"

"Want to talk about your problems?"

"Who says I have problems?"

She gave that a soft chuckle and squeezed his hand. "So let's just sit here and not talk."

They did.

After a while, he said, "This is nice."

"It is," she said with mournful surprise, "isn't it?"

Chapter Fifteen

Fix Yourself

NO SLEEP THAT NIGHT.

Every time he closed his eyes he saw the *Androphagi* walking toward him with curved blades in their hands. Or he saw the point of a bullet streaking through the dark toward the center of his forehead. He opened his eyes, heard the house creak, the walls groan, the squeak of what could be footsteps on the stairs.

Outside, the trees rustled.

The clock in the dining room struck two. Joe opened his eyes—he hadn't realized they'd been closed—and the blond boy stood in his doorway with a finger to his lips. He pointed. First Joe thought he was pointing at him, but he realized, no, he was pointing at something behind him. Joe turned in the bed and looked over his right shoulder at the fireplace.

The boy stood there now, with his blank face and sightless eyes.

He wore a white nightshirt and his bare feet were bruised purple and yellow. He pointed again and Joe looked back toward the doorway.

It was empty.

He turned back toward the fireplace.

No one there.

"FOLLOW MY FINGER."

Dr. Ned Lenox held his index finger in front of Joe's face and moved it right to left, then left to right.

Ned Lenox had been the Bartolo Family doctor since the days when Joe had run things. There were dozens of rumors about what had chased him out of a promising medical career in St. Louis—performing surgery while intoxicated, negligence that led to the death of a prominent Missourian's son, affair with a woman, affair with a man, affair with a child, theft and illegal resale of pharmaceuticals—but the rumors, varied as they were in the Tampa underworld, were all wrong.

"Good, good. Let me see that arm."

Joe held out his left arm and the frail, gentle doctor took it between pincer fingers just above the elbow and turned the inside of the arm up. He tapped a reflex hammer into the tendon where Joe's forearm met his elbow, then did the same on the other arm and each knee.

NED LENOX HADN'T BEEN CHASED OUT of St. Louis; he'd left of his own accord and with a reputation in such good standing that even now the older doctors at St. Luke's sometimes wondered aloud why he'd left in the autumn of '19 and what had become of him. There was some business, yes, about a young wife who'd died in childbirth, but the case had been reviewed by no less an authority than the State Board of Medicine, and Dr. Lenox, a tireless hero during that period of the Great Influenza, had been declared utterly blameless in the circumstances that led to the death of both his wife and child. The preeclampsia had set in with many of the same symptoms as the flu. By the time the poor man realized what ill truly beset his young bride and the child in her womb, it was far too late. People were dying at a rate of fifteen a day in those weeks, and 30 percent of the city was afflicted. Even a doctor couldn't get a hospital to answer its phone or a fellow physician to make a house call. And so Ned Lenox was home alone with his beloved wife when she was taken from him. It was assumed that he could never live with the cruel irony that he, a doctor held in the highest esteem, couldn't have saved her. In all likelihood, a team of natal specialists would have failed.

"HOW MANY HEADACHES have you had in the last week?" Ned asked Joe.

"One."

"Bad?"

"Nah."

"Any cause to which you could attribute it?"

"Chain-smoking."

"Newfangled cure for that."

"Yeah?"

"Stop chain-smoking."

"Clearly," Joe said, "you attended a top-notch medical school."

NED HAD TOLD JOE another version of his story back in '33, after a very long night patching up soldiers following one of the nastier skir-

mishes in the Rum War. Joe had lent a hand in an empty hotel ballroom they'd converted into a makeshift operating theater. After, in the morning, sitting on a pier watching the fishing boats and the rum boats head out into the bay, Ned told Joe his wife had been a poor woman when he met her, a woman far below his standing.

Her name was Greta Farland and she'd lived along Gravois Creek in a tenant farmer's shack with her rock-faced mother and hatchet-faced father and four mostly hatchet-faced brothers. All of them, with the exception of Greta, had shoulders that curled in like a crab's and pointy chins, foreheads as high and stark as the walls of a storm ditch, and grim, thirsty eyes. But Greta was full in the hips and the breasts and the lips. Her milk-white skin glowed under streetlamps, and her smile, rare as it was, was the smile of a young girl who'd just developed a woman's appetites.

"HOP OFF THE TABLE, YOUNG MAN."

Joe did.

"Walk."

"What?"

"Walk. Heel to toe. From this wall to that one."

Joe did so.

"And now back to me."

Joe crossed the room again.

GRETA HADN'T LOVED NED BACK, though he hoped that would change once she saw how much he could better her life. Their courtship was brief; her father knew a man like Ned only came around once, if that, for white-trash girls who grew up in The Basin. Greta married Ned and soon grew comfortable enough in her surroundings to learn the difference between a dinner fork and a salad fork and occasionally beat the maid. Sometimes she could be pleasant to Ned for three or four whole days before the squalls of her dark disposition returned. It was those good days that kept Ned believing she would soon wake up and realize that what she mistrusted as a dream was real—she would never want for food or shelter or the love of a decent and prominent man, and her black moods would evaporate. Her pitiless view of humanity would be replaced with empathy.

NED ADJUSTED HIS GLASSES and made a note on the form attached to his clipboard. "Relax."

Joe said, "Can I roll down my sleeves?"

"Be my guest." Another scratch of the pen. "And no earaches, no shortness of breath, no excessive nosebleeds?"

"No, no, and no."

Dr. Lenox glanced at him for a moment. "You've lost some weight."

"Is that bad?"

He shook his head. "You could have stood to lose a few pounds."

Joe grunted and lit a cigarette. He offered Dr. Lenox the pack. The doctor shook his head but produced a pack of his own and lit one.

WHEN GRETA BECAME PREGNANT, Ned felt sure a positive metamorphosis was imminent. Instead the pregnancy made her even less agreeable. The only time she was happy—and it was a hopeless, bitter happiness—was when she was with her family, because the Farland family, as a whole, was happiest when they were hopeless and bitter as well. When they came to visit, heirlooms and flatware disappeared and Ned could tell they hated him for having everything they coveted but had gone so long without they now wouldn't know what to do with it if they got it.

NED EXHALED A STREAM OF SMOKE and returned the pack to his shirt pocket. "So tell me again."

"Don't make me repeat it."

"You've been having visions."

Joe felt himself redden. He scowled. "Are they a brain tumor or not?"

"You do not show any evidence of a brain tumor."

"That doesn't mean I don't have one."

"No, but it means the likelihood is awfully minute."

"How minute?"

"About the same as being struck by lightning on a rubber plantation under a cloudless sky."

NED WASN'T SURPRISED—shocked maybe, but not surprised—the day he came home unexpectedly and found Greta in their bed, four months' pregnant, with her father grinding his dick into her from behind, the two of them rutting like hogs on a bed that had been in the Lenox family for three generations. They didn't even have the decency to stop when they saw his forlorn reflection in the dressing mirror he'd bought for her as an engagement gift.

"SO LET'S TALK ABOUT SLEEP. You getting any?"

"Not much."

He scribbled on the form again. "As the bags under your eyes would attest."

"Thanks. My hairline receding too?"

Lenox looked over his glasses at him. "Yes, but that doesn't have anything to do with our topic today."

"Which is?"

"When's the last time you saw this, uh, vision?"

"Couple days ago."

"Where?"

"My house."

"What was going on in your life at the time?"

"Nothing. Well . . ."

"What?"

"It's nothing."

"You're in my office for a reason. Tell me."

"There's a rumor that an associate of mine may be angry with me."

"Why?"

"Don't know."

"And is this associate someone you can reason with?"

"Don't know that, either. Don't know who he is."

"And in your business," Dr. Lenox said with a careful tone, "angry associates don't always deal with conflict in a . . ." He searched for the words.

"Genteel manner," Joe said.

Lenox nodded. "Exactly."

WHEN GRETA'S FATHER, Ezekiel "Easy" Farland, found Ned in the drawing room a few minutes later, he pulled a chair across from his son-in-law and chomped on a peach he'd grabbed off the dining room table.

"I know you got lots of things you think you want to say," he told Ned, "but they don't mean anything to me or mine. We got our ways. And I expect you'll learn to abide them."

"I won't abide anything of the sort." Ned's voice shook and strained like a woman's. "I won't. I will cast your daughter out of this—"

Easy put the tip of a knife to Ned's scrotum and put his other hand around his throat. "You do anything but go along, I will fuck your ass until you taste me in your mouth. Call my boys in and have them do the same, one after another. You understand? You in my family now. You part of us. That's the contract you made."

And to make his point, he made a clean slice in Ned's groin just above his testicles and to the right of his penis.

"You a doctor." He wiped the blade on Ned's shirt. "Fix yourself."

JOE THREADED A LINK through the holes in his right cuff. "So you think the vision could be connected to what?"

"Stress."

"Fuck," Joe said as his cuff link fell to the floor. "Fuck, fuck, fuck." He bent to pick it up. "Really?"

"Really do I think you're under stress? Or really do I think stress is causing you to see things? Can I speak frankly?"

Joe went back to fiddling with the cuff link. "Sure."

"Some unknown person or persons may wish you bodily harm, you're raising a son by yourself after your wife died a violent death, you travel too much, smoke too much, I presume drink too much, and don't sleep enough. I'm surprised you're not seeing an army of ghosts."

FOR THE NEXT MONTH, Ned walked, ate, went to work but did it all without conscious thought. For thirty days, to the best of his recollection, his limbs acted from memory, not because he told them to. His food—wet ash on his tongue—reached his mouth not by act but by rote.

He made house calls and kept hospital hours in a city struck asunder by the flu pandemic. Every family of respectable size had at least one member infected with it, and 50 percent of them died. And Ned tended to the sickest of them, saw some to full recovery and pronounced others officially dead. And remembered none of it. Each night, he returned home. Each morning he left it.

During the checkup he gave his wife every morning, he noted that her blood pressure had skyrocketed. He decided to think no more on it for the rest of the day and went off to work. When he returned, Greta's condition had worsened. He tested her urine and found clear evidence of kidney malfunction. He assured her she was fine. He listened to her heart and found it racing, listened to her lungs and heard the fluid sloshing within them. He held her hand and assured her that what she was feeling were the normal symptoms of a woman in the second trimester.

"SO THIS IS STRESS?" Joe said.

"This is stress."

"I don't feel stressed."

The doctor let loose a long sigh through his nostrils.

"Well," Joe explained, "I mean, not much more so than usual. Definitely not compared to, I dunno, ten years ago."

"When you were a bootlegger during the Rum War."

"Alleged," Joe repeated.

"You didn't have a child who depended on you then. Plus, you were ten years younger."

"Younger men don't fear death?"

"Some do, but most don't really believe it'll happen to them." He stubbed out his cigarette. "What can you tell me about this boy you're conjuring up?"

Joe hesitated, looking for even the slightest hint of amusement on Lenox's face. But all he saw was avid curiosity. He would have been embarrassed to admit how good the prospect of talking about the boy suddenly felt. He finished his second cuff link and took a seat across from Lenox.

"Most times," he began, "his face looks like a used eraser, you know? He's got a nose, a mouth, eyes, but I can't really see them and I can't tell you why I can't. I just can't. But once, I saw him in profile and he looked like family."

"Like family?" Lenox lit another cigarette. "Like your son?"

Joe shook his head. "No, like my father or some cousins I met once. Like a picture I saw of my brother when he was little."

"Is that brother alive?"

"Yeah. He's in Hollywood, writes for the pictures."

"Could it be your father?"

"I thought of that," Joe said, "but it doesn't feel right. My father was one of those guys came out the womb a full-grown man. Know the type?"

Lenox said, "But that's not what your mind is telling you."

"I don't follow."

"Do you believe in ghosts?"

"Well, I didn't."

Lenox waved his cigarette at that. "You didn't visit a psychic or some fortune-teller with your concerns. You came to me, a medical practitioner. You were worried about a tumor, but I'm telling you it's stress. Whatever you're conjuring up, it means something to you. Whether your father thought of himself as a boy or not, *you* may have seen fit to imagine a boyish version of him. Or maybe something happened with one of these cousins you mentioned, something in the long ago you can't reconcile with."

"Or maybe," Joe said, "it's a real fucking ghost."

"In that case, take consolation—there's a God."

Joe frowned. "Excuse me?"

"If there is such a thing as ghosts, that means there's an afterlife. Of some kind anyway. If there's an afterlife, then it stands to reason there's a supreme being. Ergo, ghosts are proof of God."

"I thought you didn't believe in ghosts."

"I don't. Hence, I don't believe in God."

WHEN GRETA BEGAN TO SCREAM TOO LOUDLY, Ned gagged her. He tied her to the bed, tied her ankles as well. She was feverish by this point, delirious and babbling, and he wiped her forehead, whispered his hatred into her ears and rattled off every statistic he'd ever learned in med school about the incidence levels of retardation, mongolism, suicidal tendencies, and severe depression in children of incest.

"The line must be broken," he whispered while nibbling on the outer edge of her ear. He fondled her engorged breasts and slapped her face or pinched her throat to keep her awake while the eclampsia first took hold and then took root. And he was certain he'd never seen a more beautiful woman than this one who died three hours and eleven minutes into labor.

Her child, product of a sin so unholy that it was the only sin outlawed by every civilization known on this earth, entered the world stillborn, its eyes scrunched tight against the horrors that would have awaited it.

LENOX LEANED BACK ON HIS STOOL and straightened his trouser crease at the knee. "Here's why I don't believe in ghosts—it's boring."

"Sorry?"

"It's boring," Lenox said. "To be a ghost. I mean, what do you do with your time? You walk through places where you don't belong at three in the morning, scare the hell out of the cat or, I dunno, the missus, and then you vanish into a wall. What's that take—a minute tops? What're you doing with the rest of your time? Because, as I said, if you believe in ghosts, then you believe in an afterlife. You have to. The two go together. No afterlife, no ghosts, we're all just decayed meat for the worms. But if ghosts, then an afterlife, a spirit world. And whatever's going on in the rest of the spirit world or heaven or limbo or wherever you are, I have to assume it's at least slightly more interesting than hanging around your house all day, waiting for you to come home so it can stare at you and say nothing."

Joe chuckled. "When you put it that way . . ."

Lenox scribbled on his prescription pad. "Take that to the pharmacist on Seventh."

Joe pocketed the prescription. "What is it?"

"Chloral hydrate drops. Don't exceed the dosage or you'll sleep for a month. But it'll help you at night."

"What about during the day?"

"If you're well rested, you won't be seeing visions, day or night." Lenox's glasses slipped down his nose. "If the visions or the sleeplessness persist, call me and I'll prescribe something stronger."

"Okay," Joe said. "I will. Thanks."

"Don't mention it."

After Joe left, Ned Lenox lit a cigarette and noticed, not for the first time, how yellow the nicotine had made the flesh between the index and middle fingers of his right hand. The nails too. He ignored the baby who sat shivering under the examining table. She'd sat there the whole of Joe Coughlin's visit, rocking and shivering in place, even as her father had lied about the afterlife being too boring a place for a ghost to live. Unlike in life, however, her eyes were open, her face unscrunched. She looked a bit like her mother, around the jawline mostly, but the rest of her was all Lenox.

Ned Lenox got down on the floor across from her because he had no idea how long she'd stay and he liked her company. In the first few years after he'd killed her and killed her mother, she had come to him nightly, crawling around the floor and the bed and even the walls a few times. For the first year, she made no noise, but by the second she was squawking, letting loose high-pitched and hungry cries. To avoid going home, Ned worked himself to the bone in his office, making house calls, and finally as the field medic to the Bartolo Family and their friends in the underworld. He enjoyed the latter the most. He had no romantic notions about men like Joe Coughlin and the life they lived—it was steeped in greed and penalty; the men who lived it died bloody or made sure others did. No overriding principle or moral code was at work except those that served self-interest while reinforcing the illusion of the opposite—that all was done for the greater good of the family.

Still, Ned found an honesty in this world that he found lacking most other places. All the men he met in this world were prisoners to their sins, hostages to their own broken parts. You didn't become a Joe Coughlin or a Dion Bartolo or an Enrico DiGiacomo because your soul was whole and your heart was untethered. You became part of this world because your sins and your sorrows had multiplied so prodigiously you weren't fit for any other type of life.

On the bloodiest day of the Tampa Rum War, March 15, 1933, twenty-five men died. Some had been shot, others hung, stabbed, or run over by automobiles. They'd been soldiers, yes, adult men who'd made their choices to live this life, but some had died screaming and others begging to live on behalf of their wives and their children.

Twelve had been massacred on a boat in the Gulf of Mexico and then kicked overboard to be consumed by sharks. When Ned Lenox had heard of the feeding frenzy, he'd prayed all twelve of those men had actually been dead by the time their bodies hit the water. Joe Coughlin had ordered their deaths. The same reasonable, kind-eyed, impeccably tailored Joe Coughlin who'd come to this office complaining of visions.

If the sins were big enough, Ned knew, the guilt didn't recede. It grew stronger. It took other forms. Sometimes, when outrage begat outrage with enough frequency, it threatened the fabric of the universe, and the universe pushed back.

Ned crossed his legs and watched his baby stare back at him, a gnarled and malignant almost-infant. When she opened her toothless mouth and spoke for the first time in twenty-four years, he wasn't surprised. Nor was he surprised that her voice was her mother's.

"I'm in your lungs," she told him.

CHAPTER SIXTEEN

This Time

AFTER HE CLOCKED OUT OF HIS JOB as a dispatcher at Bay Palms Taxi Service, Billy Kovich stopped at the Tiny Tap on Morrison for a shot and a beer. The shot was always Old Thompson, the beer was always Schlitz, and Billy Kovich never had more than one of each. From the Tiny Tap, he drove over to Gorrie Elementary and picked up his son, Walter, after band practice. Walter played the tenor drum, not so well he'd get a scholarship but not so poorly his place in the band was ever in jeopardy. With his grades, he wouldn't need a music scholarship anyway. Walter, twelve years old and nearsighted, was the biggest surprise in Billy Kovich's life. His other two children, Ethel and Willie, were in high school when Penelope became pregnant with Walter. She was forty-two at the time and Billy and the doctors had worried about a woman so small and frail delivering a child at that age. Privately, one of the doctors warned Billy the baby would probably never come to term. But come to term he did, and the delivery went quite smoothly. If Walter had been born just two months later, however, they probably would have discovered the tumor on her ovary.

She passed when Walter was barely a year old, just starting to walk, teetering from side to side like a drunken Indian at his mother's wake, a quiet boy even then, not so much introspective as insular. Smart as a whip, though. He'd already skipped a grade— third—and his teacher this year, a young man named Artemis Gayle, freshly arrived from Vanderbilt, told Billy that he might want to think about sending the boy to Tampa Catholic next fall if he thought Walter was ready for it. Intellectually there was no question he was, Gayle promised, they only had to question whether he was emotionally capable of handling the transition.

"Boy doesn't show much emotion," Billy said. "Never has."

"Well, there's not much left we can teach him here."

Driving home to the Dutch colonial on Obispo where all three of his children had grown up, Billy asked Walter how he felt about the possibility of entering high school in the fall. His son looked up from the textbook on his lap and adjusted his glasses. "That would be fine, Billy."

Walter had stopped calling Billy "Dad" when he was nine. He'd made a perfectly reasonable argument concerning the disadvantage at which a child found himself by the presumption of paternal superiority. If either Ethel or Willie had made the same argument, Billy would have told them they'd call him "Dad" for the rest of their lives and like it or he'd tan their hides. But those threats never worked on Walter; the one time Billy had spanked his son, the look of stunned outrage followed by bewildered contempt that had overtaken the boy's features had haunted Billy, haunted him still, far more than the faces of all the men he'd killed over the years.

They pulled into the carport of the house on Obispo and went inside. Walter put his drum and books upstairs while Billy fried up liver and onions and sautéed green beans and slices of potato. Billy loved to cook. Had since the army. He'd joined up in 1916, and was assigned to the kitchen at Camp Custer his first years in the military, but then war broke out and they sent him over to France, where his unit commander discovered just how good Corporal William Kovich was at killing men from great distances with a rifle.

After the war, Billy drifted to New Orleans, where he killed a man in a bar fight with his thumb. It was the kind of bar where men were often maimed, though this was the first one in six years who'd gotten himself killed. When the police arrived, every patron in the place told them the murderer of poor Delson Mitchelson there was a crazed Cajun name of Boudreaux who'd hightailed it out of there, probably right back to Algiers. Billy found out later that the Cajun in question, Phillippe Boudreaux, had been killed months before, after a card game when he'd been caught with a fifth jack. Some boys fed him to the gators during a full moon. Ever since, he'd been blamed for just about every homicide in the Quarter and two in Storyville. The owner of the bar was sitting at a table in the corner that night; he introduced himself as Lucius Brozjuola ("My friends call me King Lucius"). He told Billy he'd heard the country would be going dry soon and he had an idea how to make some money off that farther south in Tampa, was looking for a few men who knew how to handle themselves to join him.

So Billy ended up in Tampa, where he lived a quiet and respectably lower-middle-class life except when he was ordered to kill people for money. The money went into land in which he invested during the Florida Land Boom of the early 1920s. But whereas others bought swampland and oceanfront, Billy bought all his parcels in downtown Tampa, St. Petersburg, and Clearwater. He always bought near courthouses, police stations, and hospitals because he'd noticed that's where communities tended to sprout up. At some point, the community would expand and need to buy one of Billy Kovich's small plots, which were usually waiting undeveloped though properly maintained for the day someone would make an offer. Billy never made a killing on any of these deals, but he always made a sound profit and one which, most important, explained how a dispatcher for Bay Palms Taxi Service could send a daughter to Hunter Teachers College in Miami, a son to Emory University, and put himself into a fresh new Dodge every three years. No one in the cities Billy transacted with was going to look too closely into the finances of a man who gave them a fair shake on a good piece of land.

After dinner, Billy and Walter washed the dishes and discussed, as everyone did, the war Over There and how long it might take to win it.

Drying the last dish, Walter asked, "What if we don't win?"

With that Kraut asshole bogging down in Russia, Billy didn't see how the Nazis could sustain their efforts more than a few years. It was a simple matter of oil—the more they wasted in Russia, the less they could protect their supplies of the same in North Africa and Romania.

He explained this to his youngest, and Walter chewed on it thoughtfully as he did all things.

"But if Hitler takes the Soviet oil fields in Baku?"

"Well, sure," Billy said. "Then, yes, the Soviets could lose and Europe would probably fall. But what would it mean to us? It's not like they're going to head right over here."

"Why not?" the boy said.

And Billy didn't have an answer for that.

So those were the worries of young boys right now. The great boogeyman, Adolf, was on the march and willing to cross the sea eventually.

He gave the back of his son's neck a light squeeze. "Guess we'll fall off that bridge if we come to it, but that's a big *if,* and you still have homework to do."

They went upstairs together. Walter went to his room and straight to his desk, one textbook butterflied on his desk, three others stacked beside it.

"Don't read too late," Billy told his son, and the boy nodded in a way that indicated he'd ignore the advice.

Billy went down the hall to the room where all three of his children had been conceived and where Penelope had breathed her last. He had a much deeper acquaintanceship with death than most men. By his own count, he'd killed twenty-eight men in his life for sure, possibly as high as fifty, if you wanted to get picky about which bullets were his and which belonged to other members of the company during the four-day bloodbath in Soissons. His cheeks and nose had been the recipients of a half dozen final breaths. He'd watched over a dozen lights leave the eyes of other men. He'd watched it leave his wife's eyes.

And all he could tell anyone about death is that you were smart to fear it. He'd seen no indication of a world beyond this one. Never seen peace settle into the gaze of the dying nor the relief of a man whose questions were about to be answered. Just the end. Always too soon, always both a surprise and a grim confirmation of a lifelong suspicion.

In the bedroom he'd shared with his wife, he changed into an old sweatshirt with the sleeves cut off and a pair of paint-stained trousers and went downstairs to hit the bag.

It hung from a chain just past the carport and Billy hit it without finesse, though with a small measure of fluidity. He didn't hit it particularly hard or particularly fast but after half an hour his arms felt like they were filled with wet sand and his heart scampered madly in his chest and his sweatshirt was soaked through with sweat.

He showered quickly, the only way one could shower these days, and changed into his pajamas. He checked in on Walter and Walter assured him he wouldn't stay up much later and asked him to close the door behind him. He left his son to his geography textbook and went downstairs for the two beers he allowed himself after hitting the bag.

Joe Coughlin sat in his kitchen, a gun in his hand. The gun had a Maxim silencer attached. Joe had removed two beers from the icebox and placed them beside a can opener on the table in front of an empty chair so Billy would not only know where to sit but be aware that Joe had been studying his nightly routine. Joe flicked his eye at the chair and Billy sat in it.

"Open a beer," Joe said.

Billy popped a hole in the top of the can and another opposite it to help with the flow and he took a pull from it before setting it down again.

Joe Coughlin said, "We don't need to play the game where you ask why I'm here, do we?"

Billy thought about it and shook his head. Just above his right knee, strapped to the underside of the table, was a knife. It wouldn't do him much good from where he was sitting, but if he could slip it up his sleeve and then get close enough in a few minutes, keep the conversation easy, he might have a chance.

"I'm here," Joe said, "because I know you were offered the contract on me."

Billy said, "I wasn't offered it. I did hear about it, though."

"If you weren't offered it, who was?"

"My guess? Mank."

"He's in a sanitarium in Pensacola."

"So it's not him."

"Looks highly unlikely."

"Why me?"

"They wanted someone who could get close to me."

Billy snorted. "No one gets close to you. You don't think you'd have been a little suspicious if I popped into your liquor company one day or ran into you at that coffee shop you like in Ybor? You're not a get-in-close kind of hit. You're a distance kill."

"But you have long-range skills, Billy, don't you?"

They heard a soft scraping from above as Walter shifted the position of his chair. When they both looked up toward the sound, Billy dropped his right hand below the table.

"My son."

"I know," Joe said.

"What if he comes down for a glass of milk or something? You thought of that?"

Joe nodded. "We'll hear him on the stairs. They creak, particularly at the top."

If he knew that much about the house, what else did he know?

"And if you hear him coming?"

Joe rolled his shoulders slightly. "If I think you're still a danger, I'll shoot you in the face and let myself out that side door."

"And if you don't?"

"Then your son will come down and find two fellas talking."

"About what?"

"The cab business."

"You're wearing an eighty-dollar suit."

"Hundred and ten," Joe said. "We'll say I'm the owner."

Another scrape followed by footsteps. They heard the telltale squeak of Walter's door as he left the bedroom. Then his footsteps were in the hallway, heading toward the stairs.

Billy reached up for the knife.

Upstairs, Walter entered the bathroom and closed the door behind him.

Billy found nothing under the table but wood. He raised the hand and lifted his beer with it, saw Joe watching him.

"It's in your toolshed." Joe crossed his right ankle over his left knee. "So's the .22 that was behind the icebox, the other .22 on the shelf above the plates, the .38 under the living room couch, the .32 in your bedroom, and the Springfield in your closet."

Upstairs, the toilet flushed.

"If I failed to mention any weapons," Joe said, "you might want to consider whether that was on purpose. All in all, I think this would go a lot quicker if you stopped thinking about getting to a gun or a knife and just answered my questions."

Billy took a sip of beer as Walter left the bathroom and walked past the stairs. Again, the squeak of his door, this time as he closed it, followed by another scrape of his chair.

Billy said, "Ask away, Mr. Coughlin."

"Joe."

"Ask away, Joe."

"Who hired you?"

"I told you I wasn't hired. I just heard about it. Mank's the guy you should be worried about."

"Who did the hiring?"

"King Lucius, but I suspect he was subcontracting."

"For who?"

"No idea."

"And you were supposed to do it Wednesday?"

Billy cocked his head at that.

"No?" Joe said.

"No," Billy said. "First off, I didn't take the contract. I wasn't even offered it. Second, why would you have heard the date?"

"Beats me," Joe said. "But I heard the contract was supposed to go down on Ash Wednesday."

Billy laughed and drank some more beer.

"What's funny?"

"Nothing." Billy shrugged. "It's just ridiculous. Ash Wednesday? Why not Palm Sunday or Arbor Day? We want someone dead, we just kill him on It's Your Worst Wednesday Werner Day or Farewell to Fucking Freddy Friday. Christ, Joe, you're on the Commission. You know how this works."

Joe watched Billy Kovich drain his first Schlitz and use the can opener on the second. He had the most open face, Billy. A look at that face and you immediately relaxed. It was boyish and rugged at the same time, the face of a solid Working-Class Everyman. Guy who'd help you change a flat and take you up on the offer of a beer afterward, end up paying for the second and third rounds himself. If he said he was the high school football coach or the town mechanic or managed the hardware store, you'd nod and think, *Of course.*

When King Lucius wanted to send a message back in '37, Billy Kovich took Edwin Musante out on a boat, tied his hands behind his back, trussed his legs, sliced parts of both legs and his abdomen with a razor, and then tied a chain off under his armpits. Edwin Musante was alive and fully conscious when Billy Kovich tossed him into the water, played out the chain, and began motoring slowly through Tampa Bay. Paudric Dean, who five years later would himself become a victim of Billy, was also on the boat that day and would speak in a voice hushed with shock about what it had sounded like after the first two sharks showed up. How they took tentative bites

at first, given some pause by the pitch of Edwin Musante's screams.
But when the other three sharks appeared a hundred yards away, the
first two went for bigger bites. Once all five had met for the feeding
frenzy, Billy calmly cut the line to the boat and motored back to port.

Joe watched him drink his beer now, friendliest-looking guy
you'd ever come across in your life.

Billy said, "You ever think the rumor could be the point?"

"I don't follow."

"Sure you do, Joe."

"Someone wants me to *think* there's a hit on me?"

"Yeah."

"Why?"

"Get into your head, stir things up with a ladle."

"Whatever for?"

"Fuck would I know?" Billy shrugged. "I'm not the kind of guy
they bring into the boardroom, explain the whole picture to. I'm
a worker bee." He held up his empty beer. "A thirsty one actually.
Mind if I get another?"

Marston, the private investigator Joe had hired to watch the
house for the past several days, had reported that Billy had exactly
two beers every night. Never a third.

Joe mentioned this now.

Billy nodded. "Normally, yeah, I just have the two. But when a
guy sits across from me in my own home with a gun pointed at me
and my son still awake upstairs? Guy who thinks I've been hired to
kill him? That might make me break routine a bit. Get you one?"

"Sure," Joe said.

Billy went to the icebox and rummaged around in there. "You
look like you might have put on a little weight. That true?"

"Maybe a couple pounds, I don't know. Don't own a scale."

"You needed it. You were always on the thin side. You look good."

Each of his hands came out of the icebox carrying a beer. He placed them on the table. He closed the icebox. He reached for the can opener.

"How old's your boy now?" he asked.

"Nine," Joe said.

The first beer can hissed when he punctured it. "Few years younger than mine."

"Walter's quite smart, I hear."

Billy slid the beer across the table to Joe and beamed with pride. "They want him to skip eighth, go right into high school. Tampa Catholic. You believe that?"

"Congratulations."

Billy punctured his own can twice and then raised it in toast. "To our kids."

"To our kids."

Joe drank. Billy drank.

Billy said, "You notice how their natures were pretty much set on day one?"

Joe nodded.

Billy smiled softly and shook his head. "I mean, they tell you as a parent don't do this or you'll get this type of kid; don't do that, or your kid'll grow up to be that kind of kid. Truth is, they are who they are in the womb."

Joe nodded in agreement and they drank. The silence that followed was comfortable.

"I was sorry to hear about your wife," Joe said. "You know, back then."

"I remember you came to the wake." Billy nodded. "Thank you. And I was sorry to hear about yours. I would have made it to the funeral, but I was stuck out of town."

"I understood. The flowers you sent were beautiful."

"I used that florist in Temple Terrace. They do nice work."

"Yeah."

"Mind if I smoke?"

Joe said, "I wasn't aware you smoked."

"I keep it from my son. They thought it was bad for his asthma and he hates the smell. But every now and then, when I'm feeling oh, a little tense"—he laughed and Joe chuckled too—"I like to have me a Lucky."

Joe reached into his inside pocket and produced a pack of Dunhills and a silver Zippo. "You got an ashtray?"

"Sure." Billy stood and went to a drawer midway down the kitchen counter. "May I?"

Joe nodded.

Billy opened the drawer. He reached in, his back to Joe, and then turned back to the table with a small glass ashtray in hand. He placed it on the table. He closed the drawer.

"No one would want you dead, Joe. It makes no sense."

"So you're back to the theory that someone's playing a head game."

"Stirring things up in there, yeah."

Billy took his seat again and smiled across the table at Joe.

Joe opened the pack of Dunhills and proffered the pack to Billy.

"What are those?"

"Dunhills. They're English."

"They look fancy."

"I guess."

"I'm a Lucky's man. Always have been."

Joe said nothing, the pack still between them.

"May I?"

"What's that?"

"Get my pack of Lucky Strikes?"

Joe withdrew his hand. "Be my guest."

From upstairs, a small scrape of the chair.

Billy went to one of the upper cabinets. He opened it, looked back over his shoulder at Joe. Joe could see nothing in there but cereal bowls and a couple of coffee cups.

"I keep them out of sight so the boy won't know," Billy said. "I gotta reach back there."

Joe nodded.

"Ain't no reason, Joe." He dug deep and off to the right.

"What's that?"

"Anyone would want to kill you."

"Guess it's just a crazy rumor then." Joe shifted slightly to his left.

"That'd be my bet."

Billy's arm came out of the cupboard a lot faster than it went in, and Joe caught a spark of kitchen light bouncing off something metal in Billy's hand, and he shot Billy in the chest. Well, he'd been aiming for the chest, but the shot went high and the bullet took out the man's Adam's apple. Billy slid down the cupboard and sat on the floor, eyelids fluttering like mad, his gaze hungry and frantic.

Joe looked at the silver cigarette case in his hand. Billy snapped it open with his thumb to show Joe the white stubby row of Lucky Strikes.

"*This* time," Joe said.

Billy's eyelids stopped fluttering and his mouth formed an O as his chin drooped over his torn throat. Joe drained his beer can in the sink and rinsed it before putting it in the pocket of his coat. He wiped off the faucet with a dish towel and used it to open the side door off the kitchen. He put the dish towel in the other coat pocket and left the house.

He walked down the street to his car and he placed his coat on the backseat. He removed his hat and placed it on the passenger seat and then closed up the car and walked back up Obispo on the opposite sidewalk. He leaned against a telephone pole and watched the light in Walter Kovich's room.

After a few minutes, he lit a cigarette. He knew his actions were those of an insane man, certainly a wildly incautious one. He should have been ten miles away from here by now, twenty.

He thought of all the children who would grow up without fathers simply because he and men like him existed. His own son had lost his mother because of Joe's work. Ten years ago, on the bloodiest day in Tampa mob history, twenty-five men had been cut down between noon and midnight. Of those twenty, at least ten had been fathers. And if Joe died tomorrow or the day after, his own son would be orphaned. They had a rule in this business of theirs—never involve families. It was a sacred rule, trumping all except the one about making as much money as possible. It allowed them to believe something separated them from the animals. A higher moral code. A limit to their cruelty and self-interest.

They respected family.

But the truth was something different. They didn't kill families, true. They just amputated them.

He waited to see Walter Kovich's light shut off because he wanted to know the kid had one last peaceful night of sleep. After he discovered his father's body in the kitchen, peace would be a hard thing to come by for a while, and so would sleep.

Tomorrow morning, Walter Kovich, twelve years old and about to skip eighth grade, was going to walk downstairs and discover his father sitting on the kitchen floor without his throat. The splatter of blood would be black and gummy. There'd be flies. Walter would not be going into school. By this time tomorrow night, his bed would feel alien. His house would have morphed into a baffling, haunted place. He would not be able to taste his food. He would never have another conversation with his father. He would probably never know why his father was taken from him.

Nor, if Joe were to die soon, would his own son.

Did Walter Kovich have an aunt or uncle to take him in? A grandparent? Joe had no idea.

He looked back up at the window. The light was still on.

It was late. Kid must have fallen asleep at the desk, Joe decided, cheek pressed to the pages of a textbook.

Joe stepped off the curb and walked up the street to his car. The street was very quiet as he drove away; not even the bark of a dog marked his exit.

CHAPTER SEVENTEEN

Archipelagos

MONDAY, MARCH 8, 1943, two days before Ash Wednesday.

With Billy Kovich down at the morgue, Joe was surprised to wake up feeling less safe, not more. So when Dion called to convince Joe that no matter how many of Rico's bodyguards he hired, he still didn't live in a gated house, Joe put up far less of a fight than his friend would have expected.

He set off with Tomas an hour later and they drove out of Ybor and headed for Dion's. Tomas spread the morning paper out, the top half resting on the dash, the lower half on his lap. Above the fold—the battle of the Bismarck Sea. Below it, right-hand corner—the death of Billy Kovich, taxi dispatcher with suspected ties to underworld figures.

"What's an archipageo?"

Joe looked at his son. "A what?"

Tomas nodded at the newspaper. "An archipelago?" This time he pronounced it "archeep lagoo."

"An archipelago," Joe said.

"Yeah."

"Try it."

Slowly. "An archipelago."

"First try." Joe bounced his fist lightly off his son's knee. "Well done. It's what they call a group of islands."

"Why not just call it a group of islands?"

Joe smiled. "Why call a dozen things twelve? Why call a dog a canine?"

"Or a cat a feline?"

"Or a child a kid?" Joe knew once the two of them got started this way they could go all day and he was already running close to late as it was.

Luckily Tomas broke from the jokes. "New Gween-e-a?"

"New Guinea."

Tomas sounded it out, again getting it on the first try.

It's all the papers had been talking about for two days, Uncle Sam and the Australian Air Force raining hell's holy fury down on a Japanese naval convoy off the Bismarck Archipelago. And today's reports noting that a new battle had just opened nearby off Bougainville in the Solomon Islands.

"Well, they're sure giving 'em what for, aren't they?"

"I want to be a soldier someday."

Joe almost drove the car into a curb.

"Is that right?" he said lightly.

"Yeah."

"Why?"

"Fight for my country."

"Would your country fight for you?"

"I don't understand."

"You know why we live in Ybor?"

"Because we have a nice house there."

"Yeah," Joe said. "But also because it's the only place Cubans can live around here without people treating them like they're second-class. You know what 'second-class' means, right?"

Tomas nodded. "Not as good."

"Exactly. So your mother lived here and they treated her like she was second-class. She couldn't go into a lot of restaurants or hotels. If she went to the movie theater downtown? They made her drink water from the colored fountain."

Just talking about it was thickening Joe's voice.

"So?" Tomas said.

"So this country never welcomed your mother."

"I know that," Tomas said, though Joe could tell he was in a mild state of shock. Joe had never told him about the water fountains before.

"You do?"

Tomas was wide-eyed now, and the wideness made the pain all that more apparent.

Joe decided to switch tacks. "Wait—which country, by the way?"

"Which?"

Joe nodded. "Here or Cuba?"

Tomas looked at the window for a very long time, so long in fact that they'd reached Dion's and pulled past the guards at his front gate and driven down a path lined with palm trees and towering magnolias before he spoke again. It was a question Joe had never put to his son before because he'd always feared the answer. Graciela had been full-blooded Cuban. His grandmother and aunts were all Cuban. Tomas had attended first and second grades in Havana. He spoke Spanish as easily as English.

"Here," he said. "America."

The answer surprised Joe so much he almost forgot to depress the clutch as they pulled up in front of Dion's house and the car sputtered for a moment before he could slide the shift into neutral.

"America's your home?" Joe asked. "I thought—"

Tomas shook his head. "Cuba's my home."

"I'm confused."

Tomas reached for his door handle, a look on his face that said it all made perfect sense to him. "But America's worth dying for."

"I just told you how America treated your mother."

"I know," Tomas said. "But, Dad . . ."

He tried to work it out in his head, his hands moving more than usual.

"What?" Joe said eventually.

"No one's perfect," Tomas replied and opened the door.

As Tomas exited the car, Dion opened his front door, a cigar already hanging out of the side of his mouth at eight in the morning. He scooped Tomas off the patio without a word and carried him on his hip like a loaf of bread as they entered his house.

"I heard you were sick."

"Put me down, Uncle D."

"You don't look sick."

"I'm not sick. I had chicken pox."

"I heard you looked like something in the circus."

"No."

Joe followed them inside, their banter almost easing the dread that had been building in him all morning, maybe all month when he thought about it. It wasn't just dread over the assassin who could be out there, although he carried plenty of that. It wasn't just dread of the ghost boy, though he dreaded another appearance from the spooky fucking thing more than he could ever admit. It was a larger dread, a more unwieldy type. It was a feeling he'd had for the last few months that the whole world was being remade, slave-demons working tirelessly night and day at its core, reshaping, remolding. The slave-demons worked in pits of fire, and they never slept.

Joe could feel the wide swaths of ground shifting below his feet, but every time he looked, the earth appeared not to have moved at all.

"You joining the circus?" Dion asked Tomas.

"I'm not joining the circus."

"You could have your own pet monkey."

"I'm not joining the—"

"Or, say, a baby elephant. That'd be fun."

"I couldn't have a baby elephant."

"Why not?"

"He'd grow too big."

"Oh, so you're worried you'd have to clean all his poop."

"No."

"No? It's a lot of poop."

"He'd be too big to keep in the house."

"Yeah, but you got that farm in Cuba." Dion adjusted Tomas on his hip with one hand, adjusted the cigar in his mouth with the other. "You'd probably have to quit the circus, though. Elephants need a lot of attention." When they reached the kitchen, he let Tomas down.

"Got something for you." He reached into the sink and came back with a basketball. He tossed it to Tomas.

"Keen." Tomas rolled the ball between his palms. "What do I do with it?"

"You shoot it through a hoop."

A frown. "I know that. But there's no hoop."

"There wasn't a hoop," Dion said, eyebrow cocked at Joe's son until he got it.

"Christ," Joe said.

Dion shot him a look. "What?"

"Where? Where?" Tomas hopped in place.

Dion jerked his head toward the sliding glass doors. "Out back. Just past the pool."

Tomas took off running.

"Hey," Joe said.

He stopped.

"What do you say?"

"Thanks, Uncle D."

"Pleasure."

Tomas ran out the back of the house.

Joe looked out past the pool. "A fucking basketball court?"

"It's not a whole court. It's a hoop. I paved over the koi pond and a rosebush." He shrugged. "Fish and flowers—all they do is fucking die anyway. No big deal."

"You spoil that kid like he's your only grandkid."

"I'm not old enough to be a grandfather, you fuck." Dion poured some orange juice into a glass of champagne. He lifted the glass. "Want one?"

Joe shook his head as they walked into the living room. Joe gave nods to the men there—Geoff the Finn and Granite Mike Aubrey. The Finn was a great soldier when he was sober, but that was getting to be a rare condition in which to find him. Aubrey was useless. They called him Granite Mike because he looked to have been carved out of it. No one could match him in the weight room at Philo's. He could tell a good joke, and he was quick to light your cigarette or cigar, but he was all muscle and no brain. Worse than that, all muscle and no balls. Joe had seem him twitch at a car backfiring.

But Dion kept guys like these around because they made him laugh and they'd match him drink for drink and steak for steak. In

Joe's opinion, he was too chummy with his men, so when he had to knock one back into line or reprimand one, they resented it on a personal level. If Dion saw the resentment in their faces, he felt a mirror sense of betrayal or ingratitude that could trip the switch on his rage. And Dion's rage was not something you wanted to see twice, and most didn't live to.

"I know you got a lot on your mind right now, but we get any further on this rat in our house?" Dion took a drink.

"I know what you know."

"You know what I know," Dion said. "How about doing something about it?"

"I'm not your lieutenant," Joe said. "I'm your advisor."

"You work for me, you don't get to claim limited duties."

They walked into the billiards room, sat up in the chairs, and looked at the empty table.

Joe said, "With all due respect, D—"

"Oh, now I'm in for it."

"You've known for months this rat can only be coming from here."

"Or up north. Donnie's house."

"But Donnie runs Boston *for you*. So the rat's inside our house. And he's not sticking to the basement anymore. He's in the pantry."

"So take a broom and go get him."

"I'm not on the street," Joe said. "I'm in Havana, I'm in Beantown, I'm in the Apple, I'm all over the fucking place. I'm the front, D. I run the legit shops and the gambling. You're the street."

"But the rat's in the house."

"Sure," Joe said, "but he crawled from a sewer."

Dion pinched the skin between his eyebrows and sighed. "You think I need a wife?"

"What?"

Dion looked out at his garden. "You know, someone to cook and give me kids, shit like that?"

Joe had been watching Dion fuck his way through shopgirls, showgirls, and cigarette girls since they were dodging the truant officer in the streets of Boston just after the Great War. He'd never stayed with a girl more than a few weeks.

"I think women are too much of a pain in the ass," Joe said, "to move in with one unless you love her."

"You moved in with one."

"Yeah, well," Joe said, "I loved her."

Dion took a pull from his cigar. They could hear Tomas behind the house, clanging the ball off the backboard. "You ever figure on moving in with another one?"

Joe looked at Dion's monstrosity of a house. He lived alone, but his bodyguards had to sleep somewhere, so he had an eight-thousand-foot main house, and the only thing he ever used the kitchen for was to hide a basketball in the sink.

"No," Joe said, "I don't."

"She's been gone seven years."

"Are we talking as friends right now? Or boss and advisor?"

"Friends."

"I know she's been gone seven fucking years. I've counted them. I've lived them."

"Okay. Okay."

"Day by day."

"I said okay."

They sat without talking for a while and then Dion let loose a loud groan. "Like we need all this shit right now," Dion said. "I got Wally Grimes in the ground, Montooth Dix holed up in his fortress, I got more union trouble in Ybor, I got some sort of stomach flu moving through three of my whorehouses, and the war took away half our best customers."

"It's a tough job." Joe pantomimed playing a very small violin. "I'm going to go take a nap. Haven't slept in days."

"You look it."

"Fuck you."

"Take a number, sweetie."

THE NAP DIDN'T WORK OUT. If he wasn't worried about a bullet with his name on it, he was fretting over the rat in the organization. And if he wasn't fretting over the rat in the organization, he was worried about how his son would fare if something happened to his father. Which led him back to the bullet with his name on it.

To switch gears, he tried thinking about Vanessa, but that didn't carry the same comfort it used to. Something had changed between them. Or maybe just in her. With women, who knew? But it was a different Vanessa he'd sat with on the dock. An air of regret and possibly dismay—not transitory either but permanent—hung over her. They'd sat on the dock, held hands, and said almost nothing for an hour. But when she stood to walk to her car, it seemed as if an entire journey had taken place, a trek from *A* to *Z*, in the time that she'd been sitting.

Her good-bye had been a light palm placed to his cheek and eyes that darted back and forth across his face, searching, searching. But for what?

He had no idea.

And then she was gone.

So a failed nap, and Joe wandered through the rest of the day near-comatose and twitchy. He rebounded a bit after dinner, and he and Dion took brandies into Dion's study and talked about Billy

Kovich for the first time. Tomas was asleep in a bedroom upstairs.

Dion poured them each a healthy snifter and said to Joe, "What choice did you have?"

"He really was reaching for his cigarettes, though." Joe grimaced and took a long pull from his glass.

"That time," Dion reminded him.

"Yeah, yeah," Joe said. "I know, I know."

Dion went to crank open the window behind his desk, then looked back at Joe. "Okay with you?"

"Huh?" Joe looked up at his friend and then at the dark vegetation beyond the window. "Yeah, fine. I'm past worrying about myself. I just don't want someone to hit Tomas 'cause he's standing too close to me."

Dion opened the window, and the breeze that found them was pleasantly cool for March in West Florida. It sounded like schoolgirls whispering as it rustled through the palm fronds in the dark.

"Nobody's getting to Tomas," Dion said, "and no one's getting to you. You're gonna wake up Thursday morning and wonder how you ever fell for this. Bitch played a con to get you to convince Lucius to let her live. Hell, Lucius himself probably hatched the plan—he's that smart—so that he keeps ninety thousand fucking dollars and she keeps her life but thinks it was her own idea to play you. Meanwhile, you lose sleep for a week—"

"Two."

"Two. You lose weight, get bags under your eyes, fuck, your hair got thinner. And for what? To make a rich fucking devil richer and save one of his minions from getting offed, which, by the way, she deserved."

"You really think that's been the play?"

Dion sat on the edge of the desk and swirled the brandy in his glass. "What other play could there be? No one"—he leaned forward and tapped his glass off Joe's knee—"I mean, fucking *no one* wants you dead. So why do this, except to make you chase your tail so they could get what they wanted?"

Joe settled into the chair. He placed his drink on the side table and found his cigarettes, lit one. He could feel the night on his face and heard something thick and fast—a squirrel or a rat, he guessed—scuttle through the trees. "Well, if I get to Thursday at 12:01 A.M., I'll eat any crow you put before me. Do it with fucking gusto. Until then, though, I'm hearing footsteps running up behind me everywhere I go."

"Understandable." Dion poured some more brandy into their glasses. "How 'bout tomorrow you take your mind off it?"

"How would I go about doing that?"

"Montooth Dix." Dion clinked his glass off Joe's.

"What about him?"

"He's Dead Coon Walking and you know it." Dion opened the humidor on his desk. "He's gotta go. It's making me look weak, him holed up and breathing while two of my guys are already buried."

"But, like you said, he's holed up. I can't get to him."

Dion lit his cigar, puffed on it until it got going. "They respect you in Brown Town, just like they do everywhere else in this city. You can get through his front door. I know you. You get in there and you tell him to come out in the fresh air and it'll be quick. He'll never see it coming."

"And if he doesn't?"

"Then, shit, I gotta come in after him. Can't let this go on any longer. Losing too much face. He don't come out, I'll hit that building he's hiding in like the Krauts hit Leningrad. His kids are there, his wives? Ain't my fucking problem. I'll turn the whole fucking building into a parking lot."

Joe said nothing for a bit. He drank his brandy and listened to the leaves rustle and the water that bubbled from the fountain in the northwest corner of the yard.

"I'll talk to him," he said. "I'll do my best."

FAT TUESDAY, with the clock that had been ticking in his head replaced by the echoes of his own heartbeat, Joe worked the phones with Montooth's people until he'd arranged a meeting for the following morning.

He barely slept again that night. He'd nod off for fifteen minutes and then find himself wide awake once more, eyes on the ceiling. He waited for the blond boy to make an appearance, but he never did. Joe realized it was the randomness of the ghost's visits—some spaced a week apart, others occurring on the same day—that rattled him almost as much as the visits themselves. You never knew when he was going to show up. And if he had a message he was trying to transmit from the afterlife, Joe was damned if he could find it.

He went down to the room where Tomas slept. He sat on the bed and watched his son's chest—so small and fragile—rise and fall. He smoothed his cowlick with a damp palm and put his nose close to the boy's neck and breathed him in. Tomas never stirred, and Joe had to fight the urge to shake him awake and ask if he'd been a good father to him. He lay in the bed with his face across from his son's and he drifted off for a bit, had an almost-dream in which a rabbit raced along the top of a fence, though Joe couldn't see what it was running from. Then the rabbit was gone and he was staring at his sleeping son, wide awake.

The next morning, he drove Tomas to Sacred Heart and they stood in line with the other eight hundred parishioners. Father

Ruttle dipped his thumb into the chalice filled with damp ash and applied the ash to their foreheads.

Outside the church, fewer people milled around than did on a Sunday, but everyone looked slightly unsettling. Father Ruttle had a heavy thumb, and the crosses on everyone's foreheads were thick, some dripping black residue in the heat.

Back at Dion's Joe freshened up and came out into kitchen, found Dion and his son eating cornflakes at the table.

Joe crouched by his son. "I'll be back in a couple of hours."

Tomas gave him a flat look that was all Graciela. "A couple hours? Or five?"

Joe felt the guilt flood his own smile. "Be good for Dion."

Tomas nodded, mock-solemn, fidgeting.

"Don't load up on sugar. You know he's going to take you to the bakery."

"Bakery?" Dion said. "What bakery?"

"Tomas?" Joe looked his son in the eye.

Tomas nodded. "I won't load up on sugar."

Joe clapped his shoulders. "See you in a bit."

Dion spoke around a mouthful of cereal. "How you know I'm going to take him to the bakery?"

Joe said, "It's Wednesday. Isn't that your pound cake day?"

"It's not a pound cake, you ignoramus. It's a *torta al cappuccino*." He put his spoon aside and raised one finger to make his point. "Sponge cake soaked in cappuccino and layered with ricotta then topped with whipped cream. And they don't make it every Wednesday, either, 'cause of this fucking war. They make it one Wednesday a month. *This* Wednesday."

"Yeah, well, don't give too much to my boy. He's got an Irish stomach."

"I thought I was Cuban."

"You're a mongrel," Joe assured him.

"I'll give the mongrel a little taste of the *sfogliatelle* and that'll be the extent of it." He pointed his spoon at Tomas. "We playing basketball, work up an appetite?"

Tomas beamed. "Absolutely."

Joe gave his son a last kiss on the head and headed out.

CHAPTER EIGHTEEN

Men Leave

AS PREVIOUSLY AGREED UPON, Dion's bodyguards stayed behind when Joe crossed into the Negro section of Ybor City. If anyone saw two carloads of white thugs driving south of Eleventh, they'd presume the truce was off and light them all up. So he drove the final few blocks alone.

On the drive over, he'd grown increasingly angry about the way Montooth was being treated. Maybe because he genuinely liked the man. Or maybe simply because he could identify with anyone who lived in the shadow of his own noose. Joe was being asked to convince Montooth to come out into the open and die, even as Joe himself was desperately trying to stave off his own Judgment Day. And what crime had Montooth committed in the first place? He'd protected himself against men who'd come into his neighborhood to kill him.

Joe was the furthest thing from a moral pillar, but he knew an unequivocal evil when he saw it. And what was being done to Montooth fell into that category.

Montooth Dix and his family lived above the billiards parlor he owned on Fifth. The building was four stories tall and a block long. Montooth, his brood of nine children, three wives, and his phalanx of bodyguards occupied the top three floors, so much room up there it never felt crowded. So much room and so little light, you could easily get lost, Montooth having a fondness for thick dark curtains—reds and browns mostly—that covered the windows.

Joe pulled up outside the pool hall and there was a space waiting right out front, one of Montooth's men removing a cane chair that had been holding the spot, though Joe couldn't imagine anyone in this neighborhood or the whole of Tampa being stupid enough to park in front of Montooth's place. Or really anywhere near the spot where the man himself parked his ride—a canary yellow '31 Packard Deluxe Eight, a car the length of a small yacht, big enough possibly to fit all nine of Montooth's kids, though probably not the three wives, who ran big and were rumored to despise one another. Joe pulled past the Packard so he could back in behind it, and he caught pieces of his own car reflected in the gleaming spokes of Montooth's hubcaps.

Montooth's man waved Joe into the spot, the chair still in his hand. While most of the Negroes in the sporting parts of town dressed in zoot suits, two-toned shoes, and wide-brimmed hats, Montooth's men wore what they'd been wearing for ten years—crisp black suits over crisp white shirts, top button undone but never the second, no ties, black shoes gleaming from the shoeshine stand that sat out front of the billiards parlor, two of Montooth's men up in the chairs now getting the leather turned into mirrors.

Joe stepped out of his car slowly, aware of all the eyes on him—not just the eyes in front of this building but eyes that had been tracking him for blocks. Eyes that said, You don't belong and you ain't gonna start neither. Some of that, of course, was because he was white in a black neighborhood. But in Ybor any sort of racialism was unsound business. The neighborhood had been settled by Spaniards and Cubans; the Italians and coloreds had followed soon after. Joe's wife had been Cuban, her father descended from Spaniards but her mother from African slaves. Joe's son was a mixture of Irish, Spanish, and African. So Joe had no problem with the coloreds, but for the first time in a few years, he was very aware as he stepped out of his car that the last white face he'd seen had been seven blocks back.

There was no guarantee Montooth's guys wouldn't take turns banging a pipe off his skull until they got to the pink folds, leave the corpse twitching on the sidewalk. Montooth and Freddy DiGiacomo had gone to war, which meant all the black crime families and white crime families in Tampa were at war.

Montooth's man placed the chair against the brick wall beside the shoeshine stand and approached Joe to pat him down.

When he was almost done, he shot a glance at Joe's groin. "Gotta check your snake, man. Heard the stories."

Joe had once snuck a Derringer past the John brothers over in Palmetto County. Tucked it under his ball sack, pulled it out ten minutes later, and pointed it across the table at their father.

Joe nodded. "Try not to linger."

"Just so you make sure it stay the same size, hear?"

Joe thought he detected a smile on one of the guards sitting up on the shine stand as his compatriot reached between Joe's thighs and ran his palm under Joe's testicles and around his groin, the man's face turned away and twisted into a grimace.

"There." He stepped back. "I ain't lingered and you stayed small."

"Maybe that's as big as I get."

"Then God musta been drunk day he made you. My sympathies."
Joe readjusted his suit jacket, smoothed his tie. "Where's he at?"
"Up the stairs. He'll find you directly."

Joe entered the building. To his right was the door to the pool
hall. He could smell the smoke and hear the snap of the balls coming out of there at eight thirty in the morning, the place legendary
for its marathon games and fortunes won and lost. He climbed the
stairs alone. The red steel door up top had been left open wide onto
a mostly bare room with a dark wood floor that matched the walls.
The velvet drapes were closed over the windows and were a shade
of purple so dark it was almost black. Between two of the windows
near the back of the room was a pine wardrobe painted army surplus green.

There were two chairs and a table in there. Well, more
precisely—one chair, one table, and a throne.

Montooth sat in the throne, hard to miss in white silk pajamas and a white satin bathrobe, matching slippers on his feet.
He smoked cannabis from a corncob pipe, day and night, Montooth did, and he was smoking it now as he watched Joe take the
seat across from him, the chair a twin of the one that had held
Joe's parking space for him. On the table between them were two
bottles of liquor—brandy for Montooth, rum for Joe. Montooth's
brandy was Hennessy Paradis, the finest in the world, but he hadn't
scrimped on Joe's rum either, pulling out a bottle of Rhum Barban-
court Réserve du Domaine, the best bottle of rum in the Caribbean
not produced by Joe and Esteban Suarez.

Joe nodded at it. "I'm to drink my competition."

Montooth exhaled a thin stream of smoke. "Were it always so
simple." He took another small drag off his pipe. "Why all you
white people walking around town with crosses on your head?"

"Ash Wednesday," Joe said.

"All look like you found voodoo. I expect to see chickens start disappearing off the street."

Joe smiled, looked Montooth in his eyes—one the color of an oyster, the other brown as the floor. He didn't look good, not like the old Montooth Dix Joe had known for going on fifteen years now.

"No way you can win this," Joe said.

Montooth gave that a lazy shrug. "Then we go to war. I'll hit you in the streets. I'll blow up all your clubs. I'll paint the streets the color of—"

"To what end?" Joe asked. "Just get a bunch of your people killed."

"Yours too."

"Yeah, but we've got more people to spare. Meanwhile, you'll have dismantled your whole organization, weakened it beyond repair. And you'll still be dead."

"So what're my options? 'Cause I don't see any."

"Take a trip," Joe said.

"Where?"

"Anywhere but here for a while. Let everything cool down."

"This here'll never cool down long as Freddy DiGiacomo's alive."

"Can't say that for sure. Just take the wives and go for a bit."

"Take the wives." Montooth chuckled hard at that. "You ever met *one* woman who traveled well? And now you want me to put three crazy bitches on some fucking boat with me? Man, you want to kill me, you couldn't do it surer."

"I'm telling you," Joe said, "it's time to see the world."

"Shit, boy, I ain't drop outta my momma and land on this street. I was with the 369th in the Great War. Hellfighters of Harlem— heard of us? Know what we're famous for besides being the only niggers the government ever gave a weapon *to*?"

Joe did, but he shook his head so the man could tell it.

"We were under fire for six months straight, lost fifteen hun-

dred men, but we didn't lose one fucking *foot* of ground. Not one.
Never had a man taken prisoner either. You think about that. We
stood our fucking ground till they got tired of dying. Not us. Them.
Blood up to my boots. Blood inside my boots. Six months of fighting and not sleeping and scraping some asshole's meat off my bayo-
net. And you want me to be what now? Afraid?"

He tapped the ash out of his pipe into a tray on the table, refilled
it from a brass urn beside the ashtray.

"After the war," he said, "everyone said it'd be different. We'd
go home heroes, get treated like men. I knew that was just nigger
dreaming, so I lit out. Saw me Paris, saw me Germany just so I
could see why everyone had been dying. Time I got back here in
'22? I'd seen Italy and a whole shitload of Africa. Funniest thing
about Africa? No one over there ever confused me with an African.
Clear as day to them what an American looks like, no matter his
shade. Gotta come back here to get told you only half American at
best. So I seen the world, boy, and I got all I want right here. You
got anything else you offering?"

"I'm thinking. You haven't left me much to work with, Montooth."

"Back in the old days, when you were running things? You
could have worked a deal."

"I can still work a deal."

"Not for my life." Montooth leaned forward, wanting to hear
Joe say it.

"No," Joe said, "not for your life."

Montooth took that final confirmation in. He might have faced
death every day of his six months on French battlefields, but that
was over twenty years ago. This was right now, and death sat closer
than Joe. Sat on his shoulder, ran its fingers through his hair.

"I still have the big man's ear," Joe said.

Montooth leaned back. "Problem is, he might not be as big a man as he thinks anymore."

Joe smiled and scowled simultaneously at the absurd notion.

Montooth matched the smile. "Oh, you still think he is?"

"I know he is."

"You ever think what happened between me and Freddy was a play from the beginning?" He leaned back in his throne. "Which white man runs policy in this town?"

"Dion."

Montooth shook his head. "Rico DiGiacomo."

"For Dion."

"And who run the docks?"

"Dion."

Another slow shake of that big head. "Rico."

"*For* Dion."

"Well, Dion best be glad all those people doing so much *for* him because he don't seem to be doing shit for himself."

Was this the dread that had been pecking at Joe all morning? All week? All month? Did this explain the leaden weight that filled his body when he snapped awake from dreams that turned instantly elusive?

In his time on earth, he'd learned one truth above all else when it came to power—those who lost it usually didn't see it vanishing until it was already gone.

Joe lit a cigarette to clear his head. "You only got two options here. And one of them is run."

"Ain't taking that one. What else?"

"Decide what happens to the things you leave behind."

"You telling me to pick my successor?"

Joe nodded. "Or Freddy DiGiacomo gets it all. Everything you built."

"Freddy and his brother Rico."

"I don't think Rico's in on this."

"Really? You think Freddy's the smart brother, do you?"

Joe said nothing.

Montooth flung his hands at the air. "Fuck were you a month ago?"

"Cuba."

"This was a sweet town when you ran it. Hummed along like it's never hummed since. Why can't you run it again?"

Joe pointed to the freckles on his cheeks. "Wrong race."

"Tell you what," Montooth said, "you grab all the spics and micks you know, join up with me and my niggers, we take this town *back*."

"It's a nice dream."

"What's wrong with it?"

"We're mom-and-pop, they're Sears and Roebuck. We'd get a week—two, tops—before they'd come down here and crush us. Turn our bones to gravel."

Montooth poured himself a drink, nodded at Joe's bottle so Joe would know if he wanted some, he'd have to pour his own. Montooth waited as Joe did, and they raised the glasses.

"What're we toasting?" Montooth asked.

"Whatever you want."

Montooth considered the liquor in his glass and then the room around him. "To the ocean."

"Why?"

He shrugged. "I always liked looking at it."

"Good enough for me." Joe met Montooth's glass with his own and they drank.

"You look out at it," Montooth said, "it makes you feel like whatever's on the other side of it—all those worlds—are better places. Places you'll be welcome and treated like a man."

"Never quite works out that way, though," Joe said.

"Nah. But I still feel it. All that water," he said and took another drink, "all those worlds could be got to, but now they just gone by. Like anything, I guess."

"I thought you were done traveling."

"I am. 'Cause I know the truth—all those worlds ain't nothing but this one. Still, when you look at all that blue stretching to forever." He chuckled softly to himself.

"What?" Joe said.

Montooth waved it off. "You think I'm crazy."

"Try me."

Montooth squared himself, his eyes suddenly clear. "You heard the earth's mostly water, right?"

Joe nodded.

"And people think God lives up in the sky, but that don't never make much sense to me because the sky is way, way up there, not part of us, you know?"

"But the ocean?" Joe said.

"That's the skin of the world. And I think God lives in the drops. Moves through a wave like the foam itself. I look in the ocean, I see Him looking back."

"Well, shit," Joe said, "I'll drink to it a second time, then."

They did and Montooth returned his empty glass to the table. "You know I'd choose Breezy as my successor."

Joe nodded. Breezy, the second of Montooth's children, was as smart as a roomful of bankers. "I figured."

"What's the knock on him?"

Joe shrugged. "There ain't much. Same as the knock on me."

"He don't got the stomach for blood."

Joe nodded. "If Freddy *had to* deal with him, though, he would. But if he thought he could push him off the perch, take over everything with his own man running the Negro side of things, he'd do that faster."

"And Freddy's nigger is?"

Joe frowned. "Montooth, come on."

Montooth poured himself another drink. Put down the bottle, lifted Joe's and poured him one too.

"Little Lamar," he said.

Joe nodded. Little Lamar was a Negro version, some said, of Freddy DiGiacomo. They were both native sons of the area, and both had started their careers taking the jobs no one else wanted; in Little Lamar's case, he'd handled a lot of the heroin trade; he also cut his teeth double-crossing all the illegal Chinese who came over, turning half the women into opium-addicted whores working out of casitas on the east side. By the time Montooth Dix figured out Little Lamar wasn't satisfied working for him anymore, Lamar had built up too strong a gang to muscle. He'd been given his walking papers three years ago and a very shaky truce had existed ever since.

"Shit," Montooth said. "Freddy gone steal my book, cut off my head, take what I built, and give it to that high yellow shit stain?"

"'Bout the size of it."

"Then I die, they come after my *son*?"

"Yes."

"Aw now," Montooth said, "that's not right."

"I agree," Joe said. "But it's a hard world."

"I know it's a fucking hard world. Ain't have to be evil, though." He finished his drink. "They'll really kill my boy?"

Joe took a sip of rum. "I think so, yeah. Unless they have no choice but to deal with him."

Montooth looked across the table at him, said nothing.

"West Tampa don't run without Negroes," Joe said. "So Freddy has to deal with somebody. Right now, his plan probably is—kill you, then kill your son, and put Little Lamar on the throne. But can I ask you, Montooth, who could take the throne if Lamar, you, *and* Breezy were all dead?"

"No one. It'd be fucking chaos down here. Lord, would the blood spill."

"And the product would go in the toilet, and the whores would take off, and people would stop playing the *bolita* because they were too shit scared."

"All that."

Joe nodded. "Which Freddy understands."

"So if all three of us are gone . . ."

Joe held out his hands. "Disaster."

"But me, I'm dead no matter what."

Joe nodded, letting him see it now.

Montooth leaned back in his throne, stared at Joe with a stony face that grew flatter and deader by the second until the softest of smiles transformed it. "The question ain't whether I live or die. It's which other motherfucker goes down—my own son or Little Lamar."

Joe crossed his hands on his lap. "Anyone know where Lamar's at right now?"

"Up the same place as always this time of the morning."

Joe tipped his head toward the windows. "Barbershop on Twelfth?"

"Yeah."

"No civilians?"

Montooth shook his head. "Barber goes for coffee. Little Lamar take his counsel from his boys there every morning while one of them gives him a shave."

"How many of his boys?"

"Three," Montooth said. "Everyone gunned up to the chinny-chins."

"Well, Little Lamar's in a chair, and one of his men is busy shaving him. So that leaves two gunners at the front door."

Montooth gave that some thought. Eventually he nodded, seeing it.

"You send your wives away?"

"Why you say that?"

"Normally I'd have heard at least one of them by now."

Montooth stared over his pipe at him for a bit before nodding.

"Why'd you send them away?" Joe asked.

"Figured you'd find a way to kill me. If anyone could, I figured it'd be you this A.M."

Joe lied. "I haven't killed anyone since 1933."

"Yeah, but you killed a king that day. A king started out his morning with twenty men."

"Twenty-five," Joe said. "Now you know I'm not here to kill you, you want to call your women back?"

Montooth scowled. "I ain't saying good-bye to anybody but once."

"So you've said your good-byes."

"I said most of them." Muffled footsteps passed overhead, and Montooth looked up at the ceiling. Small footsteps, a child's. "I'll say a few more and then—"

"Little Lamar's got business this week in Jacksonville. He's on a train at noon. Gone." Joe shook his head. "Time he's back, who knows how the wind will have blown?"

Montooth looked up at the ceiling again, his jaw working, those footsteps gone. "You done your homework."

"I always do."

"So it's now."

"Or it's never." Joe sat back. "Which case, you sit around the rest of your days waiting for someone to come end them. No control in it, no choice in the matter."

Montooth sucked a great breath up through his nostrils and his eyes grew to the size of silver dollars. He clapped his hands on his thighs several times and stretched his neck until Joe could hear the cracks.

Then he stood and crossed to the dark green wardrobe.

He removed his bathrobe and hung it on a hanger, smoothing a wrinkle from the side. He removed his slippers and placed them inside, took off his pajama pants and folded them. Did the same with the top. He stood in his underwear for a moment, staring into the wardrobe, deciding something. "Gonna go with the brown," he said. "Brown man in a brown suit makes a harder target."

He removed a tan shirt so stiff with starch it would have stood upright if he'd dropped it to the floor. As he put it on, he looked over his shoulder at Joe. "How old's your boy now?"

"Nine."

"Needs a mother."

"You think so."

"Fact, man. All boys need mommas. Otherwise they grow up wolves, treat their ladies like shit, have no appreciation for nuance."

"Nuance, uh?"

Montooth Dix fed a dark blue tie under his collar and went to work tying it off. "You love your boy?"

"More than anything."

"Stop thinking about yourself then and give him a momma."

Joe watched him pull a pair of brown pants from the wardrobe and step into them.

"He'll leave you someday." Montooth threaded a belt through the pant loops. "It's what they do. Sit in the same room with you the rest of your life, they'll still be gone on you."

"I was the same with my father." Joe took another sip of rum. "You?"

Montooth slipped his arms into a pair of leather shoulder hol-
sters. "Pretty much. It's the process, how you become a man. Boys
cling; men leave." He added a .44 revolver to the left holster and
then another one to the right.

"You ain't going to be slipping those past anyone," Joe said.

"Ain't fixing to." Montooth added a .45 automatic to the base
of his spine. He donned his suit coat. He added a tan raincoat and
matching hat, smoothed the brim. He pulled out two more pistols
and added them to the pockets of the raincoat, then removed a
shotgun from the highest shelf, turned and looked across the room
at Joe. "How do I look?"

"Like the last thing Little Lamar's going to see on this earth."

"Son," Montooth Dix said, "you got that fucking right."

THEY TOOK THE BACK STAIRS down to the alley. The guy
who'd frisked Joe was standing down there with another guard,
and there were two guards across the alley in a car. Their heads all
spun on a swivel when they saw their boss exit the building armed
for another world war.

Montooth called out to the one who'd frisked Joe. "Chester."

Chester couldn't stop staring at his boss, that big shotgun dan-
gling by his side, the butts of the .44s sticking out of his coat.

"Yeah, boss."

"What at the end of this alley?"

"Cortlan's Barbershop, boss."

Montooth nodded.

His four men exchanged wild, desperate looks.

"Gonna get a bit messy in there about three minutes from now.
Follow?"

"Boss, look, we—"

"I asked if you follow."

Chester blinked several times, took a breath. "Yes. I follow."

"Good. About *four* minutes from now, a few of you need to head down there after me, finish off anything still moving. Hear?"

Chester's eyes filled and damn near spilled. But he looked to his right and then his left and they cleared. And he nodded. "Won't nothing be left alive, Mr. Dix."

Montooth patted his cheek and nodded at the other three. "When this is over, you listen to Breezy. Any you got a problem working for my son?"

The men shook their heads.

"Good. He gonna run a good ship, my boy. And ya'll know he's fair."

"He just ain't you," Chester said.

"Shit, boy, ain't none of us our fathers."

Chester hung his head and busied himself checking the load on his pistol.

Montooth held out his hand to Joe. Joe shook it.

"Freddy gonna know you gave me this option."

"He'll know," Joe said, "and he won't know."

Montooth held his gaze a long time, his hand still gripping Joe's. "Gonna see you on the other side someday. Teach you how to drink brandy like a civilized man."

"I look forward to it."

Montooth dropped his hand and turned without a word.

He walked up the alley, his strides growing longer, faster, the shotgun rising to port position in his hands.

CHAPTER NINETEEN

Right to Life

JOE DROVE OUT OF BROWN TOWN with some part of him wishing he could have followed Montooth Dix into that barbershop, just to see the look on Little Lamar's face if Montooth made it past his bodyguards with the shotgun. But if Joe was caught anywhere near that mess, Freddy DiGiacomo could cry foul and take up arms against the entire Bartolo Family.

Which may have been the play all along. Except that Freddy was incapable of the long game. He thought small, always had. He'd wanted to take over Montooth's policy racket, and now he was about to. If he'd had the smarts to go after the whole kingdom, Joe would have almost had to respect the asshole. Instead, he was going to wreck a dozen lives—minimum—for chump change.

Unless, as Montooth suspected, Freddy wasn't alone in this play.

But, Jesus, if Joe could pick one guy in this entire racket besides

Dion he'd call a true friend, it would be Rico. Then again, if he had to pick one guy who had the smarts and the brass to have orchestrated Montooth's downfall, it too would be Rico. But pushing out Montooth was too small a move for a guy like Rico. And pushing out Dion was a little too big.

Was it?

He's too young, Joe told the voice in his head. Charlie Luciano was young when he formed this whole thing. So was Meyer Lansky. Joe himself ran the entire Tampa operation by the time he was twenty-five.

But those were different days. Different times.

Times may change, the voice whispered, but men don't.

Joe crossed Eleventh and found the pair of Dion's bodyguards waiting for him. It was Bruno Caruso and Chappi Carpino. Joe pulled alongside them, rolling his window down while Chappi did the same from the passenger seat of the other car.

Joe said. "Weren't there two cars?"

"Mike and the Finn went back after we checked in with the boss."

"Trouble?"

Chappi yawned. "Nah. Angelo took a sick day, so the boss figured you'd still want muscle with him and your boy."

Joe nodded. "And that's where you should be too."

"We're following you."

Joe shook his head slowly. "I got a private meeting. You can't come."

Bruno Caruso leaned forward and looked across the seat at Joe. "We got orders."

"Bruno, you've seen me drive. When I put this car in gear, I'll be at the corner before you've come off the clutch. Then you gotta U-turn with all those delivery trucks double-parked over there? You really want to play cops 'n' robbers with me?"

"But, Joe—"

"I got a private thing, ya know? Man-woman kinda thing. Very hush-hush. And I'd rather you and Chappi go where you'll be useful. Tell the boss I made you say yes and I'll see him back at his house in two hours."

They exchanged looks. Joe revved his engine, shot them a smile. Bruno rolled his eyes. "You call the boss and tell him?"

"You got it."

Joe put the car in gear.

"Oh," Chappi said, "the boss said Rico's been trying to get ahold of you. He's at his office."

"Which one?"

"The docks."

"All right. Thanks. First phone booth, I'll call Dion, get you off the hook."

"Thanks."

He pulled away before they could change their minds, banged an immediate left on Tenth, and headed across town.

PULLING DOWN THE BACK ROAD behind the Sundowner Motel, he didn't have a clue what to think. She'd called him last night, all business, and said he was to meet her at noon. Then she hung up. He couldn't help feel he'd been summoned. That for all their playful lovemaking and postcoital banter, she was still a woman of considerable power and she expected those she called to appear before her without question.

Funny how power worked. Hers extended no farther than the city of Tampa and the county of Hillsborough. But that's the ground his shoes touched at the moment, so her power trumped his. Montooth Dix's power had seemed impenetrable until he killed two

men to defend it, and those men were represented by an octopus of
an organization far more powerful than himself. Poland, France,
England, Russia—all had probably thought themselves powerful
enough not to fear the ridiculous tyrant now giving them a hum-
bling lesson in power that had sucked in most of the free world.
Japan thought it was powerful enough to bomb the United States.
The United States thought it was powerful enough to retaliate
and then open a second front in Europe and a third in Africa. And
always in such struggles, one truth overrode all others—one side
had grossly miscalculated.

Joe knocked on the door to 107, and the woman who opened it
was not Vanessa, it was Mrs. Mayor. She wore a stiff business suit
and her hair was tied back severely, which only accentuated the
ashen cross on her forehead. Her face was tight, eyes distant, as if
he were delivering room service and she suspected he'd gotten the
order wrong.

"Come in."

He removed his hat as he entered, stood by the wrought-iron
bed where they'd so often made love.

"Drink?" she asked in a tone that suggested she didn't care how
he answered.

"No, I'm fine."

She poured him one anyway and freshened her own. She
handed him his glass. She raised hers in toast and clinked it off his.

"What're we toasting?"

"What we've already passed by."

"And that is?"

"Us."

She drank, but he put his glass on the edge of the dresser.

"It's good scotch," she said.

"I don't know what's going on," he said, "but—"

"No," she said, "you don't."

"But I'm not giving you up."

"That's your choice, but I'm giving you up."

"You could have done that over the phone."

"You wouldn't have accepted it. You needed to see it in my face."

"See what?"

"That I'm serious. That when a woman moves on, she doesn't look back, and I'm that woman."

"Where . . ." He couldn't seem to find the right way to hold his hands suddenly. "Where is this coming from? What did I do?"

"You didn't do anything. I've been dreaming. I woke up."

He put his hat beside his drink and reached for her hands, but she backed up.

"Don't do this," he said.

"Why not?"

"Why *not*?"

"Yes, Joe. Give me one reason why not."

"Because . . ." He waved his hand at the walls for some reason.

"Yes?"

"Because," he said, as calmly as possible, "without you . . . without knowing I have you to look forward to—and, no, not the sex, not just the sex anyway, but *you*—without that, the only thing that gets me out of bed in the morning is my son. Without you, everything's just—" He gestured at the cross on her forehead.

"A crucifix?"

"Ash," he said.

She drained her glass. "Are you in love with me? Is that what you're peddling today?"

"What? No."

"No, you're not in love with me?"

"No. No, I mean, I don't know. What?"

She poured herself another drink. "How do you see this going? You have your fun with me until we're exposed?"

"We won't necessarily be—"

"*Yes*, we will. That's what's been sinking in all week. I don't see how the fuck I never saw it before. And if that happens, you can gallivant off to Cuba for a while and by the time you return, the noise will have died down. Meanwhile, I'll have been shipped back to Atlanta where the family business will be handed over to the board of directors because no one is going to trust a dumb slut who fucked a gangster and turned her powerful husband into a cuckold."

"That's not what I want," he said.

"What *do* you want, Joe?"

He wanted her, of course. Wanted her right now, in fact, on the bed. And if they could manage it without getting caught—and why couldn't they?—he'd like to continue seeing her a few times a month until either they found themselves so swept up in each other that it made sense to consider some kind of bold break from the pack or they discovered their passion had been a hothouse flower, the bloom already curdling.

"I don't know what I want," he said.

"Great," she said. "Magnificent."

"I do know that I can't get you out of my head no matter how hard I try."

"How burdensome for you."

"No, no. I just mean, look, we could try, couldn't we?"

"*Try?*"

"To see where this takes us. It was working so far."

"This?" She pointed at the bed.

"Yeah."

"I'm married. To the mayor. This can't take us anywhere but disgrace."

"Maybe it's worth the risk."

"Only if there's a reward for losing everything you know."

Women. Jesus.

Maybe he was in love with her. Maybe. But did that mean he was supposed to ask her to leave her husband? That would be a scandal for the ages. Turn the handsome young mayor into a public cuckold? If they did that, Joe would go from outlaw to outcast. He'd never be able to do business in West Central Florida again. Possibly the whole state. They smiled more down south, Joe had learned, but they forgave less. And a man who stole the wife of the war hero son of one of Tampa's oldest families would find every door in town shut to him. Joe would have to go back to being a full-time gangster; problem was, he was thirty-six and too old to be a soldier, too Irish to be a boss.

"I don't know what you want here," he said eventually.

He saw in her eyes that his answer confirmed something for her. He'd failed some kind of test. Hadn't even known he'd been taking it, but he'd failed it all the same.

As he looked across the bed at her, a voice whispered in his head, *Don't speak.*

He didn't listen to it. "Am I supposed to put a ladder up to your window? We run off into the night?"

"No." Her fingers shook slightly on her lap. "It would have been nice to know you considered buying it, though."

"Do you want to run away?" Joe said. "Because I'm wondering how your husband and all his powerful cronies will respond to that. I'm wondering—"

"Stop talking." She looked across the bed at him, her lips pursed.

"What?"

"You're right. I agree with you. There's nothing to discuss. So please stop talking."

He blinked at that. Several times. Then he took a sip of the drink she'd poured him and awaited sentence for a crime he couldn't remember committing.

"I'm pregnant," she said.

He placed the glass back down. "Preg."

"Nant." She nodded.

"And you know it's mine."

"Yes, I do."

"You're sure?"

"I'm positive."

"Would your husband know?"

"Undoubtedly."

"He could get the math wrong. He could—"

"He's impotent, Joe."

"He's . . . ?"

She gave him a tight smile and a tighter nod. "Always has been."

"So you've never . . . ?"

"Twice," she said. "Once and a half, really, when I think about it. The last time was over a year ago."

"So what are you going to do?"

"I know a doctor." She said with false brightness. She snapped her fingers. "Problem solved."

"Hang on," he said. "Hang on."

"What?"

He stood. "You're not killing my child."

"It's not a child yet, Joe."

"Sure it is. And you're not killing it."

"How many men have you murdered, Joseph?"

"That has nothing to do with—"

"If even half the stories I've heard are true, I'll assume several," she said. "Either personally or on your orders. But you think you're going to—"

He came around the bed so fast, her chair toppled as she stood.

"You're not doing this."

"Oh, yes, I am."

"I know every abortionist in this town. I'll blackball you."

"Who said I'm doing it here?" She looked up into his face. "Would you kindly take a step back?"

He held up his hands, took a breath, and did as she asked.

"All right," he said.

"All right what?"

"All right. You leave your husband, come with me. We raise the child together."

"Catch me," she said. "I'm swooning."

"No, listen—"

"Why would I leave my husband to live with a gangster? Your chances of being alive this time next year aren't much better than a soldier's in Bataan."

"I'm not a gangster."

"No? Who's Kelvin Beauregard?"

Joe said, "Who?"

"Kelvin Beauregard," she repeated. "A local businessman in Tampa back in the thirties. Owned a cannery, I believe?"

Joe said nothing.

Vanessa took a drink of water. "Rumored to be a member of the Klan."

Joe said, "What about him?"

"My husband came to me two months ago and asked if you and I were intimate. He's not a fool, you know. I said, 'No. Of course not.' He said, 'Well, if you ever do become intimate, I'll send him to jail for the rest of his fucking life.'"

"That's smoke," Joe said.

Vanessa shook her head slowly, sadly. "He has two signed affidavits from witnesses who place you in Kelvin Beauregard's office the day someone shot him through the head."

Joe said, "He's bluffing."

Another head shake. "I've seen them. According to both affidavits, you nodded to the gunman just before he pulled the trigger."

Joe sat on the bed and tried to figure a way out of the box. But he couldn't. After a while, he looked up at her, his hands hanging off his knees.

Vanessa said, "I'm not getting tossed out of the mayor's mansion and tossed out of my family, so I can land on the street and give birth in the poorhouse to a child who will grow up seeing his father through bars. That is"—she smiled sadly at him—"if one of the judges in my husband's pocket doesn't sentence you to death instead."

They sat in silence for five minutes. Joe tried to find an escape hatch and Vanessa watched his search fail.

Eventually Joe said, "Well, when you put it that way."

She nodded. "I thought you'd come around."

Joe said nothing.

Vanessa gathered her purse and velvet cloche. She looked back at him, her hand on the door. "For a smart man, I've noticed you have a lot of trouble seeing what's directly in front of your nose. You might want to work on that." She opened the door.

By the time he looked up, she was gone.

After a few minutes or so, he retrieved the drink he'd left on the dresser and sat in the chair by the window. He couldn't think through a gray cloud that settled in his head and seeped into his blood. He understood on some fundamental level that he was in shock, but he couldn't identify which stimulus—her pregnancy, her plan to abort it, her severing of the relationship, or the paper her husband held on Joe's freedom—had most directly caused his paralysis.

To clear his head or at least get blood flowing to it again, he picked up the phone and asked for an outside line. He'd forgotten to call Dion and let him know that he'd relieved Bruno and Chappi of their responsibilities. It would be just his luck today that he got them fired.

There was no answer at Dion's and then he remembered that it was Wednesday, which always meant a trip to Chinetti's Bakery. Joe decided he'd just head back there after his next call; everyone would have returned by then and the sponge cake would probably still be warm.

He hung up, picked up the phone again, and got another outside line. He called into work and asked Margaret if he had messages.

"Rico DiGiacomo called twice. Said it was urgent you return his call."

"Okay. Anything else?"

"That gentleman from Naval Intelligence?"

"Matthew Biel."

"That's the one. He left an odd message."

Margaret had been Joe's secretary since 1934. In that time she'd heard plenty of odd.

"Relay it to me," Joe said.

She cleared her throat and her voice dropped an octave. "What will happen next has already happened." Her voice returned to normal. "Know what he means?"

"Not exactly," Joe said. "But these government types sure do love making threats."

When he hung up, he smoked a cigarette and worked his way, as best he could, through his one conversation with Matthew Biel. It didn't take him long to recall the moment when Biel had promised that Joe wouldn't like "what we do next."

So whatever that act, it had already been executed.

Do your worst, Joe thought, as long as you're not trying to put me in the ground.

Speaking of which . . .

Joe called over to Rico DiGiacomo's, got his secretary, who put him right through.

"Joe?"

"Yeah."

"Fuck, where you been?"

"What? Why?"

"Mank's not in a sanitarium."

"Sure he is."

"No, he isn't. He's back in Tampa. And he's looking for you. He was seen a block up from your house. Two hours before that, he cruised the block outside your office. Wherever you are, you need to stay there. Hear?"

Joe looked around the room. At least Vanessa had had the decency to leave behind the bottle of scotch.

"I can do that," Joe said.

"We'll hunt him down. Okay. We'll put him in the ground if we have to."

"Fair enough."

"You just sit on your hands until we can fix this."

Joe thought of Mank out there, trolling, him and his rheumy eyes and flaky scalp, breath smelling of rotgut and salami. Mank didn't play a finesse game the way Theresa or Billy Kovich had. Mank just came at you, engine revving and guns blazing.

"All right," he told Rico. "I'll sit tight. You call me as soon as it's done."

"You bet. Talk soon."

"Rico," Joe said.

Rico's voice came back on the line. "What? What?"

"You need the number here."

"Huh?"

"To call me back."

"Right. Shit." Rico laughed. "Right. Let me get a pen. Okay. Go."

Joe gave him the direct line to the room.

"Okay, okay. Be back in touch," Rico said and hung up.

The curtains in the room were drawn, but Joe noticed there was a gap between the ones that covered the window that overlooked the jetty. He lay on his stomach on the bed and tugged the hems of the curtain panels until they crossed over each other.

Then he got off the bed in case Mank was out there right now, trying to ascertain his position in the room.

He sat on top of the dresser and stared at the tan walls and the painting of the fishermen casting off from a storm-drenched shore. The Cantillions had placed reproductions of the same painting in every room. In this room it hung too low, and two weeks ago Vanessa had accidentally knocked it askew, trying to find purchase as Joe entered her from behind. Joe could see the scratch the back of the frame had nicked into the paint. He could also see her hair again, its ends damp against the side of her neck. He could smell the liquor on her breath—it had been gin that day—and hear the slap of their flesh as their movements grew more frantic.

He was surprised how acute the memory was, how much it hurt to explore it. If he sat here all day and thought about her with nothing but a bottle of scotch and no food, he'd come out of his skin. He needed to think about something else, anything else. Like—

Who took a contract to kill someone and then entered a sanitarium in the middle of the job?

Had that been some kind of ploy to throw Joe off the scent?
Or an actual moment of madness? Because whoever had put the
contract out on Joe would have been more than a little dismayed
when Mank bugged out and checked into the cuckoo house. In
that case, the man who'd taken out the contract would have hired
somebody else to clip both Joe *and* Mank. No, killers on an active
contract didn't take time off to get their brains unfried and then
pop back up on the day of the hit to finish the job. It made zero
sense.

Joe had half a mind to go out on the street right now and talk to
whichever of Rico's men had seen Mank, because he'd bet a thousand dollars they'd mistakenly seen someone who looked like him.
Make it two thousand dollars, that's how sure he was.

His life, though? Would he bet that? Because those were the
stakes. All he had to do was stay in this room—or this box, as he was
already starting to think of it—and pretty soon this would be over.
Rico and his guys would track down this Mank impersonator—or,
okay, possibly Mank himself—and Joe could start sleeping again.

Until then, stay in the box.

He raised his drink to his lips, but stopped before it got there.
The box is the point.

What was it Vanessa had said in her parting shot? He saw
everything but what was directly in front of his nose.

If someone had been trying to kill him these past two weeks,
he should be dead by now. Until he'd actually been made aware of
the alleged plot, he'd walked the streets blithe and ignorant. An
easy target. Even after he'd been appraised of the potential danger,
he'd tried running the rumor down; he'd bartered for Theresa's life;
gone on the boat with King Lucius and twenty drug-poisoned kill-

ers. He could have been easily killed on any of several drives—to Raiford, to the Peace River, hell, just tooling around town.

What was the killer waiting for?

Ash Wednesday.

But why wait?

The only possible answer was because they weren't waiting. There was no "they." Or if there were, "they" weren't trying to kill Joe.

They were trying to keep him on ice.

He picked up the phone, got an outside line, and asked to be connected to the Lazworth Sanitarium in Pensacola. When he got through to the switchboard there, he told the girl who'd answered that he was Detective Francis Cadiman of the Tampa Police Department and he needed to speak with the chief of staff immediately in regards to a murder.

The girl put him through.

Dr. Shapiro got on the line and asked what this was about. Joe told him there'd been a murder last night in Tampa and they'd need to speak with one of his patients about it.

"We believe," Joe told the doctor, "that this man could kill again."

"Kill my patient?"

"No, Doctor. Quite frankly, our suspect *is* your patient."

"I don't follow."

"We have two eyewitnesses who place a Jacob Mank at the scene of the crime."

"That's impossible."

"I'm sorry, but it isn't, Doctor. We'll be coming by directly. I thank you for your time."

"Don't hang up," Shapiro said. "When was this murder?"

"Early this morning. Two fifteen actually."

"Then you have the wrong man. The patient in question, Jacob Mank?"

"Yes, Doctor."

"Tried to kill himself two days ago. He sliced his own carotid with a shard of glass from a broken window. He's been in a coma ever since."

"You're positive?"

"I'm staring at him right now."

"Thank you, Doctor."

Joe hung up.

Who had the most to gain by removing Montooth Dix?

Not Freddy DiGiacomo. Freddy just got the policy racket.

Rico got the territory.

Who suggested he take Tomas and go to Cuba?

Rico.

Who just tracked him down to give him the one name guaranteed to keep him from sticking his head up?

Rico.

Who was shrewd enough to sideline Joe so he could make a play for the throne?

Rico DiGiacomo.

Where had Rico not wanted Joe to be on Ash Wednesday?

Church.

No, that wasn't it. Joe had come and gone without incident . . .

The bakery.

"Jesus," Joe whispered and reached for the door.

CHAPTER TWENTY

The Bakery

WHEN UNCLE DION'S DRIVER, Carmine, pulled up outside Chinetti's Bakery, it was twelve thirty and the day had grown sticky, though the sun hid behind a woolen sky caught somewhere between light gray and dirty white. Uncle Dion patted Tomas's leg and said, "The *sfogliatelle*, right?"

"I can come with you."

Mike Aubrey and Geoff the Finn pulled up to the curb behind them.

"No," Dion said, "I got this in hand. *Sfogliatelle*, right?"

"Right."

"Maybe I'll see if they'll throw in a *pasticiotti*."

"Thanks, Uncle D."

Carmine came around and opened the door for his boss. "I'll see you in."

"Stick with the kid."

"Boss, you don't want me to just go in for you?"

Tomas looked up at Uncle Dion's jowly face as it turned purple.

"I ask you to learn French?" he said to Carmine.

"What?"

"Did I ask you to learn French?"

"No, boss, no. Of course not."

"Did I ask you to paint the hardware store across the street?"

"No, boss, you sure didn't."

"I ask you to fuck a giraffe?"

"What?"

"Answer the question."

"No, boss, you didn't ask me to—"

"So, I didn't ask you to learn French, paint the store across the street, or fuck a giraffe. What I did ask you to do is stay with the car." Dion patted Carmine's face. "So stay with the fucking car."

Dion walked into the bakery, fixing the line of his suit and smoothing his tie. Carmine sat back behind the wheel and adjusted the rearview mirror so he could see Tomas.

"You like bocce?" he asked Tomas.

"I don't know," Tomas said, "I never played it."

"Oh," Carmine said, "you gotta. What do they play in Cuba?"

"Baseball," Tomas said.

"You play?"

"Yes."

"You any good?"

Tomas shrugged. "Not as good as the Cubans."

"I started playing bocce when I was about your age," Carmine said, "back in the Old Country. Most people think my father taught me, but it was my mother. You picture that? My mother in her brown dress. She loved brown. Brown dresses, brown shoes, brown dinner plates. She was from Palermo, which my father said meant she lacked imagination. My father was from . . ."

Tomas tuned Carmine out. His own father had told him on numerous occasions that a man who listened to other men—truly listened to them—gained their respect and often their gratitude. "People just want you to see them as they hope to be seen. And everyone wants to be seen as interesting." But Tomas could only pretend to listen when the speaker was clearly a bore or simply a poor conversationalist. There were times when he wished he was half the man his father was and other times when he knew his father was simply wrong. On the matter of suffering fools, however, he wasn't sure who was right, though he suspected they both might be.

As Carmine prattled on, the postman's bell rang and he rode past them on his yellow bicycle. He parked it against the wall just past the bakery and went sifting through his bag for the block's mail.

A tall man with sunken cheeks and an ashen cross on his pale forehead stopped just past the postman and bent to tie his shoe. Tomas noticed that the man's shoelaces were already tied. But he remained there, even as he looked up and locked stares with Tomas. His eyes sat high in the sockets and Tomas noticed the top of his collar was damp. The man dropped his eyes and went back to fiddling with his shoelace.

Another man, a much shorter, stockier man came up the sidewalk on Seventh Avenue from behind their car and walked into the bakery with fast, certain strides.

Carmine was saying, " . . . but my aunt Concetta, she was . . ." and then his words faded away to nothing, his head turning toward something in the street.

Two men in dark purple raincoats stepped off the opposite sidewalk. They paused in the street to allow a car to pass, then walked in unison, their raincoats loosely belted, but both of them reaching for the belts.

Carmine said, "Stay here a sec, kid," and got out of the car.

The car moved a little bit when Carmine thumped back against it and Tomas stared at the man's back as the fabric of his coat changed color and the echo of the gunshots revealed themselves to Tomas for what they were. They shot Carmine again and he fell away from the window. Some of his blood speckled the glass.

Mike Aubrey and Geoff the Finn never even got out of their car. The two men in the street took care of Aubrey, and Tomas heard the boom of a shotgun and then all that was left of Geoff the Finn was a shattered passenger window and blood splattered on the inside of the windshield.

The two men in the middle of the avenue held Thompson machine guns. They turned toward Tomas, one of them squinting in surprise—*Is that a kid in there?*—and the muzzles of their Thompsons came with them.

Tomas heard shouts and loud cracks in the air behind him. Shattered glass fell from the storefronts. A pistol report was followed by another and then something louder that Tomas took for a shotgun. He didn't turn to look but he didn't drop down into the foot well, either, because he couldn't take his eyes off his own death. The muzzles of those Thompsons remained pointed at him and the men were looking at each other, deciding something unpleasant without exchanging a word.

When the car hit them, Tomas threw up. Just a little—a hiccup of shock and bile. One of the men flew high out of view and then crashed back down on the hood of Uncle Dion's car. Landed on his head. The head turned in one direction while the rest of the body turned in the other. Tomas had no idea what happened to the other man, but the one on the hood looked in at him, the right side of his face and chin looking over his left shoulder like it was the most natural thing in the world. It was the one who'd squinted when he'd looked in the car at Tomas, and Tomas felt the bile rising up the center of his chest as the man continued to stare, his pale eyes as dead as they'd been when he'd been alive.

Bullets moved through the air like squalls of wasps. Again, Tomas knew he should get down behind the seat, get as low as he could, but what he was witnessing was so far beyond his comprehension or experience that the only thing he knew for sure was that he'd never see it again. Everything unfolded in jagged bursts. Nothing seemed connected but everything was.

The car that had hit the two men had crashed into the side of a truck and a man in a pale silk suit fired into it with a machine gun.

On the sidewalk, the man who had pretended to tie his shoe fired a pistol into the bakery.

The postman lay crumpled across his toppled bicycle, his bright blood spilling all over the mail.

The man who'd pretended to tie his shoe screamed. It was a scream of shock and denial, as high pitched as a girl's. He dropped to his knees and lost his grip on his handgun. He covered his eyes with his fingers, the ashen cross on his forehead beginning to leak in the heat. Uncle Dion staggered out of the bakery with blood all over the lower half of his blue shirt. He held a cake box in one hand and a gun in the other. He pointed the gun at the kneeling man and fired a bullet straight through the cross in his head and the man fell over.

Uncle Dion wrenched open the car door. He looked like something that had emerged roaring from a cave to eat children. His voice was the growl of a dog.

"Get on the fucking floor."

Tomas curled up in the foot well and Dion reached over him and dropped the cake box behind the driver's seat.

"Do not move. Hear me?"

Tomas said nothing.

"Hear me?" Dion screamed.

"Yes, yes."

Dion grunted and slammed the door and pings of hail hit the side of the car, Tomas knowing it wasn't hail, it wasn't hail.

The *noise*. Rifles and pistols and machine guns all erupting. The high-pitched squeals of grown men being shot.

The slap of shoes on pavement, men running now, most in one direction—away from the car. And the sound of gunfire dropped away to almost nothing—a stray shot coming from up the street, another from the front of the car. But it was as if a chain had been pulled and the noise snapped off.

Now the street bore that echoing silence of streets that had just hosted a parade.

Someone opened the door and Tomas looked up, expecting to see Dion, but a stranger stood there. A man in a green raincoat and dark green fedora. He had very thin eyebrows and a matching mustache. Something about him was familiar, but Tomas still couldn't place him. He smelled of cheap aftershave and beef jerky. He'd wrapped a handkerchief around his bloody left hand but held a pistol in the right.

"It's not safe," he said.

Tomas said nothing. Upon a second look, though, he realized this was the same man who stood in the playground sometimes after Sunday mass with the witchy old lady who always wore black.

The man poked Tomas's shoulder with his damaged hand. "I saw you. From across the street. I'm taking you somewhere safe. It's not safe here. Come with me, come with me."

Tomas clenched even more tightly into a ball on the floor.

The man poked him. "I'm saving you."

"Go away."

"Don't tell me to go away. Don't. Don't tell me. I'm saving you." He patted Tomas's shoulder and head like a dog, then pulled at his shirt. "Come on."

Tomas batted at his hand.

"Sssshhhhhh," the man said. "Listen," he said. "Listen, listen. Just listen. We don't have much—"

"Freddy!"

The man's eyes bugged at the sound of his name.

And the man out on the sidewalk called again, "Freddy!"

Tomas recognized his father's voice and the relief was so overwhelming he wet his pants for the first time in five years.

Freddy whispered, "Right back," and straightened. He turned toward the sidewalk. "Hi, Joe."

"That my son in there, Freddy?"

"Is that *your* son?"

"Tomas!"

"I'm here, Dad!"

"You all right?"

"I'm okay."

"You hit?"

"No. I'm okay."

"He touch you?"

"He touched my shoulder, but—"

Freddy danced in place.

Tomas found out later his father fired his gun four times but the shots came so fast he never would have guessed the number. All he knew was that suddenly Freddy DiGiacomo's head was lying on the seat above him, the rest of him splayed on the sidewalk.

His father reached into Freddy's hair and yanked his head out of the car. Dropped him in the gutter and reached for Tomas. Tomas wrapped his arms around his father's neck and without warning began to wail. He howled. He could feel the tears pouring out of his eyes like bathwater and he couldn't stop, he couldn't stop. He just kept wailing. Even to his own ears, it sounded alien. It was a cry of such outrage and terror.

"It's okay," Joe said. "I got you. Daddy's here. I got you."

CHAPTER TWENTY-ONE

Lighting Out

JOE HELD HIS SON and surveyed the carnage around him on Seventh Avenue. Tomas shook in his arms and wept like he hadn't wept since he'd suffered a dual ear infection when he was six months old. Joe's car—the one he'd used to run over Anthony Bianco and Jerry Tucci—was totaled. Not from the crash with the light pole but from Sal Romano running up and unloading a full drum of Thompson rounds into it. Joe had come around the trunk of a car two spaces back and shot Romano in the hip while he was reloading. He could still hear him moaning in the middle of the street. Romano had played quarterback for his high school back in Jersey. Still lifted weights and did five hundred push-ups a day, or so he claimed. Joe had blown his left hip into the next block, though, so future push-ups were looking iffy.

As he'd crossed the street, Joe had shot a guy in a capeskin jacket.

The guy had been firing a shotgun into the bakery, so Joe had popped a round into his back and kept walking. He could hear him too—screaming from the sidewalk about fifteen yards back, asking for a doctor, asking for a priest. Sounded like Dave Imbruglia, actually. Looked like him from the back too. Joe couldn't see his face.

His son had stopped wailing, was trying to get his breath back.

"Ssshh." Joe stroked Tomas's hair. "It's okay. I'm here now. I'm not letting go."

"You . . ."

"What?"

Tomas leaned back in Joe's arms and looked down at Freddy DiGiacomo's corpse. "You shot him," he whispered.

"Yup."

"Why?"

"A lot of reasons, but mostly because I didn't like how he looked at you." Joe looked deep into his son's brown eyes, into his late wife's eyes. "You understand?"

Tomas started to nod, then shook his head slowly.

"You're my son," Joe said. "That means nobody fucks with you. Ever."

Tomas blinked, and Joe knew he was seeing something in his father he'd never seen before—the arctic fury Joe had spent his life learning to hide. His father's fury, his brothers', the Coughlin male's birthright.

"We gotta find Uncle Dion and get out of here. Can you walk?"

"Yeah."

"You see your uncle?"

Tomas pointed.

Dion was sitting on the windowsill of the women's hat shop, the glass blown out in the gunfire, staring at them. He was white as new ash, shirt covered in blood, breathing heavily.

Joe put Tomas down and they walked over, the glass crunching under their feet.

"Where you hit?"

"My right tit," Dion said. "Went through, though. I fucking felt it exit. Believe that?"

"Your arm too," Joe said. "Shit."

"What?"

"Your arm, your arm." Joe pulled off his tie. "That's an artery, D."

The blood was spitting straight out of the hole in the inside of Dion's right arm. Joe tied his tie off just above the wound.

"Can you walk?"

"Barely breathe."

"I can hear that. Can you walk, though?"

"Not far."

"We're not going far."

Joe slung an arm under Dion's left arm and pulled him off the window. "Tomas, open the back door again. Okay?"

Tomas ran to Dion's car. He froze, though, when he reached Freddy's corpse, as if it might wake up and lunge for him.

"Tomas!"

Tomas opened the door.

"Good boy. Hop up front."

Joe sat Dion on the seat. "Lie back."

He did.

"Pull up your legs."

He pulled his legs onto the seat and Joe shut the door.

As he came around to the driver's side, he saw Sal Romano across the street. Sal was up on his feet. Well, one foot. The other dangled as he leaned against what had been Joe's car, breathing heavy. Hissing actually. Joe kept his gun on him.

"You killed Rico's brother." Sal winced.

"Sure did." Joe opened the driver's door.

"We didn't know your kid was in the car."

"Yeah, well," Joe said, "he was."

"Won't save you. Rico's going to cut off your head and light it on fire."

"Sorry about the hip, Sal." Joe shrugged, nothing left to say, and got in the car. He backed out of the space and then backed down the street, hearing the sirens now, the sound coming from the west and the north.

"Where we going?" Tomas asked.

"Just a couple blocks," Joe said. "We have to get this car off the street. How you doing, D?"

"World's my oyster." Dion let slip a soft groan.

"Hang in there." Joe backed around the corner onto Twenty-Fourth Street and put the car into first, headed south.

"Surprised you showed up," Dion said. "You always hated getting your hands dirty."

"Ain't about my hands," Joe said. "It's my hair. Look at it. And I'm all out of Brylcreem."

"Such a nance." Dion closed his eyes with a soft smile.

Tomas had never known fear like this. It turned his tongue and the roof of his mouth to dust. A ball of it pulsed in his throat. And his father was making *jokes*.

"Dad," he said.

"Yeah?"

"Are you a bad guy?"

"No, son." Joe noticed specks of vomit on Tomas's shirt. "I'm just not a particularly good one."

. . .

HE DROVE THEM to a Negro veterinarian on a dinged-up stretch
of Fourth in Brown Town. In an alley out back, the veterinarian
had a carport that easily got lost in the cowls of rusted Cyclone
fencing and razor wire the vet shared with his neighbors, an auto
salvage yard and a pest exterminator. Joe told Tomas to stay with
Dion, and before his son could reply, he ran up the back walk and
let himself in through a white door warped by the heat.

Tomas looked into the backseat. Uncle Dion was sitting up, but
his eyes were half closed, his breathing very shallow. Tomas looked
at the door where his father had gone, then out at the alley, where
two stray dogs loped along the fence line, snarling at each other
whenever one got too close.

Tomas leaned over the seat. "I'm really scared."

"Be a fool not to be," Dion said. "We ain't out of this."

"Why'd those men want to kill you?"

Dion chuckled softly. "In our thing, kid, you don't get fired."

"Our thing," Tomas repeated carefully, his voice still shaky.
"Are you and Father gangsters?"

Another soft chuckle. "Well, we were."

Joe and a colored man in a white smock came back out through
the door pushing a gurney. It was a short gurney, maybe only as
long as Tomas, but Joe and the colored man got Dion out of the car
and onto it. His legs dangled off the end as they pushed him up the
walk and inside.

The veterinarian was Dr. Carl Blake, and he'd been a practic-
ing physician at a colored clinic in Jacksonville before he'd lost
his license and arrived in Tampa to work for Montooth Dix. He
patched up Montooth's men and kept his whores healthy and clean,
and Montooth had paid him in the opium he'd lost his license over
in the first place.

Dr. Blake smacked his lips a lot and moved with a strange

stilted grace, like a dancer trying not to knock over the furniture. Tomas noticed that his father always called him Doctor, while Dion, before they knocked him out, called him Blake.

After Dion passed out, Joe said, "I'm going to need a lot of morphine. Probably clean you out, Doctor."

Dr. Blake nodded and poured water over the gash in Dion's arm. "Nicked his brachial. Man should be dead. Is that your tie?"

Joe nodded.

"Well, you saved his life with it."

Joe said, "I'm going to need something stronger than sulfur."

Dr. Blake looked across Dion at him. "With the war? Son, good luck."

"Come on. What can you give me?"

"Prontosil's all I got."

"Then Prontosil will have to do. Thank you, Doctor."

"Hold that light right there, would you?"

Joe moved the lamp over the exam table so the doctor could get a closer look at Dion's arm.

"Boy going to be okay?"

Joe looked over at Tomas. "You want to go in another room?"

Tomas shook his head.

"You're sure? This could make you sick."

"I won't get sick."

"No?"

Tomas shook his head again, thinking, *I'm your son.*

Dr. Blake poked around inside Dion's arm until he said, "It's a clean cut. Nothing foreign in there. Let's put this artery back together."

They worked for a while in silence, Joe handing the doctor instruments as he asked for them or adjusting the lamp or wiping the doctor's forehead with a cloth when the doctor requested it.

Tomas grew certain of one thing—he would never be as calm under strain as his father. He flashed on his father's face as he'd backed the bullet-riddled car out onto Twenty-Fourth Street, the sirens growing louder in the background, Dion groaning in the backseat, and his father squinting at the nearest street sign like a man out for a Sunday drive who found himself slightly turned around.

"Did you hear about Montooth?" Dr. Blake asked Joe.

"No," Joe said lightly. "What about him?"

"Took out Little Lamar and three guns. Didn't get a scratch."

Joe laughed. "He *what*?"

"Not a scratch. Maybe that voodoo shit's true." Dr. Blake finished sewing up Dion's arm.

"What'd you say?" Joe asked sharply.

"Huh? Oh, you know, all those rumors over the years that Montooth practices voodoo in a special room somewhere in that fortress of his, puts hexes on his enemies, all that. Man walks into that barbershop and walks back out the only survivor, maybe there's some truth to it."

A curious look passed over Joe's face. "Can I use your phone?"

"Sure. Right over there."

Joe removed the plastic gloves he'd been wearing and made his phone call as Dr. Blake moved on to the wounds in Uncle Dion's chest. Tomas heard his father say, "You get over here in fifteen, okay?"

He hung up, put on a fresh pair of gloves, and rejoined the doctor.

Dr. Blake asked, "How much time you think you have?"

Joe's face grew dark. "A couple of hours at best."

The door to the exam room opened and another colored man dressed in dungaree overalls stuck his head in. "All set."

"Thank you, Marlo."

"Sure thing, Doctor."

"Thank you, Marlo," Joe said.

When he was gone, Joe turned to Tomas. "There's some pants and underpants for you in the car. Why don't you go get them?"

"Where?"

"In the car," Joe said.

Tomas left the exam room and went back down the hall where the caged dogs barked at his scent. He opened the back door onto the white day and walked back up the path to where they'd left the car. It was still in the same place but it wasn't the same car. It was a Plymouth four-door sedan from the late '30s, no paint, just primer, as forgettable as a car got. On the front seat, Tomas found a pair of black trousers in his size and a pair of underpants and he remembered only now that he'd wet himself just before his father shot the man with the foul breath and the milky eyes. He wondered how he could have forgotten because he could smell himself suddenly, and he could feel the cold stickiness of his own urine turning his thighs raw. But he'd sat in it for over an hour without realizing it.

When he exited the car, he saw his father speaking to a very small man in the alley. The man was nodding over and over as his father talked. As Tomas neared them he heard his father say, "You still related to Boch?"

"Ernie?" The little man nodded. "Married my older sister, divorced her, and married my younger sister. They're happy."

"He still a master?"

"There's a Monet been hanging in the Tate in London since '35 that Ernie painted in a weekend."

"Well, you're gonna need him on this. I'm paying premium."

"You don't pay me anything. Just don't call that witch doctor."

"I'm *not* paying you, but I am paying your brother-in-law. He doesn't owe me shit. So you make sure he knows, he's getting full market value. But this is a rush order."

"Got it. That your boy?"

They turned and looked at Tomas, and something sad passed through his father's eyes, a leaden regret. "Yeah. Don't worry. He's seen the world today. Tomas, say hi to Bobo."

"Hi, Bobo."

"Hey, kid."

"I gotta change," Tomas said.

His father nodded. "Go on then."

He changed into the clothes in a bathroom at the back of the clinic. He wet the lower leg of his old pants in the sink and cleaned his thighs as best he could. He rolled up the piss-stained pants and underpants and brought them back into the exam room with him, found his father pressing a stack of bills into Dr. Blake's hands.

"Just throw them away," his father said when he saw the old clothes. Tomas found the barrel in the corner of the room, tossed the clothes in with the bloody gauze and scraps of Dion's bloody shirt.

He heard Dr. Blake tell his father that Dion had a collapsed lung and that his arm should remain immobile for at least a week.

"By immobile you mean he shouldn't move?"

"He can move, but I wouldn't want him bouncing around much."

"What if I can't control how much bouncing he does in the next few hours?"

"Then the suture in the artery could tear."

"And he could die."

"No."

"No?"

Dr. Blake shook his head. "He will die."

Dion was still out when they put him in the backseat and filled the foot wells with old dog blankets so he couldn't roll off and hurt himself. They kept the windows rolled down, but even so the car smelled like dog hair and dog piss and sick dog.

Tomas said, "Where are we going?"

"Airport."

"We're going home?"

"We're going to try to get to Cuba, yeah."

"And the men will stop trying to hurt you?"

"I don't know about that," Joe said. "But they won't have any reason to hurt you."

"Are you afraid?"

Joe smiled at his son. "Little bit."

"How come you don't show it?"

"Because this is one of those times when thinking is more important than feeling."

"So what are you thinking?"

"I'm thinking we've got to get out of the country. And I'm thinking the man who tried to hurt us, he embarrassed himself. He tried to kill Uncle Dion and he failed. He planned to kill another friend of mine, but that friend got the advantage over him too. And the police are going to be very angry about what happened at the bakery today. The mayor and the chamber of commerce too. I'm thinking if I can get us to Cuba, this man might be willing to negotiate a peace."

"What about his cake?"

"Huh?"

Tomas was kneeling on the front seat, looking at the dog blankets in back. "Uncle Dion's *torta al cappuccino*?"

"What about it?"

"It was in the backseat."

"I thought he got shot in the bakery."

"He did."

"So . . . Wait a minute, what?" Joe looked over at his son.

"But he put the cake in the car."

"*After* the shooting started?"

"Um, yeah. He came over to tell me to get down. He yelled at me. He said get on the floor."

"Okay," Joe said, "okay. But, but this was during the shootout?"

"Yeah."

"And then what?"

"And then he put the cake on the floor of the car and went back outside."

"That doesn't make any sense," Joe said. "You're sure you're remembering it right? There was a lot going on and you were—"

"Father," Tomas said, "I'm sure."

CHAPTER TWENTY-TWO

Flight

COUGHLIN-SUAREZ IMPORT/EXPORT transported much of its product on a Grumman Goose seaplane. Back in the late 1930s, Esteban Suarez had purchased the plane from Joseph Kennedy, the banker, ambassador, and movie producer, after Kennedy decided to distance himself from the illegal liquor business that built his fortune.

Joe had met Kennedy on a couple of occasions. They were both Irishmen named Joseph from Boston, Joe from the south side of the city, Kennedy from the east. They were both hustlers and bootleggers. Both ambitious men.

They hated each other on sight.

Kennedy, Joe assumed, hated Joe because he embodied the worst stereotypes of the Irish bootlegger and made no attempts to hide it. Joe disliked Kennedy for precisely the opposite reason—because he'd embraced the street life when it suited his greed but now that he wanted respectability, he acted as if the fortune he'd amassed had been bequeathed from on high as reward for his piety and moral fiber.

His plane had served them well for five years now, though, aided by the aeronautic gifts of Farruco Diaz, one the most insane men to ever put on a pair of pants but a pilot so talented he could thread the Goose through a waterfall without getting wet.

Farruco was waiting for them at Knight Airfield on Davis Islands, a ten-minute drive out of downtown and over a squeaky bridge that swayed in the softest breeze. Knight Airfield, like most airfields in the country right now, had leased a lot of its land and its runways to the government, in this case as an auxiliary landing field for the Third Army Air Force Group out of Drew and MacDill. Unlike those airfields, however, Knight remained primarily under civilian authority, although that authority could be superseded on a dime by Uncle Sam, something Joe was unfortunately reminded of when he pulled down the main road and saw Farruco on the other side of the fence standing by the Goose.

Joe pulled over and got out. He and Farruco met at the fence.

"Why isn't the engine warming?"

"Can't do it, boss. They won't let me."

"Who?"

Farruco pointed at the control tower, which rose from behind the single-story Quonset hut where the passengers waited. "Guy up there. Grammers."

Lester Grammers had taken at least a hundred bribes from Joe or Esteban over the years, particularly when they picked up marijuana loads in Hispaniola or Jamaica. But since the war started, Lester had started spouting off at the mouth a bit too much about his patriotic responsibilities as an air warden, a neighborhood watch captain, and a reborn believer in the racial superiority of Anglo-Saxons.

He still took their money, of course, but he showed more contempt as he did.

Joe found him up in the tower with the two traffic controllers, and thankfully no uniformed personnel in sight.

"Is there a weather front I don't know about?" Joe asked.

"Not at all. Weather's fine."

"So, Lester . . . ?"

Lester dropped his heels off the edge of his desk and stood. He was a tall man and Joe was not, so Joe had to look up at him, which was probably Lester's intention.

"So," Lester said, "you can't leave. Good weather or bad."

Joe reached into his pocket, careful to keep the flaps of his trench coat closed over his bloody shirt. "What'll it take?"

Lester held up his hands. "I wouldn't know what you're talking about."

"Sure you would." Joe kicked himself for not asking Blake's guy, Marlo, to grab him a clean shirt when he'd gotten the fresh clothes for Tomas.

"I sure would not, sir," Lester said.

"Lester, listen." Joe didn't like the smug pleasure he saw in Lester's eyes. Didn't like it one bit. "Please. I need to fly out right now. Name a price."

"There is no price, sir."

"Stop calling me sir."

Lester shook his head. "I don't take orders from you, sir."

"Who do you take orders from?"

"The United States of America. And they don't want you flying tonight, sir."

Shit, Joe thought. Matthew Biel of Naval Intelligence. You vengeful motherfucker.

"Fine." Joe looked Lester up and down, took his time about it.

"What?" Lester said eventually.

"Sizing you up for an infantryman's uniform, Lester."

"I'm not joining any infantry. I serve the war effort right here."

"But after I take your job, Lester? You'll be serving the war effort on the front fucking lines."

Joe gave him a clap on the shoulder and left the tower.

VANESSA EXITED THE HOTEL SERVICE DOOR into the alley. Joe had pushed back the flap of his trench coat to fish for his lighter and she saw the blood on his shirt and suit jacket.

"You're hurt. Are you hurt?"

"No."

"Oh my God. The blood."

Joe crossed the alley to her, took her hands in his. "It's not mine. It's his."

She looked over his shoulder at Dion slumped in the backseat. "Is he alive?"

"At the moment."

She dropped his hands and scratched nervously at the base of her throat. "There are dead people all over the city."

"I know."

"A group of Negroes shot in a barbershop. And six—I heard six?—men shot in Ybor. Maybe more."

Joe nodded.

"You were involved?" She looked up at him.

No point in lying. "Yup."

"The blood is—"

"I don't have much time here, Vanessa. They're gonna kill me and my friend and maybe even my son if they decide he saw too much. I can't stay another hour in the United States."

"Go to the police."

Joe laughed.

"Why not?"

"Because I don't talk to cops. And even if I did, some of them are on his payroll."

"Whose?"

"The guy trying to kill me."

"Did you kill people today, Joe?"

"Vanessa, look—"

She wrung her hands. "Tell me. Did you?"

"Yes. My son was in the middle of that shootout. I did what I had to do to pull him out. Kill a dozen more men if they were threatening my son."

"You say that with pride."

"It's not pride. It's will." He exhaled a long slow breath. "I need your help. And I need it now. Sand's almost out of the hourglass."

She looked past him at his son kneeling on the front seat and Dion slumped in the back.

When she looked back at him, her eyes were bitter and sad. "What'll it cost me?"

"Everything."

UP IN THE TOWER, Joe kept his trench coat belted as Mrs. Vanessa Belgrave asked Lester Grammers to consider his options.

"That plane isn't just carrying corn and wheat," she said. "It's carrying a personal gift from the mayor of Tampa to the mayor of Havana. A private gift, Mr. Grammers."

Lester looked anxious and pained. "The government man was explicit, ma'am."

"Can you get him on the phone?"

"Ma'am?"

"Right now. Can you get him on the phone?"

"Not this time of night."

"Well, I can get the mayor on the phone. Would you like to explain to him your hostility toward his wife?"

"It's not hos— Jesus."

"No?" She sat on the edge of the desk and removed her right earring as she lifted the receiver off the cradle. "Could I have an outside line, please?"

"Mrs. Mayor, please listen to—"

"Hyde Park 789," she told the operator.

"I need this job, Mrs. Mayor. I—three kids, all in high school."

She patted his knee in agreement, crinkled her nose at him. "It's ringing."

"I'm not a *soldier.*"

"Brrring," Vanessa said. "Brrring."

"My wife, she . . ."

Vanessa raised her eyebrows, then turned back to the phone.

Lester reached across her lap and depressed the cradle.

She looked at him, at his arm hovering over her lap.

He removed the arm. "We'll clear Runway Two."

"Stellar choice, Lester," she said. "Thank you."

"SO WHAT IS THIS?" Vanessa stood in front of Joe at the base of the runway, both of them shouting over the clack and roar of the propellers.

Farruco had helped Joe load Dion inside; they'd lain him on

a pile of the dog blankets while Tomas took one of the seats by the window. Joe had removed the blocks from the wheels, and the plane was starting to shimmy a bit in a sudden warm gust off the Gulf.

"This?" Joe said. "It's the rest of your life. It's me and you and that baby."

"I barely *know* you."

Joe shook his head. "You've barely spent time with me. You know me. I know you."

"You're . . ."

"What? I'm what?"

"You're a killer. You're a gangster."

"I'm mostly retired."

"Don't joke."

"I'm not. Look," he shouted, the gusts and the propellers blowing his coat and hair all around, "there's nothing left for you here. He'll never forgive you for this."

Farruco Diaz appeared in the doorway of the Goose. "They're telling me to wait, boss. The tower."

Joe waved him off.

Vanessa said, "I can't just get on a plane and *vanish*."

"You won't be vanishing."

"No." She shook her head, trying hard to convince herself. "No, no, no."

"They're telling me to put the blocks back in front of the tires," Farruco called.

"I'm older than you," Joe said to Vanessa, his words rushed and desperate, "so I know you don't regret the things you do in this life. You regret the things you don't. The box you didn't open, the leap you never took. Don't look back ten years from now from some drawing room in Atlanta and think, 'I should have gotten on that plane.' Don't. There's nothing left for you here and the whole *world* is waiting over there."

"But I don't know that world," she yelled.

"I'll show it to you."

Something stricken and merciless entered her face. Something that immediately covered her heart in black rock.

"You won't live long enough," she said.

Farruco Diaz called, "We gotta go now, boss. Now."

"One second."

"No. Now!"

Joe held out his hand to Vanessa. "Come."

She stepped back. "Good-bye, Joe."

"Don't *do* this."

She ran to the car and opened the door. She looked back at him. "I love you."

"I love you." His hand still hung in the air. "So—"

"It won't save us," she called and got in her car.

"Joe," Farruco called, "the tower's telling me to shut the engines."

Joe saw the headlights on the far side of the fence then—at least four pairs of yellow eyes, floating up the airport road through the heat and dust and dark.

When he looked back at Vanessa's car, she was driving away.

Joe hopped into the plane. He slammed the door closed and threw the bolt.

"Go," he called to Farruco and sat on the floor. "Just go."

CHAPTER TWENTY-THREE

A Matter of Recompense

WHEN CHARLIE LUCIANO WENT TO PRISON IN 1936, control of the outfit was divvied up between Meyer Lansky of New York and Havana, Sam "Jimmy Turnips" Daddano of Chicago, and Carlos Marcello of New Orleans. These three men, plus three junior officers, Joe Coughlin, Moe Dietz, and Peter Velate, presided over the Commission.

A week after his flight from Tampa, Joe was summoned to meet with the Commission on *El Gran Sueño*, a yacht owned by Colonel Fulgencio Batista but, as often as not, on loan to Meyer Lansky and his associates. Joe was met by Vivian Ignatius Brennan at one of the United Fruit Company piers and boarded a launch for the ten-minute ride out to the yacht in Havana Harbor. They called Vivian "Saint Viv" because more men had prayed to him just before they died than had ever prayed to Saint Anthony or the Blessed Mother. He was a trim, short man with pale hair and pale eyes and unimpeachable manners and taste in wine. Since his arrival in Cuba with Meyer Lansky back in '37, he tended to dress like a Cuban—short-sleeved silk shirts that flared moderately at the waist, silk trousers, two-toned shoes—and he'd even taken a Cuban woman for a wife. But he was all Outfit when it came to his loyalties. A native of Donegal who'd grown up on New York's Lower East Side, Saint Viv discharged his duties without complaint or error. When Charlie Luciano came up with the concept of Murder Inc.—hit men with no affiliation to the towns in which they killed people—he put Vivian Ignatius Brennan in charge of it until Meyer talked Lucky into letting him take the Saint to Cuba with him, whereupon the reins were handed off to Albert Anastasia. But even now, if Charlie or Meyer wanted absolute certainty that someone walking upright today was going to quit that practice by tomorrow, they sent Saint Viv to fulfill the contract.

Joe handed Viv the satchel he was carrying and Viv opened it and looked at the two matching binders inside. He removed them and patted the satchel all over until he was satisfied. He placed the binders back inside and stepped back so Joe could board the launch. Once he was aboard, Vin handed him the satchel.

Joe said, "How you doing?"

"I'm grand." Vivian gave him a sad smile. "I hope it goes well out there."

A small laugh escaped Joe's lips. "I hope it does too."

"I like you, Joe. Hell, everyone does. Break my heart if I had to see you out."

See you out. Jesus.

Joe said, "Let's hope it doesn't come to that."

"Let's." Vivian steered the launch away from the pier, the clanging motor exhaling small clouds of blue smoke up toward the greasy orange sky.

Heading toward what could be his death, Joe realized he didn't fear dying so much as he feared orphaning his son. Yes, he'd made provisions. There was plenty of money socked away for Tomas to live a life without want. And, yes, the boy's grandmother and aunts would raise him as their own. But he wouldn't be their own. He was the product of Graciela and Joseph, his parents. And with both of them gone, he would be an orphan. Joe, who'd grown up an orphan even though his biological mother and father lived full lives under the same roof, wouldn't wish a parentless life on anyone, not even Rico DiGiacomo or Mussolini.

Another launch approached, heading back toward the UFC piers. There was a family in it—father, mother, child—all standing ramrod straight. Joe recognized the blond hair on the boy. It didn't surprise him that the ghost had reappeared now of all days; it actually made a kind of sense.

What did surprise him was the man and the woman in the boat, who refused to look at him as the two launches passed each other. The man was trim and fit, his flaxen hair cut tight to his scalp, his eyes the same pale green as the shallows. The woman was also thin, pinched, her hair piled up in a tight bun, her features so stern with terror disguised as propriety and self-loathing masquerading as imperiousness that it took a second look to realize how pretty she must have once been. She too ignored Joe. Which was the least surprising aspect of the whole experience, since she'd spent the whole of his childhood ignoring him.

His mother. His father. And the boy with the featureless face. Crossing Havana Harbor with the grim fortitude of Washington crossing the Delaware.

They passed, and Joe turned to watch their backs and the core of him shriveled. Their marriage, by the time he came along, was a sham. Their parenting, by the time he came along, was an afterthought, a burden to be borne with self-righteous irritation and short fuses. They spent eighteen years trying to break his spirit of any spark of joy, ambition, or reckless love. And all they produced because of that was an unstable and insatiable organism.

I'm here, he wanted to yell after them. *Maybe not for long. But I was here, and I lived fucking large.*

You lost, he wanted to yell after them.

But yet . . .

You won.

He faced forward again and *El Gran Sueño* loomed before them, a blaze of white against smudged blue sky.

"Good luck in there," Vivian said when they reached the yacht. "I wasn't kidding when I said it would break my heart."

"Break your heart to stop mine, uh?" Joe said.

"Something like that, yes."

Joe shook his hand. "Some business we're in."

"Ah, beats a dull life, sure, though, doesn't it? Watch your step on the ladder. It gets wet."

Joe climbed the ladder and stepped onto the deck and Vivian handed his satchel up after him. Meyer was waiting there, smoking as always, four other men with him—button guys or bodyguards by the look of them. Joe only recognized Burt Mitchell, a Kansas City gun monkey and bodyguard for Carl the Bowler. No one acknowledged Joe. They might be feeding his body to the sharks in half an hour, so there was no point in getting cozy.

Meyer indicated the satchel. "This it?"

"Yup." He handed it to Meyer, who passed it off to Burt Mitchell. "See that gets to the accountant in my stateroom." He put a hand on Burt's shoulder. "No one but the accountant."

"Yes, Mr. Lansky. Absolutely."

When Burt walked off, Joe shook Meyer's hand, and Meyer gave him a hard pat on the shoulder. "You're a talented orator, Joseph. I hope you can bring all your skill to bear today."

"You talk to Charlie?"

"A friend did on my behalf, yes."

"What'd he say?"

"He said he doesn't like publicity."

There'd been way too much of that coming out of Tampa in the past week. There was talk the Feds were commissioning another board to investigate organized crime in Florida and New York. The papers had plastered Dion's face on the front pages for days, along with garish pictures of the dead Joe had left on Seventh Avenue and the four dead in the Negro barbershop. A couple of newspapers had even linked Joe to the shootings, though they were careful to use words like *purportedly*, *allegedly*, and *rumored to*. It was noted in all news reports, however, that neither Joe nor Dion had been seen since the afternoon of the bakery shootout.

"Charlie say anything else?" Joe asked Meyer.

"He'll say it by proxy at the end of this meeting."

So Meyer was the final judge. Ironic that the guy who might pass the death sentence on Joe had been his partner and biggest benefactor these last seven years.

Then again, not the exception but the rule in their thing. Your enemies rarely got close enough to kill you. So the dirty work usually fell to your friends.

Down in the stateroom, Sam Daddano and Carlos Marcello sat with Rico DiGiacomo. Meyer came in behind Joe and closed the door after him. So, besides Rico, the only other three men present were the lords on high of the Commission, which meant this was as serious as a meeting got.

Carlos Marcello had been running New Orleans since the teens; he'd inherited it from his father and grew up with the business in his blood. If you stayed out of his territory, which also included Mississippi, Texas, and half of Arkansas—Carlos was a perfectly pleasant human being to deal with. But if, on the other hand, you sniffed for money anywhere near his turf, the bayous occasionally burped up parts of someone who'd confused where Marcello borders began and their right to breathe ended. Like most of the men on the Commission, he was known for a calm demeanor and a desire to be reasonable until reason had exhausted itself as a business model.

Sam Daddano had been the Outfit's entertainment and union guy for a decade before his success there got him bumped up to the top Chicago slot when old man Pascucci had himself a stroke in Lincoln Park one rainy spring morning. Sam had advanced the Outfit's interests out west and had pulled all the movie unions into the fold. He'd even gotten out ahead of the record business. They said if Sam glanced at a nickel it turned into a dime. He was very thin and had been going bald since his teens. He was only in his early fifties but he looked fifteen years older, always had, his skin flaky and mottled with liver spots, as if their business consumed all the fluid inside of him, just sucked him dry all day long.

Meyer took his seat on the other end of the table. He placed his briefcase down and neatly laid out his cigarettes, gold lighter, gold pen, and the notebook where he occasionally scribbled an idea— never a fact, never a fact—and always in code and always in Yiddish. The Little Man himself, Meyer Lansky. The architect of all they'd built, and as unflappable as any man with a pulse could get. The closest thing Joe had to a mentor in this business. He'd certainly taught him most of what he knew about the casino business, while Joe had taught Meyer most of what he knew about Cuba. As soon as this fucking war ended, they'd be able to make some real money here.

Or would have been able to. Meyer might be making that money all by himself if Joe didn't convince his jury that he was worthy of more days in the fresh air.

Joe took his seat across from Rico, who stared at him with his true face for the first time. In it, Joe saw the bottomless appetite for empire that he should have seen the first time he'd met him fifteen years ago, when Rico had still been mostly a boy. But even then Rico had possessed the most priceless gift for a man of his ambition—people couldn't see into him; they only saw their own images reflected in his eyes. Rico managed to keep you out by making you feel as if all he dreamed of was for you to let him in. Now he stared across the table at Joe, an open smile on his open face, and looked like he might just dive across the table and tear Joe's limbs off with his bare hands.

Joe had no illusions about his own physical capabilities—he'd been in three fistfights in his life and he'd lost them all. Rico, on the other hand, grew up in Port Tampa, the son, grandson, and nephew of longshoremen. Joe looked across the table at his betrayer and Dion's usurper and showed no fear because anything less would have been an admission of guilt or lack of balls, both of which would seal his fate in this room. But the truth was, if he made it back out of here alive, he knew that Rico would never stop wanting him dead.

"The concern," Carlos Marcello said to open the meeting, "is how much damage you did last week, Joe."

"*I* did," Joe said, looking at the table. "How much damage I did."

Sam Daddano said, "You met with the nigger Dix, and ten minutes later he killed four nigger associates of Rico's. Was this a coincidence, Joe?"

"I told Dix he couldn't talk or fight his way out of the jam he was in and he needed to make peace with his maker. I—"

"Might end up being good advice for you." Rico smiled across the table at him.

Joe ignored him. "I didn't know Dix was going to take that to mean he should shoot up a barbershop and kill Little Lamar."

"And yet," Meyer said, "it happened. And then this business at the bakery."

"He's dead by the way," Rico said to Joe.

Joe looked over at him.

"Montooth. Got in his car yesterday morning and that car went *boom*. Somebody found his nutsack melted to the side of a hydrant across the street."

Joe said nothing. Just gave Rico flat eyes as he lit a cigarette. Last week, Joe had made his peace with Montooth Dix's death. But it hadn't happened. So, unbeknownst to him, his heart had opened to the possibility that Montooth could stay aboveground a few more years.

Now he was dead. Because a serpent cloaked in a man's body decided he wasn't satisfied with the chips on the table, decided he was owed the whole fucking casino. Fuck you, Rico. And everyone like you. Make you a prince, you want to be a king. Make you a king, you want to be a god.

Joe turned back to the man at the head of the table. "You wanted to discuss the bakery."

"Yes."

"Was the hit sanctioned, by the way?"

Sam Daddano held his gaze for several seconds. "It was."

"Why wasn't I consulted? I'm part of this Commission."

"With all due respect," Meyer said, "you couldn't be trusted.

You've described Dion Bartolo on several occasions as your brother. Your judgment would have been clouded."

Joe took that in. "And that plot to assassinate me? That was all smoke?"

Meyer nodded.

"My idea," Rico said, helpful as ever, hands folded on the table in front of him, voice soft. "I wanted to get you clear of the danger when the hit went down. Believe that? I figured you'd grab your son and light out for here, sit the whole thing out. I was looking out for you."

Joe couldn't think of a reply to that, so he turned back to the room. "You sanctioned a rubout on my friend and boss. Then my son got caught in the crossfire when all these hitters came down from . . . Brooklyn, I'm assuming? Midnight Rose's Candy Store?"

An affirmative flick of the eyelids from Carlos Marcello.

"Bunch of out-of-towners standing in my territory taking shots at my boss while my son's in a car on the same street, and I'm somehow to blame for my reaction?"

"You killed three of our friends that day," Daddano said. "You crippled another."

Joe narrowed his eyes at that, confused.

"Dave Imbruglia."

So that had been Dave he'd shot in the back.

Rico said, "Shit in a bag the rest of his life, the poor bastard."

"I pulled onto that street," Joe said to the bosses, "and the first thing I see besides a bunch of guys firing away like it's St. Valentine's Day all over again is my son's head poking out of the backseat of Dion's car."

"We didn't know he was there," Rico said.

"So that makes it okay? I saw Slick Tony Bianco and Jerry the Nose air out Carmine Orcuioli and then turn their Thompsons on *my* son? You're fucking right I ran them over. I shot Sal Romano because he unloaded his machine gun into my car. And I shot Imbruglia in the back because he was firing a shotgun at my boss. As for Freddy, yes, I shot him. I—"

"Four fucking times."

"—shot him because he was pointing a gun at my son."

"Sal says Freddy's fucking gun wasn't pointed at your son."

Meyer Lansky nodded. "Says it was pointed at the ground, Joe."

Joe nodded, as if it made perfect sense. "Sal was on the other side of the car, sitting on the other side of the street. Actually, he wasn't sitting. He was lying there in a ball because I'd blown his fucking hip off. How's he see anything?"

Carlos Marcello held up a placating hand. "So why did you think Freddy wanted to kill your son?"

"*Think,* Carlos? Would you be thinking if that was your son in the car?" He looked at Sam Daddano. "Your boy Robert?" He looked at Meyer. "If it was Buddy? I wasn't thinking. I saw a man pointing a gun at my son. And I pulled my trigger so he couldn't pull his."

"Joe," Rico said quietly, "look at me. Right into my eyes. Because I'm going to kill you someday. I'm going to do it with my bare hands and a spoon."

"Rico," Carlos Marcello said, "please."

"We're adults here," Meyer said. "Men discussing a difficult piece of business. Seems clear that Joe's not trying to back off anything he did. He's not making excuses."

"He killed my brother."

Carlos Marcello said, "But your brother had a gun pointed at his son. That doesn't seem to be in much dispute. Guns pointed at white children, Rico, that's an *infamnia,* and you shouldn't be fucking arguing otherwise."

Rico had boarded the boat thinking the only guy who wasn't

getting back off was Joe, but now he was seeing his own corpse reflected in Carlos Marcello's black eyes.

Sam Daddano looked down the table at Joe. "On the other hand, you killed a made guy and two valued associates. You cost us a lot of money."

"A lot of money," Meyer agreed.

"And not just now," Sam said, "but for years down the road with all this bad publicity. That's food off our table, money out of our pockets. Money we were counting on. And there's no way you can make that up to us."

"I think I can," Joe said.

Carlos Marcello shook his big head. "Joseph, that's wishful thinking. The mess you and Rico created last week in Tampa will drain us."

Joe said, "What if I could spring Charlie from Dannemora?"

Meyer's lighter paused halfway to his cigarette.

Carlos Marcello's head froze in a cocked position.

Sam Daddano stared directly at Joe, his lips parted.

Rico looked around the room. "That all? Why don't you part the Gulf of Mexico while you're at it?"

Carlos Marcello waved at the air between him and Rico like he was batting away a fly. "Speak plain, Joseph."

"I met with a guy from Naval Intelligence two weeks ago."

"But we understand it didn't go well," Meyer said.

"It didn't. But I could tell he was close to the hook. He just needed a little more convincing. The U.S. has lost ninety-two ships—military and commercial—in the last five months. They're scared shitless but they're telling themselves, 'Well, at least it's never happened along the shore.' But if we could convince them that the only thing standing between them and Hitler parading down Madison Avenue is *us*? They'll let Charlie out after the war.

At the very least, they'll leave us alone and let us make money."

"And how do we show them they need us?"

"We sink a boat."

Rico DiGiacomo exhaled loudly. "What's with this guy and boats? Didn't you blow one up ten years ago?"

"More like fourteen," Joe said. "The government has a boat in Port Tampa right now, an old luxury liner they're retrofitting into a warship."

"Used to be *The Neptune*," Rico said. "I know it."

"And you got guys working on it, right?"

Rico nodded at the rest of the men. "We do all right, but it's no cash cow. A little scrap metal here, some copper there, lotta old metal beds not ending up where they were supposed to, that sorta shit."

"United States government wants that liner turned into a troop transport ship by June. Am I right?"

"You're not wrong."

"So . . ."

The corners of Carlos Marcello's lips twitched. Sam Dadanno let loose a short bark of a laugh. Meyer Lansky smiled.

"Someone sabotages that ship? Make it look like Krauts did it or could have?" Joe sat back, tapped an unlit cigarette off the side of his brass Zippo. "Government will come to us on their knees." He met the eyes of each man in the room. "And you'll all be the men responsible for springing Charlie Luciano from prison."

Nods from the table, a tip of the imaginary hat from Meyer Lansky.

Joe's pulse slowed in his throat. He might make it back off this boat after all.

"Okay, okay," Rico said. "Let's say he's right and this works. And I'm not pretending it's not a good plan. No one ever questioned this guy's brain, only his stomach for the grim stuff. What about here?"

"Excuse me?" Joe said.

"Here." Rico stabbed a finger into the table. "He gets to build a kingdom with Meyer here, now that I pushed him out of Tampa and he got caught with his dick in the mayor's wife." He looked over at Joe. "Yeah, Romeo, everyone knows about that now. Big to-do back home." He raised his eyebrows a couple times, then looked back at the bosses. "Do I get any of his action here? A little something to tide me over?"

Joe looked down the table at Meyer. Cuba was Meyer's and Joe's pampered princess-child; they protected her from everything in the world that could soil her. Now here came Rico DiGiacomo, pawing at her with grime and germs all over his hands. Meyer looked at Joe with a fatalistic fury that said, For this, I blame you.

"You want a piece of Cuba?" Carlos asked.

Rico DiGiacomo held his index finger and thumb a hair apart. "Tiny piece."

Carlos and Sam looked over at Meyer.

Meyer threw it right at Joe. "Joe and I own that land we're turning into a hotel once this war's through. Hotel, casino, the works. You all know this."

"How much a piece you own, Joe?"

"I got twenty, Meyer's got the same. Pension fund's owning the rest."

"You give five to Rico."

"Five," Joe said.

"Five's fair," Rico DiGiacomo said.

"No," Joe said, "three's fair. I'll give you three."

Rico took the temperature of the room before he replied. "Three it is."

Joe shared another look with Meyer. They both knew what had just happened. Even if they'd only given Rico half a percentage point, the result was still the same—his foot was now in the door. As he'd just done in Tampa, he could someday do in Havana.

Fuck.

Rico wasn't done. "There's still the matter of personal recompense."

"Giving you credit for springing Charlie from Dannemora and a slice of the Cuban operation ain't enough for you?" Marcello asked.

"It's enough for me, Carlos," Rico said solemnly. "Is it enough for my brother, though?"

The men looked at one another.

"His point's fair," Meyer finally admitted.

"What can I do?" Joe asked. "I can't put the bullets back in the gun."

"Rico lost a brother," Daddano said.

"But I don't have a brother to give him in return," Joe said.

"Sure you do," Rico said.

It took Joe less than half a second to see what should have been obvious from the moment this meeting had been arranged. He looked across the table to see Rico smiling at him.

"A brother for a brother," Rico said.

"You want me to give up Dion."

Rico shook his head.

"No?"

"No," Rico said. "We want you to kill Dion."

Joe said, "Dion's not—"

"Don't insult us," Carlos Marcello said. "Joseph, don't."

Meyer lit a cigarette from the butt of his previous one, Meyer capable of filling an ashtray faster than a roomful of junkie gamblers. "You know the Commission doesn't give a death sentence lightly. Don't dishonor us or embarrass yourself by pleading his case."

"He's a real piece of shit," Daddano said, "and he's gonna fucking go. Only questions left are how and when."

A pause, particularly a contemplative one, would be read immediately as weakness, so Joe didn't skip a beat. "Then it'll be done first thing tomorrow. Over and done. You want to pick him up? You want me to send him to a spot?"

If they gave him the night, he'd figure something out. He had no idea what, but something. If, instead, they sent somebody back with him, he had no clue what miracles he could work. Or couldn't.

"Tomorrow's fine," Meyer said.

Joe made his face blank, as if the answer meant nothing to him.

"It doesn't even have to be done in the morning," Daddano said. "By the end of the day's fine."

"Just so long as it gets done," Carlos Marcello said.

"By you." Rico's chair creaked when he leaned back in it.

Joe kept his face still. "Me."

Four nods.

"You," Rico said. "You do him like you did my brother. Same gun. That way every time you look at it, you piece of . . . every time you look at it, you think of my brother and you think of yours."

Joe looked at each of the men in the room again. "Done."

"Sorry," Rico said, "I didn't hear that."

Joe looked at him.

"Seriously. I get that tinnitus sometimes, like kettles going off in my ears. What'd you say?"

Joe let a few ticks come off the clock above the door.

"I said I'll kill Dion. Consider it done."

Rico slapped the table lightly. "Well, then, I'd call this meeting a success."

"You don't call this meeting anything," Carlos Marcello said. "We call meetings and we adjourn them."

As Rico sat back down, three men walked into the room. Saint Viv came through the doorway first and walked down the left side of the table toward Joe, his brokenhearted eyes locked on him the whole way. When he reached Joe, he stood directly behind his chair, and Joe could hear his breathing.

The second man, Carl the Bowler, came down the other side of the table and stopped between Sam Daddano and Rico DiGiacomo, his hands crossed over his waist. Rico looked at Saint Viv the Executioner standing behind the man who'd killed his brother. He met Joe's eyes and couldn't help himself—he smiled.

The third man who entered the room was a stranger. He was very thin and nervous and kept his eyes on the floor until he reached Meyer. He placed the satchel in front of him and removed one black binder and put it on the table. He spoke low into Meyer's ears for a full minute, and when he was done, Meyer thanked him and told him to get something to eat.

The man followed the carpet back out of the room, his scrawny shoulders hunched, his balding head catching the light.

Meyer slid the binder across the table to Rico. "Yours, right?"

Rico opened it and leafed through it. "Yup." He closed it, slid it back. "What's it doing all the way over here?"

Meyer said, "This is your ledger? This is everything you make for us?"

Rico's eyes were moving a bit when he lit his cigarette. For the first time in a while, Joe suspected, he found himself a step behind the play. "Yeah, Meyer. It's the one I send out to you guys with the cash every month. Same ledger Freddy used to bring in that alligator skin briefcase of his."

"And that's your handwriting, no question?" This from Carlos Marcello.

Rico didn't like where this was going at all, but there wasn't much he could do but answer. "Yes. All mine."

"No one else could have scribbled anything in here?"

"No. No. Definitely not. You've seen my chicken scratch; it's not pretty but it's definitely mine."

Meyer nodded, as if that settled everything, tied it off with a bow. "Thank you, Rico."

"No problem. Happy to help."

Meyer reached into the satchel and came back with the second binder. He tossed it onto the table.

And Rico caught up to the play.

"Ho," he said. "Fuck is this?"

"This is a second ledger." Meyer slid it across the table to him. "Recognize the chicken scratch?"

Rico opened it up, his eyes flying back and forth as he leafed through the pages. He looked across at Meyer. "I don't get it. Is it a copy?"

"Appeared to be at first. Then we had the accountant look it over. According to him, you've been cooking it."

"No."

"To the tune of thirty thousand this year, forty last."

"No, Meyer. No." Rico looked around the room and then his eyes fell on Joe and he knew. *"NO!"*

When Carl the Bowler placed the plastic bag over his head, Rico raised his arms, but Sam Daddano grasped them at the wrist. He and Carl the Bowler turned Rico in his chair and Carl twisted the plastic at the back of Rico's head into a knot.

Carlos Marcello said to Joe, "Who can replace him? Can't be you."

When Joe had hired Bobo Frechetti to break into Rico's office, he'd honestly thought there would be a second ledger. But just in case, he'd had Bobo's brother-in-law, the forger's forger, Ernie Boch, on standby if the need arose.

The need arose.

Rico's lit cigarette rolled into the center of the table and Meyer reached for it, put it out in the ashtray before him.

"You know that guy hangs at the Italian Social Club in Ybor?" Joe said.

"Trafficante?" Marcello said.

"Yeah. He's ready."

Bobo had handed off the ledger to his brother-in-law, and Ernie duplicated Rico's handwriting—its looping capital letters, its undotted *i*'s and *j*'s, its slanted *t*'s and flat-lining *n*'s. The rest was just a matter of shaving off a number here, some zeroes there.

Rico's feet kicked Sam Daddano's chair hard enough to lift the man out of it, but he held on to Rico's wrists.

"Trafficante's a good earner," Daddano managed, already a little out of breath.

Marcello looked at Meyer and Meyer said, "I've always found him reasonable."

Marcello said, "Then Trafficante it is."

Rico's body voided and the smell of it found the room. He stopped kicking. His arms went limp.

Carl the Bowler kept the bag on for another two minutes just to be sure as Joe watched the other men file out.

When Joe stood to leave the room, he gave the corpse one last look as he gathered up his cigarettes. He waved his hand at the stink that emanated from it.

That's all you did with your time on this earth, Rico—you soiled the air.

And fucked with the wrong Irishman.

CHAPTER TWENTY-FOUR

Send You a Postcard

DRIVING TO AN APARTMENT he kept in the Old City, Joe considered his options.

He came up with two:

Kill Dion, his oldest friend.

Or don't kill him and die.

Even if he did kill Dion, the Commission could still vote to kill Joe. He'd cost them money and he'd left a big mess behind. Just because he walked off that boat didn't mean he was safe.

His driver, Manuel Gravante, said, "Boss, Angel drove by while you were on the boat, told me there's another package back at the place for you."

"What package?"

"Angel said it was a box." Manuel held his hands about a foot apart and then put them back on the wheel. "Said it was sent to the palace in your name. The Colonel's men brought it over."

"Who sent it?"

"Somebody named Dix."

One of his last acts aboveground apparently.

Christ, Joe thought. When all this is over, will any of us be left?

EVEN THOUGH HE'D BEEN EXPECTING THE PACKAGE, he still opened it in the courtyard behind his apartment building just in case. If Joe did, as many suspected, have nine lives, he lost two when he opened the flaps on the box and the smoke poured out. He jumped back, stood there with fresh sweat running into a suit that had already been sweated through, as the white vapor poured off the dry ice and over the flaps and dissipated into the palm fronds above him. Once he'd ascertained that the source was, in fact, dry ice, he waited until the last of the vapors had cleared, then reached in and lifted the smaller box out of the package and placed it on the stone table.

It was dented on all four corners. Oily stains on one side of the cardboard where the contents had rested. Spots of blood speckled the words on top: CHINETTI BAKERY, CENTRO YBOR. The twine still crisscrossed the carton, and Joe cut it with the same pair of scissors he'd used to open the shipping box. Inside was the *torta al cappuccino,* although you could barely recognize it as such. It was collapsed and green with mold on one side. It reeked.

Every week for the past two years, rain or shine, hot and humid or cold and rainy, Dion had gone to the bakery and walked back out with a cardboard box with a cake inside.

But was that all that had been inside?

Joe lifted the ruined pastry.

All that lay below it was soiled wax paper and a circular piece of cardboard. He'd been wrong. He could feel his heart still pounding in his chest while all around it a warm river of relief flooded his body. His suspicions shamed him now. He looked up at the window of the bedroom where Dion had stayed the first night before Meyer confirmed that Rico was sending hitters over from Tampa. They'd moved Dion that morning, had him tucked away under the Colonel's care and the Colonel's guards about thirty miles south, which was running Joe a pretty penny.

Joe sent a silent apology to his friend.

Then he turned back to the cake box and listened to the darkest part of his heart. He reached in and lifted the wax paper out and then the cardboard circle.

And there it was.

An envelope.

He opened it. He shuffled through the small stack of hundred-dollar bills inside and then found the slip of white paper at the end of the stack. He read what was on it—one name, nothing more. But then there didn't have to be. The content of the note was irrelevant. The note itself told the whole story.

Every week for the past two years, Dion had gone to Chinetti's Bakery on Seventh to eat his fill of pastry and get his marching orders from either a Fed or a cop as to which of his guys he was going to rat out next.

Joe folded the note and placed it in his wallet and then put the cardboard, the wax paper, and the cake back in the carton. He closed the carton and took a seat by his rosebushes and the knowledge that he was alone in this business—truly fucking alone—threatened to knock him off his chair. So he stood and he buried his sorrow and buried his fury in a fresh pocket of himself. At thirty-six, after twenty years on the wrong side of the law, he had a lot of those pockets. They were sealed and stored all over his interior. He wondered if they'd ever burst all at once and that's what would kill him.

Either that or he'd run out of space for them and choke from the lack of air.

HE FELL ASLEEP IN HIS STUDY, sitting upright in the big leather armchair. In the middle of the night he opened his eyes, and the boy stood by the fireplace, the fire mostly embers behind him. He wore red pajamas similar to a pair Joe had worn as a child.

"Is that it?" Joe asked. "You my twin who died in the womb? Or are you me?"

The boy crouched and blew on the embers.

"I never heard of someone having a ghost of himself," Joe said. "I don't think that's possible."

The boy looked back over his shoulder at Joe, as if to say, *Anything's possible.*

In the shadows of the room, there were others. Joe could feel them, even if he couldn't see them.

When he looked at the fireplace again, the embers were out and it was already dawn.

THE HOUSE WHERE HE'D STASHED Dion and Tomas was in Nazareno, smack in the center of the interior of Habana Province. Behind it lay Havana and the Atlantic, beyond it were mountains, jungles, and then the sparkle of the Caribbean. It was deep in sugarcane country, which is how Joe had discovered it. The house had been originally built as the estate of the Spanish *commandante* who'd headed the army brought in to crush a rebellion by the Cuban field hands back in the 1880s. The barracks of the soldiers who'd done the crushing had long since been abandoned and retaken by the jungle, but the *commandante*'s estate remained in its original state of glory—eight bedrooms, fourteen balconies, high iron fences and gates surrounding it.

El Presidente himself—Colonel Fulgencio Batista—had provided Joe with twelve soldiers, enough to repel any attack from Rico DiGiacomo and his men, should they have discovered the location. But Joe knew the real danger wouldn't have come from Rico, even if he had survived his trip to the boat. It would come from Meyer. And not from the outside, but from one of the well-armed soldiers already inside.

He found Tomas and Dion in Dion's bedroom. Dion was teaching the boy chess, a game Dion himself was barely adequate at, but at least he knew the rules. Joe placed the paper shopping bag down on the floor. In his other hand, he carried the medicine bag Dr. Blake had given him in Ybor. He kept it in his hand as he stood in the doorway and watched them for a while, Dion telling Tomas all about the origins of the European conflict. He told him about the anger over Versailles, about Mussolini invading Ethiopia, about the annexation of Austria and Czechoslovakia.

"That's where his shit should have been stopped," Dion said. "Once you tell a man it's okay to steal, he won't stop until you cut off his hand. But if you threaten to cut off his hand before he reaches for that piece of bread, and he sees in your eyes that you're serious? He'll figure out how to get by on less."

"Will we lose?" Tomas asked.

"Lose what?" Dion said. "We don't own real estate in France."

"But then why're we fighting?"

"Well, we're fighting the Japs because they attacked us. And Hitler, little Kraut bastard, kept going after our ships, but the real reason we're fighting is because he's just nuts and he's gotta go."

"That's it?"

"Pretty much. Sometimes, a guy's just gotta go."

"Why're the Japanese mad at us?"

Dion opened his mouth to answer, then closed it. After a minute, he said, "You know, I don't even know. I mean they're Japs, so they're not like you or me, but I don't know why their panties got in a bunch originally. Want me to look into it?"

Tomas nodded.

"Deal. By our next game, I'll know all there is worth knowing about Japs and their sneaky ways."

Tomas laughed and said, "Checkmate."

"Sneak attack, uh?" Dion looked down at the board. "You might be half Jap yourself."

Tomas looked back at Joe. "I won, Father."

"I see that. Well done."

Tomas got off the bed. "Are we leaving here soon?"

Joe nodded. "Soon, yeah. Can you go wash up? I think Mrs. Alavarez is making you lunch downstairs."

"Okay. See you, Uncle Dion."

"See ya."

"Checkmate," Tomas said as he was leaving. "Ha."

Joe placed the shopping bag near the foot of the bed and the doctor's satchel on the nightstand. He removed the chessboard from Dion's thighs. "How you feeling?"

"Better every day. Still weak, you know, but getting there. I got a list of guys I think we can trust. Some are in Tampa, but a lot of them are guys from our Boston operation. If you could get up there, convince them to get down to Tampa in a month, maybe six weeks, we could take the town back. Some of these guys are going to be expensive. You know, like Kevin Byrne ain't picking up his eight kids and leaving his empire there in Mattapan out of pure loyalty. We'll have to pay him boxcar numbers. And Mickey Adams, he ain't going to be cheap either, but if they say yes, their word is gold.

And if they say no, they'll never tell anyone you were ever in town. Guys like that are—"

Joe placed the chessboard on top of the dresser. "I had a meeting yesterday with Meyer, Carlos, and Sammy Turnips."

Dion resettled his head against the pillows. "You did, uh?"

"Yup."

"And how'd that go?"

"I'm still breathing."

Dion snorted. "They wouldn't have clipped you."

"Actually," Joe said and sat on the side of the bed, "they had the burial spot all picked out. I was floating above it for a good hour."

"You met on a *boat*? What are you, insane?"

"I didn't have a choice. The Commission says come, you better well come. If I hadn't, they'd have clipped us all by now."

"Get past *those* guards out there? I don't think so."

"Those are Batista's guards. Batista takes money from me and he takes it from Meyer. That means if there's a beef between the two of us, he'll take the biggest cut from whoever gets it to him first and let the gods sort it out. Nobody has to get through these guards. It would be the guards who'd kill us."

Dion shifted some more in the bed and pulled half a cigar out of his ashtray and relit it. "So you met with the Commission."

"And Rico DiGiacomo."

Dion's eyes rose around the cigar smoke as the flame finally caught and the tobacco cackled. "He's a little irate about his brother, I'd guess."

"That's a mild way of putting it. He came in wanting my head."

"How'd you leave with it then?"

"I promised them yours."

Dion shifted in the bed again, and Joe realized he was trying to get a look in the bag. "You promised them mine."

Joe nodded.

"Why would you do that, Joe?"

"Only way I walked back off the boat."

"What's in the bag, Joe?"

"They made it clear to me that the hit on you wasn't something Rico just thought up and did. It was sanctioned."

Dion sat with that for a while, his eyes gone small and inward, his face pale. He continued to puff on his cigar, but Joe wondered if he was even aware of it. After about five minutes had passed, he said, "I know revenue's been declining the last couple years on my watch. I know I play the horses too much, but . . ." He fell silent again, took a few more puffs on the cigar to keep the coal hot. "They say why they want me cooked?"

"No. But I got a few theories." Joe reached into the bag and pulled out the box from Chinetti's. He placed it on Dion's lap and watched his friend's face drain.

Dion said, "What's that?"

Joe chuckled.

Dion said it again. "What's that? That from Chinetti's?"

Joe reached into Dr. Blake's bag, removed a full syringe of morphine. Enough to dope a herd of giraffe. He tapped it against the heel of his hand and considered his oldest friend.

"Dirty box," Dion said. "Got blood all over it."

"It's dirty," Joe agreed. "What'd they have on you?"

"Look, I don't know what you—"

"What'd they have?" Joe tapped the syringe off Dion's chest.

"Hey, Joe, I know it looks like one thing."

"Because it is."

"But sometimes things aren't what they seem."

Joe tapped the syringe down Dion's leg. *Tap tap tap.* "Most times they are, though."

"Joe, we're brothers. You're not going—"

Joe placed the point of the needle against Dion's throat. He didn't do it with any sort of flourish—one second the syringe was tapping against Dion's shin, the next the point was pressed against the artery just to the left of his Adam's apple. "You betrayed me once before. I spent three years in prison because of it. And not just any prison—Charlestown. And still I stood by you. Second time I had this choice given to me, they killed nine of my guys because I chose not to give you up. Remember Sal? Remember Lefty and Arnaz and Kenwood? Esposito and Parone? They're all dead because I didn't turn you over to Maso Pescatore in '33." He scratched the needle point down Dion's throat and then back up the other side. "Now, here comes the choice again. Except I got a son now, D." He tipped the point of the needle into the skin and placed his thumb on the plunger and kept his voice steady. "So why don't you fucking tell me what the Feds have on you?"

Dion gave up trying to see the needle and looked into Joe's face. "What do they always have on guys like us? Proof. They had me on the phone ordering a knee-capping of that turd in Pinellas last year. Had pictures of me when we off-loaded that boat you sent from Havana back in '41."

"You went to an off-load? What the fuck is wrong with you?"

"I got sloppy. I was bored."

It was all Joe could do not to plunge the needle into his fucking eye.

"Who made contact?"

"He worked for Anslinger."

The Bureau of Narcotics, under the zealot Harry Anslinger, was the only law enforcement group out there that could tell the difference between its ass and a hat. And there had long been a suspicion that this could be due to Anslinger having someone feeding him information from the inside.

Dion said, "I would never have turned on you."

"Yeah?"

"Yeah. You *know* that."

"I do, uh?"

Joe reached over and dumped the stale cake out onto Dion's lap.

"The fuck you doing?"

"Ssshhh." Joe removed the envelope he'd found under the cake last night. He threw it up the bed, where it hit Dion in the chin. "Open it."

Dion's fingers trembled as he did. He pulled out the sheaf of bills—two thousand in hundreds—and the slip of paper below it. He opened the piece of paper and closed his eyes.

"Show it to me, D. Show me the name on it."

"Just because they were asking, doesn't mean I would have given it to them. Plenty of times, I don't."

"Show me the name. Show me who their next target was."

Dion turned the piece of paper outward:

Coughlin.

"I never would have—"

"How many lies you want me to believe? How long you want this dance to go on? You keep saying you wouldn't this, you'd never that, you couldn't the other thing. What do you want me to do—fucking agree with you? Okay, fine, I agree with you. You're a man of principle pretending to be a man without honor. Me, I'm just the sap who lost everything—my home, my standing, could still lose my life—to protect a rat."

"You were protecting a friend."

"My son was in the car. You took my son to your contact point with federal fucking cops. My son."

"Who I love like a—"

Joe came forward in a rush, put the needle under Dion's left eye. "Don't you say the word *love* again. Not in this room."

Dion breathed heavily through his nostrils but said nothing.

"I think you rat on people because it's your nature. Gives you a thrill. I can't say for sure, but that's my guess. And if you do a thing enough times, you are that thing. All your other characteristics are just bullshit."

"Joe, listen. Just listen."

Joe was humiliated when he saw a warm tear hit Dion's face and realized it had come from his own eye. "What am I supposed to believe in now? Huh? What's left?"

Dion didn't answer.

Joe sucked a wet breath through his nostrils. "There's a sugar plantation a few minutes' walk from here."

Dion blinked. "I know. You and Esteban showed it to me about five years ago."

"Angel Balimente is going to meet us there in a couple hours. I'll hand you off to him and he'll lead you out of the province to a boat. You'll be off the island by tonight. I ever hear from you again or I ever hear of you popping your head up somewhere, I'll put you down. Like a fucking goat with a foaming mouth. We clear?"

"Listen—"

Joe spit in his face.

Dion scrunched his eyes and now he was weeping too, his chest heaving.

"I said are we clear?"

Dion kept his eyes closed and waved his arm at the air above his face. "Clear."

Joe got off the bed, walked to the door. "Do what you need to do. Pack, say good-bye to Tomas, have a meal, whatever. If you're seen outside the house before I come back for you, the guards have orders to shoot you on sight."

He left the room.

OUT ON THE STONE PORCH, Tomas was bewildered. "When will I see you again?"

"Oh," Dion said, "soon enough. You know."

"I don't know. I don't."

Dion knelt by him. It took some effort, would probably take more to get back up. "You know what business your father and me are in."

"Yes."

"What is it?"

"Illegal."

"Well, yeah, but it's more than that. We call it our thing because that's what it is—a few guys like me and your father involved in a, whatta ya call it—enterprise. And it's just ours. We don't bother nobody outside it, we don't invade your country or steal your land because our eyes are bigger than our plates. We make money. And we protect other people who are trying to make money the same way for a fee. And if we get in trouble, we can't cry to the police or the mayor. We're on our own, like men. And sometimes that's a tough pill to swallow. So, yeah, now I gotta go away. Because you saw what happened back in Tampa. You saw how it can get when we have a disagreement in our thing. It can get a little serious, right?"

He laughed and Tomas laughed too.

"Very serious, right?"

"Yes," Tomas said.

"But that's okay—the serious stuff is what makes life worthwhile. The other stuff—the dames, the laughs, the silly games and lazy days—it's all fun, but it doesn't stick. The serious stuff—that sticks, makes you feel alive. So it's pretty serious right now, and your father he's got a way to get me out but I gotta go now, and I might have to go forever."

"No."

"Yeah. Listen to me. Look, look at me." He gripped Tomas's shoulders, locked their gazes. "Someday you're going to get a postcard. Ain't going to be anything written on it. Just the card. And the place on that card? That won't be where I am, but it will be where I *was*. And you'll know your uncle Dion is living the life somewhere. He's getting by."

"Okay. Okay."

"Your old man and me, Tomas, we don't believe in kings or princes or presidents. We believe we're all kings and princes and presidents. We're all whatever we decide to be and no one tells us different. You understand?"

"Yes."

"Don't ever take a knee for nobody."

"You're on your knee now."

"That's because you're family." He chuckled. "Now help me up, would ya, kid? Shit."

"How can I help you up?"

"Just keep your head right there and don't move it."

He clamped his big paw on top of Tomas's head and pushed up. "Ouch."

"Stop your bellyaching and be a man, for Christ's sake." He said to Joe, "Gotta toughen this kid up." He pinched Tomas's biceps. "Right? Right?"

Tomas swatted at his hand.

"Bye, kid."

"Bye, Uncle Dion."

He watched his father lift Dion's suitcase off the stone porch and then watched them walk out of the yard toward the slope that led down to the plantation, and he hoped this wasn't what life was—a series of departures.

But he suspected it was.

CHAPTER TWENTY-FIVE

Cane

JOE AND DION WALKED DOWN A ROW that cut through the center of the plantation. The workers called the row Little House Lane; at the end of it stood a small yellow house the previous owner had built as a playhouse for his daughter. It was no bigger than a tool-shed but had been constructed to look like a Victorian. The owner had sold the plantation to Suarez Sugar Ltd., Joe's and Esteban's company, back in the early 1930s, during the boom years of rum-running, when sugar was at a premium. The owner's daughter had long since grown up and left the island, and the little house she'd left behind had been used as storage and occasionally as sleeping quarters for smaller men. One year, they'd removed the window in the west wall and fixed a shelf below it and turned the house into a cantina with a few small wooden tables placed out front. It proved an ill-fated act of benevolence, however, when the drunken workers became prone to fighting, and the experiment ended for good when two got in a machete battle that left both men maimed and unemployable.

Joe carried Dion's suitcase for him. There wasn't much in it—a few shirts and pairs of pants, socks and underwear, one pair of shoes, two bottles of cologne, a toothbrush—but Dion was still too weak to carry it the length of a sugarcane field in the late afternoon heat.

The cane stood seven to eight feet tall. The rows were spaced about two and a half feet apart. Off to the west, workers burned a field. The fire consumed the leaves but not the stalks and their precious sugar juice, which would be transported up to the mill. Luckily the warm breeze crossed the plantation from the east and kept the smoke from covering the rest of the fields. Some days, it worked the opposite—you'd think the sky had been stripped from the world and replaced with a ceiling of roiling clouds as big as airships and dark as cast iron. Today, however, the sky was bold and blue, though hints of orange were beginning to encroach on the edges.

"So that's the plan?" Dion said. "Angel, he takes me out through those hills?"

"Yup."

"Where's the boat?"

"I assume it's on the other side of the hills. All I know for sure is it'll take you to Isla de Pinos. You stay there for a bit. Then someone will pick you up again, take you to Kingston or Belize."

"You don't know which."

"Nope. And I don't want to."

"I'll take Kingston. They speak English there."

"You speak Spanish. What difference does it make?"

"I'm tired of speaking Spanish."

They walked in silence for a while, the soft soil making everything cant. The mill sat on the highest hill before them, overlooking the ten-thousand-hectare plantation like a stern parent. On the next highest hill was the housing for the managers—colonial-era villas with verandas stretching the length of the second stories. The field supervisors lived in similar structures a little farther down the hill, but theirs had been sectioned off to house six to eight units. Ringing the field edges were the tin-roof shacks of the workers. Dirt floors mostly, a few with running water, most without. Outhouses spaced behind every fifth shack.

Dion cleared his throat. "So, let's say I'm lucky, I end up walking around Jamaica, then what? What am I supposed to do after that?"

"Disappear."

"How am I supposed to disappear without money?"

"You've got two grand. A hard-earned two grand."

"That won't last long on the lam."

"Hey, you know what? That's not my fucking problem, D."

"Seems like it is, though."

"How you see that?"

"If I don't have money, I'll stick out more. I'll be more desperate too. Probably more inclined toward rash behavior. Plus—Jamaica? How much business did we do down there in the 1920s and 1930s? You don't think I'll be recognized at some point?"

"Maybe. I'd have to give it some more—"

"No, no. You would have figured on that. The Joe I know would have stashed bricks of money in a bag for me along with a few passports. He'd have people waiting to change my hair color, maybe give me a fake beard, that sorta thing."

"The Joe You Know doesn't have time for that. The Joe You Know needs to get you the fuck out of this region."

"The Joe I know would have already figured out how he was going to get funds to me in Isla del Pinto."

"Isla de Pinos."

"Stupid name."

"It's Spanish."

"I know it's Spanish. I just said it's a fucking stupid name. You understand me? It's fucking stupid."

"What's stupid about Isle of Pines?"

Dion shook his head several times and said nothing.

The next row over, something brushed against the cane stalks. A dog surely, tracking its prey. They moved constantly along the perimeter and down the rows—dun-colored terriers that killed rats with their razor teeth and gleaming dark eyes. The dogs were sometimes so adept at their job, they'd attack workers in packs if they smelled rat on them. One, a mottle-flank bitch named Luz, was such a legend—she'd killed 273 rodents in one day—that she'd been allowed to sleep in the Little House for a month.

Armed men watched the fields, ostensibly to protect the plants from thieves, but really to keep the workers in line or the ones with debt from running off. And all the workers carried debt. This isn't a farm, Joe thought the first time he and Esteban walked around it, it's a prison. I own shares in a prison. Which is why Joe had no need to fear the guards; they all feared him.

"I was speaking Spanish," Dion said, "two years before you were. Remember when I told you it was the only way you could survive in Ybor? And you said, 'But this is America. I want to speak my own damn language.'"

Joe had never said that, but he nodded just the same as Dion looked back over his shoulder at him. He heard the dog again off to their right, its flank brushing cane.

"I was your guide there back in '29. 'Member? You're off the train from Boston with your chalk skin and your prison haircut.

You wouldn't have been able to find your ass with two hands and both heels if it wasn't for me."

Joe watched him look up past the tall stalks at the orange and blue sky. It was such an odd mix of colors—the blue of the day trying so hard to hang on as the orange blush of evening began its march toward bloodred dusk.

"The colors down here don't make sense. Too many of 'em. Same in Tampa. In Boston, what'd we have? We had blue, we had gray, we had some yellow if the sun was out. Trees were green. Grass was green and didn't grow ten fucking feet tall. Things made sense."

"Yeah." Joe suspected Dion needed to hear the sound of his voice.

The yellow house was about a quarter mile off now, a five-minute walk on a dry road. Ten minutes in the soft earth, though.

"He built that for his daughter, uh?"

"That's the story."

"What was her name?"

"I don't know."

"How do you not know?"

"Easy—I simply don't know."

"You never heard it?"

"I might have. I dunno. Maybe when we bought the place and heard the story for the first time. His name was Carlos, the previous owner, but the daughter? Why the fuck would I know her name?"

"It just seems wrong, you know." He raised an arm to the fields and the hills. "I mean, she was here. Played here, ran here, drank water here, ate." He shrugged. "Seems like she should have a name." He looked back over his shoulder at Joe. "Whatever happened to her? You know that much?"

"She grew up."

Dion turned forward again. "Well, no shit. But what *happened* to her? She live a long life? She book passage on the *Lusitania?* What?"

Joe removed the gun from his pocket, let it hang down by his right leg. He still carried Dion's suitcase with his left hand, the ivory handle growing slick in the heat. In the movies, when Cagney or Edward G shot a man, the victim grimaced and then politely folded over and died. Even if they shot them in the stomach, a wound Joe knew made a man claw the air, kick the ground, and scream for his mother, his father, and his god. But what he didn't do was die right away.

"I don't know anything about her life," Joe said. "Don't know if she's alive or dead or how old she'd be. I just know she left the island."

The yellow house grew closer.

"You?"

"What?"

"Gonna leave the island someday?"

A man shot in the center of the chest didn't automatically die right away either. It often took time for bullets to do their work. A slug might bounce off a bone and nick the heart instead of entering it. And the victim didn't lose consciousness during that process. He moaned or writhed like he'd been dropped in a tub of boiling water.

"Not sure there's anyplace I can go right now," Joe said. "This is the closest there is to safe for me and Tomas."

"Christ, I miss Boston."

Joe had seen guys with head shots walk around scratching the wound before the body began to shut down and the legs finally gave way. "I miss Boston too."

"We weren't meant for this."

"Meant for what?"

"All these hot wet climates. Mush your brain, get you all turned around."

"That's why you betrayed me—humidity?"

The only sure kill shot was if you placed the muzzle directly to the back of the skull at the base of brain. Otherwise, bullets could wander quirky paths.

"I never betrayed you."

"You betrayed us. You betrayed our thing. That's the same."

"No, it's not." Dion looked back at Joe, his eyes noting the gun in his hand without surprise. "Before there was our thing, there was *our* thing." He pointed from his chest to Joe's. "Me, you, and my poor, dumb brother, Paulo, God rest him. Then we became—we became what, Joe?"

"Part of something bigger," Joe said. "And, Dion, for eight years, you ran the company store in Tampa, so don't start playing violins about the old days, getting all sappy about a three-story walkup on Dot Ave with no icebox and a toilet on the second floor that didn't work."

Dion turned his head forward and continued walking. "What's the word for when you *know* one thing but you still *believe* the opposite?"

"I don't know," Joe said. "A paradox?"

Dion's shoulders rose and fell. "That'll have to do. So, yes, Joseph—"

"Don't call me that."

"—I know I just spent eight years running the company store and ten years before that climbing the company ladder. And maybe if I had a chance to do it all over, I'd do the exact same thing. But the para . . ." He looked back at Joe.

"Dox," Joe said. "Paradox."

"The paradox is that I really wish you and me were still sticking up payroll rooms and casing out-of-town banks." He looked back with a sad smile. "I wish we were still outlaws."

"But we're not," Joe said. "We're gangsters."

"I never would have given you up."

"What else are you going to say?"

Dion looked up at the hills ahead of them and the words came out of him like a moan. "Oh, shit."

"What?"

"Nothing. Just shit. Aww shit. It's all shit."

"It's not all shit. There's good in this world." Joe dropped Dion's suitcase to the earth.

"If there is, we ain't part of it."

"No." Joe extended his arm behind Dion and watched his shadow do the same in front of him.

Dion saw it too. His shoulders hunched and his next step was a stutter step, but he kept walking.

"I don't think you can do this," he said.

Joe didn't think he could either. The twitches had already begun rippling the skin around his wrist and thumb.

"I've killed before," Joe said. "Only lost sleep over it once."

"Killed, yeah," Dion said. "But this is murder."

"You've never had trouble with murder." Joe found it harder to talk with the beats of his heart punching up against the base of his throat.

"I know. But this ain't about me. *You* don't have to do this."

"I think I do," Joe said.

"You could let me run."

"To where? Through the jungle? You'll have a price on your head big enough for any man in these fields to buy his own sugar plantation. And I'll be dead in a ditch half an hour after you."

"So it's about your life."

"It's about you being a rat. It's about you threatening everything we built."

• "We've been friends over twenty years."

"You ratted on us." Joe's voice was even shakier than his hand. "You lied to my face every day and it almost got my son killed."

"You were my brother." Dion's voice was shaking now too.

"You don't lie to your brother."

Dion stopped. "But you can kill him, huh?"

Joe stopped too, lowered the gun, closed his eyes. When he opened them, Dion was holding his right index finger aloft. There was a scar there, a pink so faint you had to be standing in direct sunlight to see it.

"You still got yours?" he asked.

When they were kids, they'd cut their right index fingertips with a razor blade in an abandoned livery stable in South Boston and pressed the fingertips together. A silly ritual. A laughable blood oath.

Joe shook his head. "Mine faded away."

"Funny," Dion said. "Mine didn't."

Joe said, "You wouldn't get half a mile."

"I know it," Dion whispered. "I know."

Joe pulled a handkerchief from his pocket and mopped his face with it. He looked past the worker shacks and the plantation homes and the mill itself to the dark green hills beyond. "Not half a mile."

"So why didn't you just kill me back at the house?"

"Tomas," Joe said.

"Ah." Dion nodded and scuffed at the soft earth with his shoe. "You think it's already written, like under a rock somewhere?"

"What's that?"

"How we end up?" Dion's eyes had gone hungry now as they tried to consume everything—drink the sky, eat the fields, inhale the hills. "From the moment the doc pulls us out of our old lady's womb, you think maybe somewhere it's written 'You will burn in a fire, you will fall off a boat, you will die in a foreign field'?"

Joe said, "Jesus," and nothing more.

Dion seemed spent suddenly. His arms drooped, his hips sagged.

After a while, they started walking again.

"You think we'll see our friends in the next life? All be back together?"

"I don't know," Joe said. "I hope so."

"I think we will." Dion glanced up at the sky again. "I think . . ."

The breeze shifted and small rags of smoke floated past them from the west.

"Charlotte," Joe said.

"What?"

A terrier bolted across their path—startling Joe because it came from the left, not the right, where he'd heard it a couple times on their walk. It leaped into the cane, snarling. They heard its prey squeak. Just once.

"It came back to me. That was the girl's name. The previous owner's daughter."

"Charlotte." Dion smiled firmly. "That's a good name."

From somewhere over the hills came the faintest rumble of thunder, though the air didn't smell of anything but burning sugar leaves and moist earth.

"It's pretty," Dion said.

"What?"

"The yellow house."

They were about fifty yards away.

"Yeah," Joe said. "It is."

He pulled the trigger. He closed his eyes at the last moment but the bullet still left the gun with a sharp crack and Dion fell to all fours in the earth. Joe stood over his friend as the blood spilled out of the hole in the back of his head. It coated his hair and dripped off the left side of his head, down his neck, into the soft ground. Joe could see brain but Dion continued to breathe, a desperate huffing, an unquenchable greed for air. He sucked in a watery breath and turned his face toward Joe, one glassy eye finding him, the knowledge already beginning to rush out of it—knowledge of who he was and how he'd come to be here on his hands and knees, knowledge of a life lived, the names of so many simple things already vanished. His lips moved, but no words left them.

Joe fired the second bullet into his temple and Dion's head snapped hard to the right and he sprawled on the ground and made no sound.

Joe stood in the row of cane and his gaze fell on the small yellow house.

He hoped souls were real and Dion's was now rising through the blue and orange sky. He hoped the little girl who'd played in the little yellow house was somewhere safe. He prayed for her soul and prayed for his own soul even though he knew it was damned.

He looked out at the fields, at the breadth of them, and he could see the full breadth of Cuba beyond, but it wasn't Cuba. Everywhere he lived, everywhere he traveled, everywhere he walked from now on was the land of Nod.

I am damned. And alone.

Or am I? he wondered. Or is there a path I can't see yet? A way out. A road that inclines.

The voice that replied was weary and cold:

Look at the body at your feet. Look at him. Your friend. Your brother. Now ask that question again.

He turned to head back—disposal of the corpse had already been arranged—and froze. There, about thirty yards up the row, Tomas knelt in the soft earth, mouth open, face wet. Bewildered. Broken. Lost to him forever.

CHAPTER TWENTY-SIX

Orphans

A WEEK LATER, as they were packing up the apartment in Havana, Manuel told Joe an American woman was asking for him downstairs.

As he left the apartment, Joe passed Tomas sitting on his bed, all packed. He caught his eye and gave him a nod, but Tomas looked away.

Joe stood in the doorway. "Son."

Tomas looked at the wall.

"Son, look at me."

Tomas eventually obeyed the order, stared at him with the same look he'd worn for a week. It wasn't enraged—Joe had been hoping for the sadness to turn into rage; rage he could work with. But instead, Tomas's face was a map of despair.

"It will get better," Joe told him for maybe the fiftieth time since the cane field. "The hurt will pass."

Tomas's mouth opened. The muscles worked under his skin. Joe waited. Hoping.

Tomas said, "Can I look away now?"

JOE WALKED DOWNSTAIRS. He passed the guards in the foyer and then the two outside the front door.

She stood in the street, just short of the curb, the lazy afternoon traffic kicking up dust behind her. She wore a pale yellow dress and her red-black hair was tied back in a bun. She held a small suitcase in each hand and seemed to cling to her prim and proper posture, as if to relax a muscle would cause the whole lie of herself to crumble.

"You were right," she said.

"About what?"

"Everything."

"Come off the street."

"You're always right. How does that feel?"

He thought of Dion lying in soft soil splattered black with his blood.

"Awful," he said.

"My husband threw me out, of course."

"I'm sorry."

"My parents said I was a whore. Said if I showed my face in Atlanta, they'd slap it in public and never look at me again."

Joe said, "Please step off the street."

She did. She placed her suitcases on the sidewalk in front of him. "I have nothing."

"You have me."

"Won't you wonder if I came because I love you or because I'd exhausted my options?"

"I might." He took her hands. "But not enough to keep me up nights."

That elicited a small, black laugh, and then she took a step back, still holding his hands but holding them by the fingertips. "You're different."

"Yeah?"

She nodded. "You're missing something." She searched his face. "No, no. Wait. You've *lost* something. What is it?"

Just my soul, if you believe in that sort of thing.

"Nothing I'll miss," he said and lifted her bags off the sidewalk and led her inside.

"Joseph!"

He put Vanessa's bags down on the floor of the vestibule and turned toward the sound of the voice because whoever had called him had sounded a lot like his late wife.

Not a lot like her, actually. Exactly like her.

She was at the next corner, walking with the oversize hat she'd favored in summer and a pale orange parasol. She wore a simple white dress, a peasant dress, and she looked over her shoulder once at him, and turned the corner.

Joe stepped out on the sidewalk.

From the vestibule, Vanessa said, "Joe?" but he continued walking toward the street.

The blond boy stood on the far sidewalk in between the apartment building and the movie theater. Once again he wore an outfit that was at least twenty to twenty-five years out of date, a gray serge knickerbocker suit with matching golf cap, but this time his features were clear—blue eyes sunk back a little bit into their sockets, thin nose, sharp cheekbones, hard jawline, medium height for his age.

Even before he smiled, Joe knew who he was. He'd known it

the last time he'd seen him, though it hadn't made any sense. Still didn't.

The boy matched the smile with a wave, but all Joe could see was the Cumberland Gap where his two front teeth should have been.

His father and mother passed by on the curb. They were younger and they held hands. Their clothes were Victorian and of poorer quality than they'd worn by the time he'd been born. They didn't look at him, and even though they held hands, they didn't look particularly happy.

Sal Urso, dead ten years, propped his foot on a hydrant and tied his shoelace. Dion and his brother, Paulo, played craps against the wall of the apartment house. He saw people from Boston who'd died in the flu pandemic of '19 and a nun from Gate of Heaven School who he hadn't known was dead. All around him were the nonliving—men who'd died at Charlestown Prison, men who'd died in the streets of Tampa, those he'd killed personally and those he'd ordered killed. He saw some women he didn't know, suicides judging by the wrists of one or the ligature ring around the neck of another. Down the end of the block, Montooth Dix beat the shit out of Rico DiGiacomo, while Emma Gould, a woman he had loved once but hadn't thought of in years, staggered down the sidewalk with a bottle of vodka in her bluing hand, her hair and dress soaking wet.

All his dead. They filled the street and clogged the sidewalks.

He lowered his head in the middle of the busy street in Old Havana. Lowered his head and closed his eyes.

I wish you well, he told his dead. *I wish you good things.*

But I will not apologize.

When he looked up again, he saw Hector, one of his bodyguards, walking in the wrong direction, disappearing around the same corner where he'd last seen Graciela.

All his ghosts, though, were gone.

Except the boy. The boy cocked his head at Joe, as if surprised he was coming closer.

Joe said, "You're *me?*"

The boy seemed confused by the question.

Because he wasn't the boy anymore. He was Vivian Ignatius Brennan. Saint Viv. The Gatekeeper. The Undertaker.

"There were just too many mistakes," Saint Viv said kindly. "Too late to go back and fix them all. Too late."

Joe didn't even see the gun in his hand until Vivian fired the bullet into his heart. Didn't make much noise, just a soft pop.

The impact swept Joe's legs out from under him, and he fell in the street. He put one hand to the cobblestone and tried to stand, but his heels wouldn't grip the stone. Blood left the hole in the center of his chest and spilled onto his lap. His lungs whistled through the hole.

The getaway car pulled up behind Vivian and a woman screamed hopelessly from somewhere close by.

Tomas, if you're seeing this, for Christ's sake, look away.

Vivian pointed the pistol at Joe's forehead.

Joe placed the heels of both hands to the cobblestone and tried to put some fire in his eyes.

But he was afraid. So afraid.

And he wanted to say what they all said: *Wait.*

But he didn't.

The flash that left the muzzle looked like a shower of falling stars.

When he opened his eyes, he was sitting on a beach. It was night. All around him was darkness except for the white of the surf and the white of the sand.

He stood and walked toward the water.

He walked and walked.

But no matter how much he walked, he never got any closer. He couldn't see the water itself, just the impact of the waves when they broke up in the black wall before him.

After a while, he sat down again.

He waited for others to come. He hoped they would. He hoped there was more to this than a dark night, an empty beach, and waves that never quite reached the shore.